AN OTTER CREEK BOOK

Marcus Chandler is a reclusive film producer who seems to have a rare disease that has left him with bleached skin and a heightened sensitivity to light. The Graveyard Armadillas are convinced he is a vampire. Since vampires can't be photographed, they decide to get a picture of Chandler to make their case. Fifteen-year old Scooter Keyshawn, who wants to prove himself to the Armadillos, agrees to snap the photo. Whether Chandler's vampirism is real or imagined, there are still plenty of disappearing and eventually turning up dead. It's up to Scooter and his friends to clear the innocent and trap the real vampires. The atmospheric writing and the harrowing quest will keep the pages turning and the simple prose and the emphasis on action rather than character development will make the book a good choice for reluctant readers. . . .

-Booklist (American Library Association)

This is a young adult vampire thriller about a group of youngsters who decide to solve the mystery surrounding a series of gruesome deaths. There's a farm in town whose perimeter consists of half buried pickup trucks, and the kids suspect that the recently returned resident is a blood-sucker. They unwisely pursue their investigation and encounter Mister Shade, a nasty vampire whom they eventually defeat. There's lots of adventure in this. . . .

-Science Fiction Chronicle

While staying with his grandparents, fifteen-year old Jonathan "Scooter" Keyshawn tries to join the Graveyard Armadillas, the nearest thing to a gang available in Gunstock, Texas. The Armadillas, an uneven assortment of some half-dozen local youths, have planned a novel first exploit for him: helping to prove that a reclusive moviemaker Marcus Chandler is a vampire. Chandler avoids the sun and is unnaturally pale; and in the words of ringleader Garrett Brashear: "Never seen a white African-American." But, Chandler's explosive reaction when Scooter catches him in a Polaroid's flash sends the group scattering upon the nighttime swamp . . .and not quite all of them come out.

The abilities of the vampire himself offers a few interesting twists (he's quite the shapeshifter), but for the most part the appeal of The Vampire Hunters is not in gratuitous novelty but in a few kids' determination to overcome the odds and set things right.

Sounds good to me. . . .

-The Vampire's Crypt

When Scooter is asked to join the Graveyard Armadillas, he is thrilled, even when he learns that to be accepted he is expected to "prove" that moviemaker Marcus Chandler is a vampire. Along comes a strange man who sets into motion a series of events that change the residents of Scooter's small town. . . .

-School Library Journal

Fleeing Pickup Ranch

"Ahh. . . ." the front door opened slowly, allowing a faint light to be cast across the porch. Scooter jumped a foot and almost screamed — barely managing to swallow it. He darted behind the bushes near the gate, then peered around the corner.

At first, Chandler's shadow was crisp, his slender form distinctly outlined against the interior light. The backlit darkness couldn't totally conceal his pale complexion. Chandler's face and arms held a gleaming quality, reminding Scooter of how the house had radiated an eerie luminescence earlier. Dressed in navy clothing, Chandler appeared disembodied, his bald head and bare arms floating along as though unattached.

Scooter was amazed. Was he really black? African-American? How could anyone tell? Marcus Chandler was whiter than sun-bleached bones.

Scooter took a deep breath, crossed his fingers, then jumped in front of the infamous director. With quivering hands, Scooter snapped picture after picture, the flash illuminating the night as though lightning from a storm.

"AWWW!" Chandler screamed, his hands going to his face and covering his eyes.

In the flashing white light, Scooter could see Chandler's gaunt face. It was transformed into something horrible, contorted and twisted, as if he were in sheer agony. His flesh appeared to take on an even brighter, unholy illumination. His eyes were amazingly bright — blazing red embers within deep black pits.

"Who's there? Damn you! Damn the Press! Why won't you leave me alone?" Chandler suddenly swung at Scooter, who stumbled backwards to avoid the blow.

Almost dropping the camera, Scooter turned and ran toward the Armadillos.

"You're dead meat!" Chandler cried.

THE VAMPIRE HUNTERS

—William Hill—

OTTER CREEK PRESS, INC.

F L O R I D A

The Vampire Hunters
by William Hill

Copyright © 1998 by William Hill

ISBNs:1-890611-02-6 (softcover)
      1-890611-05-0 (hardcover)
Library of Congress Card Number: 97-76112
Retail Price: $12.95 (trade softcover)
             $14.95 (softcover — Canada)
             $19.95 (hardcover)
             $24.95 (hardcover — Canada)

All inquiries should be addressed to

Otter Creek Press, Inc.
P. O. Box 416
Doctors Inlet, FL 32030-0416
(904) 264-0465
(800) 326-4809

Interior Design: Betsy Lampé
Cover Design: Rod Volkmar and Mandy Davis

First Printing 1998

DEDICATION

In thanks to W. W. "Dub" Hill, my father and a great grandpa. He surprised me by taking an interest in my "unconventional" tales. Without him, this novel would not exist in published print.

Titles by William Hill

Fiction for the Young in Spirit
>
> *The Magic Bicycle*
> *The Magic Bicycle II: Stealing Time*

Young Adult Fiction
>
> *The Vampire Hunters*

Fiction
>
> *Dawn of the Vampire*
> *Vampire's Kiss*
> *California Ghosting*
> *Hunting Spirit Bear**
> *The Wizard Sword**
> *Dragons Counsel**

*forthcoming

ACKNOWLEDGMENTS

The following people unselfishly helped improve
THE VAMPIRE HUNTERS:
Kat Hill, Ellen Hill, Dub Hill,
Lynne Crankshaw, Evan Crankshaw,
Rainbow Betty & Betsy, and Lewis G. Adler.

Chapter One

THE INITIATION

"Can't be much farther," Scooter Keyshawn panted as he and his young golden Labrador charged through the darkening woods, racing the rapidly setting sun. The redheaded boy gasped, his breath short, his heart hammering loudly in his ears. His eyes stung from the sweat that dripped down his face.

What would happen when darkness descended? he wondered. His canine companion, Flash, whined in response, as though he'd heard Scooter's thoughts.

Scooter put on a burst of speed. His gaze flicked about as he searched the woods. Flash had no trouble keeping up, loping alongside Scooter. Except for their crashing strides echoing in the silence, the air was unnaturally still, the twilight, eerily calm. Even the crickets and frogs were silent, the woods absent their usual lullabies.

A faint mist gathered near the small stream to their left, threatening to obscure part of the darkening woods. Scooter knew the fog could get thicker than smoke from a chili cook-off. If that happened, he might get confused, unable to find his way back to the abandoned house where he'd left his bicycle.

Scooter shivered. He'd better slow down. He certainly didn't want to get lost out here in the woods.

He paused and wiped the sweat from his brow. He was thoroughly soaked, the humidity suffocating. The evening air draped itself about him like a wet blanket.

Beyond the forest and above the lake, the setting sun sat teasingly upon the flat Texas horizon. The high cirrus clouds were crimson stains smeared against the golden twilight. The waning light was low, angled and weak, barely touching the shadow-filled forest. Any moment now, the sun would disappear, plunging the woods into darkness.

"Come on!" Scooter encouraged Flash, then started running again. The Lab needed no encouragement; the pure joy of running radiated from his sparkling eyes. His ears flapped like wings, and his flailing tongue seemed to reach all the way to his lively tail.

Despite the ninety-plus heat, fear chilled Scooter to the bone. Where were they? What would they do to him? Again, Scooter cursed the flat tire he'd had to fix in front of the old Pilot Point Cemetery. His new-found friends would be mad with him for being late.

Getting into the Graveyard Armadillos meant a lot to him. Heck, until two months ago, the only friend he'd ever had, besides Flash, was Russell Knight, the sheriff's son. Then he'd met Garrett Brashear and the rest of the Armadillos. Today at lunch, Garrett told Scooter that if he wanted to join the Armadillos, he should meet them outside the fence on the woods' side of the Pickup Ranch.

Scooter hoped that Jo wouldn't call him a "wimp" — afraid

of fun and scared of adventure. Cause it just wasn't true! It wasn't! He'd show her! Show them! Tonight was the first night of summer! The first evening of three months free of school! Free of time constraints! Full of long days and total freedom!

At last, off to his right, Scooter saw a trio of white buildings beyond a cluster of tall mesquite and oak trees. The ranch was quiet, unearthly still even for sunset, as if holding its breath, waiting for something strange to happen.

In many ways the old place looked the same as other Texas farms — mostly used for livestock with a huge garden along the side and a modest-sized chicken coop out back.

In other ways the Chandler's Pickup Ranch was very different. A line of pickup trucks spread out from the driveway, as though it might be a metal picket fence. It halfway surrounded a barn and a single-story house. The back acres ended in water; the grazing field sloped along the backside of Lake Tawakoni's earthen dam.

A moat and a metal castle wall, Scooter thought. He studied the line of trucks buried nose-first and hood-deep in the dirt. Most were in good condition as though repainted before being buried. All their windows were intact, and their rear bumpers were shiny. The oldest models started at the road with the newer makes farther away from the driveway.

Why would anyone do that? Scooter wondered. A Texas-sized picket fence? A historical museum of pickups? He'd always heard the Chandler folks were peculiar. Some people were glad they had died. Well, most of them were dead, he thought.

The barn to his left was being repainted; it had been all red once, faded and peeling, but now bone white swathes covered it. Against the pink sky, a star-shaped weather vane stood starkly atop the rusted corrugated metal roof. The hayloft door slowly swung back and forth as if moved by an invisible hand.

A gentle lake breeze brushed Scooter; he smelled hay, dung, and freshly-mown grass.

A pigpen was on the left side of the barn, and a horse corral surrounded the back of the building. Strangely enough, Scooter didn't see any livestock. Where were all the animals?

As though compelled, Scooter's gaze was drawn to the house. The place caught the last light of day and appeared to radiate an odd, hypnotizing glow. The shadows seemed darker than normal. Cave dark. Tomb dark. The strange sight mesmerized Scooter.

He was still running, but he felt as though he weren't moving. Yet, the house continued to grow larger and larger, looming and distorted; the details becoming sharply defined as if magnified. He had never before experienced such a weird feeling.

The house was painted off-white with green trim and shutters. The massive chimney stretched into the twilight like a blunt finger — pointing out that this was someplace special. Across the front of the house was a covered porch where the waning light failed to reach. The shadows seemed strangely opaque and foreboding.

He saw something move, at least he thought he did. The dark swaths seemed to writhe as though striving to break free. Scooter sensed the shadows were waiting for something. Waiting for darkness. Waiting for release. Waiting for a victim to come near. Too near. Scooter grew closer . . . and closer. He told himself he should cut back on his favorite comic book, SPAWN. His imagination was getting the best of him, again.

Scooter and Flash suddenly burst out of the woods and into the row of pickups. Scooter immediately slid to a stop. "Oh —"

"Quiet!" someone shushed and grabbed Scooter, pulling him to the ground behind a blue `74 Ford pickup. The hands shifted quickly, one clamping across Scooter's mouth. He smelled garlic . . .

Flash barked, ready to defend Scooter. A familiar voice off to their right spoke the Lab's name. Flash grew quiet.

"You're late, Scoot boy," came a voice from behind him.

"And you brought your big ugly mutt!" There was a heavy sigh. "Not a good way to start . . . if you still want to join the Graveyard Armadillos."

"We do! I do!" Scooter mumbled. "And so does Flash."

"No dogs allowed," the handsome, dark-haired boy snapped, implying a double meaning as he released Scooter.

Flash stiffened, glanced up, then cocked his head as if understanding. With a highly insulted look, the Labrador took a couple of steps forward. Now Flash began gagging, then suddenly threw up on Garrett's boots.

Garrett didn't step back in time, getting the toes of his boots sullied. "Hey! Damn your mutt!" Garrett reared back preparing to kick Flash.

The Lab looked up with shining eyes and an expression of wonderment — an angelic face of innocence.

"Don't kick my dog!" Scooter said forcefully.

"Shut up!" Garrett snapped. "You still want to join the Graveyard Armadillos, don't you?"

Scooter nodded.

"Then listen up and keep your mutt away from me. Tonight's your initiation, and you'll do exactly what I tell you to do or you're gone!"

Flash chuffed; then with tail and nose in the air, the Lab returned to Scooter's side. "He's not a mutt, and I will." Scooter leaned down to the Lab and whispered, "Always a comedian, aren't you?" Flash grinned.

"Don't be a smart-ass, or you'll be out on your butt," Garrett said. "Hey, I'm talking to you, you know."

Scooter nodded to the older boy.

With piercing blue eyes, a charming smile and the looks of a movie star, Garrett was the heart-throb of Tawakoni High; and he reveled in it; he was as proud as a strutting peacock. Despite the heat, Garrett wore a dark leather jacket without breaking a sweat. "Listen up. We need to get in gear. That movie-guy ought to be coming soon."

"I'm tired of waiting," Scooter heard someone drawl, then noticed BJ Mochrie. Below his black cowboy hat, he was scowling. As far as anyone could remember, Byron Jefferson Mochrie had always worn a look of barely restrained impatience. It went along with his arrogant walk that proclaimed he wasn't afraid of anything. With his curly, white-blond hair, green-blue eyes, and the build of a rodeo champion, BJ drew lots of attention from girls, although none of them seemed to stay around for long.

With BJ and Garrett were the other members of the Graveyard Armadillos; BJ's twin and bespectacled brother, CJ; the stout tomboy Jo Gunn; skinny Russell Knight and his coldly beautiful sister, Racquel, who had a crush on Garrett; and redheaded Kristie Candel, the minister's pretty daughter.

They all nodded at Scooter. Russell smiled, looking as though he wanted to wave but unsure if it was cool. Scooter shot Russell a look that said, "You didn't mention Kristie was a member!" Scooter tried not to stare but wasn't succeeding; Kristie was very, very cute.

Flash went over to Russell, was petted for a moment, then moved to Kristie, settling in her lap as if it were his new home.

Kristie smiled warmly as though she'd read Scooter's thoughts and patted Flash. The Labrador's eyes rolled back, as his tongue lolled lazily.

Scooter smiled back at Kristie, his flush hidden in the twilight. Never in his wildest dreams would he have imagined that the minister's daughter would be part of this group.

She'd changed a lot in the past year, no longer gangly, but tall and pretty — on the verge of being beautiful. In some ways, she reminded Scooter of himself, tall and trim with auburn hair. Beyond that, the similarities ended. She was pretty and looked composed. He was awkwardly gangly and felt very out of place.

"Ouch!" Scooter slapped at his neck. "Damn mosquitoes!"

"Here!" Kristie tossed him a plastic bottle. "It keeps the `skeeters at bay." Her voice was lilting, reminding him of the times he'd heard her singing in the church choir.

"Really?" Scooter asked. Kristie nodded, so he applied some to his exposed skin.

Scooter found himself wishing she'd offer to help, and that thought surprised him. Embarrassed, he avoided eye contact and stared at the others. They were all dressed in dark clothing and, to his surprise, wearing homemade necklaces of garlic. Each absently clutched a crucifix as though it were a life preserver they might need at a moment's notice. What was going on here? Certainly not a prayer session.

"This is gonna be great! We're gonna prove there's a vampire in Gunstock!" CJ announced. BJ's nearly identical twin wore thick glasses and a cowboy hat similar to his brother's. Calvin Jefferson was a little taller, but the main difference between the brothers was their expressions. CJ's face projected so much innocence that no one could possibly believe he'd ever done anything wrong — was even capable of doing wrong.

"A vampire?" Scooter wondered dumbly. What was he missing? Oh, that explained the garlic and crucifixes. But he didn't believe in vampires. They were a myth or characters in a fictional tale.

"Yep, a vampire," Jo Gunn began. "We're gonna make the TV big time!" Her already wide face stretched with a crooked, toothy smile. Her brown cowboy hat pulled down tight, its shadow all but hid her doubled chin. Jo was thick everywhere, through the face, neck and shoulders with legs the size of tree trunks.

"You . . . see, S . . .Scooter," Russell Knight began, stuttering as usual, "Garrett believes . . . .that the moviemaker, Marcus Chandler, isn't sick like the paper says, but actually a v . . . vam . . . vampire."

Russell was tall, dark-haired, tanned and as skinny as a tent pole. His expression and gray eyes were placid and unreadable. Russell was half-Hispanic and rarely showed any emotion, especially his frustration over stuttering. He compensated by singing — which never led to stuttering — or humming Grateful Dead songs. He wore a t-shirt with a skull on the back and dancing skeletons on the front.

"He came back last month to kill his parents," Garrett explained, "and now that they're dead, he's hungry again. Ready to prey on someone else."

"I guess that line of metal didn't protect them like they thought," BJ chuckled, giving reason to the strange museum of pickups.

"That's why people have been disappearing," Garrett continued.

"By revealing Chandler's a vampire, we'll show everybody we're not kids anymore," Racquel said bitterly. "We're adults."

Other than their coloring, Racquel and Russell looked very little alike, Scooter thought. Racquel was a blossoming beauty with nearly flawless features and cold, uncaring eyes the color of obsidian.

"Soon, Chaquita." Garrett looked at her, then Scooter. "This is gonna be fun — and memorable." With a wicked smile, Garrett pulled out a Polaroid and handed it to Scooter.

Made uneasy by Garrett's expression, Scooter licked his lips as he accepted the camera. "What do you want me to do?"

"When he comes out for his evening walk, you'll be hiding nearby, ready to snap some pictures. Vampires can't be photographed, so when the picture's blank, except for the background, we'll know he's truly one of the legion of undead."

"How can you be so sure he'll come out now?" Jo asked.

"He always comes out after the sun sets," Garrett replied.

"H . . . how do you . . . know?" Russell asked.

"Been watching him," Garrett replied. "There's something very, very strange about him. I've seen his picture. He's one weird looking dude! Never seen a white African-American."

CJ said, "This Chandler fella looks like he's been bleached!"

"Yeah," Garrett continued. "His face is pasty white, almost colorless. His eyes are red, sorta like a rabid wolf's. Boy howdy, he is ugly! Butt ugly! The kicker is he can't stand the daylight. It blisters and burns his skin. What did I tell ya? He's a vampire. Why else would he look like that and make movies about the living dead?" Garrett asked. "He knows all about being one with the darkness. It's a perfect cover!"

"Maybe he's related to Michael Jackson," BJ snickered.

Scooter didn't believe any of this and was fairly sure none of them did, either.

" P . . . paper says he's an anemic albino and has vitiligo," Russell responded. "Don't ask me to s . . . spell it."

"What's that?" Jo asked.

"A lie to cover up for the fact that he's a vampire," Garrett persisted.

"Maybe he has AIDS," CJ suggested.

"And notice," Garrett went on, "there's no livestock around. No pigs, cows or chickens. Not even a horse! He probably sucks the blood from them when he can't get ahold of a person!"

"I got a b . . . bad feeling about th . . . this." Russell stammered.

Scooter looked at the camera again. Ever since Marcus Chandler returned to his hometown, Scooter had wanted to meet him — to talk to him about writing — but not like this! Scooter started to ask a question, but Garrett interrupted him.

"I got something that'll make the waiting easier. And fun!" Garrett reached underneath his shirt, pulling out a bottle.

"What's that?" BJ asked.

"Red Hot Cinnamon Schnapps, buddy boy," Garrett said as he unscrewed the top. He took a slug, then licked his lips.

Scooter's apprehension grew stronger. Flash felt it and returned to his side. Scooter began scratching him between the ears, seeking comfort in the contact.

"Well, I'd like to try some," BJ replied. Taking the open bottle, he repeated Garrett's actions, then smiled broadly. "Yee-ha! Smooth!" He took another slug and gargled.

Jo's smile was huge as she followed suit.

Trying unsuccessfully to imitate his brother, CJ drank, then choked and began coughing.

"QUIET!" Garrett whispered harshly.

BJ smiled broadly, then took the bottle from his brother, holding it out to Russell. "First beer. Now schnapps, Russ ole buddy."

Scooter was surprised. Russell never said anything about trying beer. Scooter looked at Russell who just shrugged. Was Russell starting to keep secrets from him? Scooter didn't know if he was upset because he hadn't been told or had been missing out.

Russell hesitated.

"You ready, Russ?" Garrett asked. "Or afraid your papa will find out?"

Russell snatched the bottle from BJ and took a sip. With wide eyes and a beet-red face, he looked as though he'd swallowed liquid fire.

With a defiant and disdainful expression, Racquel took the bottle and managed a big swallow. She coughed delicately, then smiled, her eyes watering.

Garrett snorted, then said, "Good shot, Chaquita! Another step in getting y'all out from under your old man's law-biding thumb! Learn about life! Be your own person, I always say! Kristie?"

With a slight frown, Kristie took the bottle from Racquel and drank. She reddened immediately and had trouble breathing. Tears rolled down her face. She held the bottle away as if it was a viper.

"You'll get used to it," Garrett told her. "Your turn, Scoot. It's part of the initiation. Part of being one of us — one of the Graveyard Armadillos." Garrett gave Scooter the bottle.

He remembered Russell's expression and Kristie's reaction. He didn't want to "get used to it." Trying to appear cool, Scooter casually took a swig. It tasted of cinnamon and medicine, then lava ripped down his throat, exploding and expanding throughout his stomach. He grew dizzy and began to cough quietly, then uncontrollably louder, hacking harshly as if his lungs were tearing free.

Everyone but Kristie shushed him. Understanding completely, Russell patted his friend on the back. Scooter finally got it under control, coughing apologetically only now and then.

"Got something special to show y'all," BJ said as he reached into his backpack. He pulled out something metallic. "I just bought it. It's sweet!"

"A . . . gun!" Russell squeaked.

Scooter bristled. A gun? For hunting, he hoped.

"A .38 special. Just in case there's an emergency. 'Course I only shoot what I'm gonna eat."

"He eats lots of stop signs," CJ joked.

They all laughed. "Then we're set!" Garrett said as he pulled out his knife. "I've got Trusty here ready for trouble."

The knife reminded Scooter of the ones in the Rambo movies.

"Me, too!" Jo announced, pulling out her switchblade and clicking it open.

The tension that had been welling inside Scooter suddenly bubbled free. He couldn't stop laughing. It grew louder and louder.

"Damn it, Scooter," said Garrett. "Be quiet! We don't want him to know we're here!"

Kristie looked at Scooter, their gazes locked, then she began to snicker. Russell, unable to control himself, began to do the same.

"I'm warning all y'all . . . " Garrett whirled, looking directly at Scooter. His face tightened and his nostrils flared as he slowly spoke. "If you can't shut —"

A kitchen light in the back of the house came on.

"Time to get rolling," Garrett said. "You ready, Scoot?" He pointed to the camera in Scooter's trembling hand.

Scooter really didn't want to do this. There was no way Chandler was a vampire, but for some reason, he was suddenly scared, couldn't stop shaking. "Wh . . . what am I supposed to do again?" Scooter almost choked on the words.

"Like I said, you're gonna get proof that Chandler's a vampire by taking pictures of him!" Garrett repeated. "Hide by the front gate, and when he steps out, jump in front of him and start taking pictures. The flash will blind him long enough for you to escape. Trust me. Besides, I hear nobody can outrun the Scooter."

"Y . . . you can . . . do it," Russell said.

Scooter tried to smile back and failed. At his feet, Flash whined.

"C . . . come here, Flash," Russell called quietly.

Flash looked at Scooter who nodded. The golden Labrador reluctantly moped over to Kristie.

"I'll take care of him," Kristie promised.

Scooter nodded, tried to smile and failed again. He felt miserable.

Trying to relax, Scooter breathed deeply several times, then scampered off toward the house, staying low to the ground and hidden in the tall grass and weeds. He could barely see anything in the dusky light.

As he climbed over the split-rail fence behind the trucks, he wondered what would happen if he tripped, fell down and broke the camera? What was he doing out here, anyway? Did he really want to be in the group this badly? Oh, well, it was a harmless prank. Nobody really believed Chandler was a vampire, did they? He suddenly wished he had a crucifix. Just in case.

The silence was stark and unnerving. Scooter's heartbeat and breathing was almost deafening. As he climbed the fence and headed across the hard-packed dirt, Scooter felt his laughter rising again. He was almost shaking.

Chapter Two

ALL FOR NONE AND NONE FOR ALL

"Check this out!" Scooter heard Garrett say.

"Wow! A mallet and a stake!" BJ whispered loudly. "You really believe this, don't you?"

"You bet! All you have to do is just look at Chandler! If he isn't a vampire, he's an abomination. He doesn't deserve to live!"

"Abomination?! Hey, nice word there! You been payin' attention in English?" Jo asked.

Scooter groaned. Garrett did believe! And they were being so loud he was going to get caught! Scooter wanted to leave, but he couldn't. If he left, he couldn't join the Graveyard Armadillos.

Nervous beyond words, Scooter began to snicker. Chandler's not a vampire. Chandler's not a vampire, Scooter repeated to himself.

"Ahh. . . ." the front door opened slowly, allowing a faint light to be cast across the porch. Scooter jumped a foot and almost screamed — barely managing to swallow it. He darted behind the bushes near the gate, then peered around the corner.

At first, Chandler's shadow was crisp, his slender form distinctly outlined against the interior light. The backlit darkness couldn't totally conceal his pale complexion. Chandler's face and arms held a gleaming quality, reminding Scooter of how the house had radiated an eerie luminescence earlier. Dressed in navy clothing, Chandler appeared disembodied, his bald head and bare arms floating along as though unattached.

Scooter was amazed. Was he really black? African-American? How could anyone tell? Marcus Chandler was whiter than sun-bleached bones.

Scooter took a deep breath, crossed his fingers, then jumped in front of the infamous director. With quivering hands, Scooter snapped picture after picture, the flash illuminating the night as though lightning from a storm.

"AWWW!" Chandler screamed, his hands going to his face and covering his eyes.

In the flashing white light, Scooter could see Chandler's gaunt face. It was transformed into something horrible, contorted and twisted, as if he were in sheer agony. His flesh appeared to take on an even brighter, unholy illumination. His eyes were amazingly bright — blazing red embers within deep black pits.

"Who's there? Damn you! Damn the Press! Why won't you leave me alone?" Chandler suddenly swung at Scooter, who stumbled backwards to avoid the blow.

Almost dropping the camera, Scooter turned and ran toward the Armadillos.

"You're dead meat!" Chandler cried as he blindly pursued the young redhead.

Scooter scrambled onward.

"Hear me! Dead meat! You're not in Hollywood any more! You're in TEXAS! Hear me? Texas! And you're trespassing on my property!"

Kristie and Russell looked at each other, their thoughts the same: RUN!

Straining at his collar, Flash barked. Scooter raced past them, not even pausing as he tossed Garrett the camera and the Polaroid prints.

The golden Lab jerked free and joined his friend in flight. Russell and Kristie bolted together, following in Scooter's wake.

"Nothing to worry about, Chaquita," Garrett told them.

"Race ya to the wheels," CJ suggested eagerly.

"Yeah!" BJ agreed. Holding their hats, the brothers fled. Jo was just a few slow steps behind.

Garrett knelt to pick up a fallen photo, then sneered, looking from the completely gray picture to Chandler. As Garrett watched, the infamous director sprinted through the grass, unerringly heading toward the truck they hid behind as if guided by radar. Racquel's fingernails dug painfully into Garrett's arm. "Let's go!" she whispered.

Garrett's sneer was short-lived, his expression slowly becoming doubtful. He wasn't afraid of anything . . . unless this guy really was a vampire. Could that be? Impossible. But . . . he looked like a vampire! And the way he moved gave pause for thought.

"Come on, Chaquita," Garrett breathed, scared for the first time in a long time. As Chandler hurdled the fence, Garrett grabbed Racquel and ran as fast as he could, dragging her along with him.

"Please! So help me, God, I'll never do this again!" Russell gasped as he ran, holding his arms in front of his face — protection from the ripping branches. He could barely see Scooter and Flash ahead of him, darting in and out of the trees with surprising agility.

Russell knew nobody could outrun the Scooter. He'd reach the bicycles first. But what about the rest of them? If he got caught and his dad found out . . . Russell sprinted as if slavering Dobermans were breathing hot on his heels.

Huffing and grunting, Jo ran as fast as she could, rumbling through the woods. She wanted to be far away from here. Jo liked to believe she was like her three brothers — one tough *gringa*. But now all she wanted was to cruise the back roads on her Harley, the wind in her face blowing away her fear and sweat.

Something grabbed at Jo's feet, and she stumbled. Unable to recover, she fell forward.

When she looked up, she said, "Hey, what are you doing here! You following me?"

Darkness swept forward from the figure, engulfing her. Jo felt a biting pain, then the last thing she heard was a haunting chuckle.

Nearby Kristie came to a halt. Was that a scream? She strained to listen, but couldn't hear anything besides the thundering of her heart and the gasping of her ragged breath. She couldn't see anything, either. What if something happened to one of them? She was unexplainably afraid for Scooter. Should she use her flashlight? Or would it give her away? She wished she had never come along — wished she were elsewhere.

Unable to control her fear, Kristie fled. The boys would take care of themselves. Boys always did. In the distance, she heard a dog bark and wondered about Scooter. She said a heartfelt prayer for him as she ran.

"Man, oh, man, oh, man . . . " Scooter breathed, sprinting all out and easily outdistancing the others. He barely noticed Flash running smoothly alongside.

Scooter ran through a low-hanging branch that nearly decapitated him. He hardly noticed. He had only one thought in mind. ESCAPE! Unless he was lost, the chain-link fence should be coming up soon. Then he'd be at the deserted house, on his bicycle and long gone.

Scooter thought he heard the crack of a stick behind him.

Worried about his friends, Scooter glanced over his shoulder. "Russell?"

As Scooter turned around, something bit sharply and painfully into his leg. He somersaulted head over heels, his world abruptly crashing to black. Flash began barking wildly.

"Where's Russell?" Racquel asked Garrett.

"He'll be fine," Garrett replied. She looked doubtful, so he kissed her on the cheek and said, "Probably ahead of us. He left before we did. Trust me, Chaquita." Racquel didn't smile, so he said, "Come on, or I'm gonna leave ya." Racquel hesitated only a moment before following.

Elsewhere in the woods, BJ grabbed CJ by the arm. "The bicycles are this way."

"No way, bud. Your sense of direction sucks," CJ disagreed; but BJ dragged him along anyway.

They quickly moved toward a thicket where a colossal oak had fallen long ago. The night was draped in fog so thick it might have been poured like syrup. A gentle breeze wafted through, and the mists around the tree shifted as though the downed colossus was going to arise.

"We're lost!" CJ cried. "And I lost my glasses! Hey, I thought I saw something," he said as he pointed ahead.

"Right, son of Helen Keller. Ya don't even have — " BJ started, then he too saw the cloud of dark fog. It drifted toward them, gathering and assuming a human form. Its arms stretched forward, claws reaching for them.

"Let's get out of here!"

They ran, stumbling along, missing trees but tripping over rocks, stumps and fire ant mounds. All around the fog continued to grow thicker and thicker, entrapping the duo within its misty borders.

"Wish you hadn't dropped the flashlight," BJ gasped.

"Yeah, yeah, yeah," CJ retorted. "It won't do us any good anyway."

They came to a line of buried pickups that stretched to the left and right. The row was truncated at four trucks as though the rest of the world didn't exist.

"We're going in a circle!" BJ cursed.

"I told you!"

The mists suddenly billowed and roiled. Something slid out from between the upended trucks. The boys reversed directions, bolting into the woods with fear driving them on.

After a seemingly endless time of flight, the brothers finally paused near an old rusted pickup sitting alone in the woods. They bent over with hands on their knees, their breathing harsh and raspy. Cold sweat ran down their faces, and their shirts were soaked. They hoped they'd outraced whatever was pursuing them.

"I'm exhausted," CJ gasped. "I swear he's either Carl Lewis, or two things are chasing us!"

BJ simply nodded, unable to speak.

Something suddenly appeared in the fog, quickly moving in and out of the tall grasses. As it grew closer, for a moment, BJ thought he recognized the figure. "Dad?" he whispered incredulously.

A sharp snapping of a stick sounded from behind the brothers.

"COME ON!" CJ cried.

BJ looked for the familiar figure — one that couldn't have been there — and found nothing in the mists. He must have been imagining things — hoping his dad would come back. Heavy footfalls sounded behind them.

"COME ON!" CJ cried again, grabbing his brother this time. "I see him! He's here! Chandler's here!"

The Mochrie brothers fled at a dead run.

Shortly BJ and CJ arrived at a narrow creek bed where the fog was even heavier and more opaque. CJ paused, but BJ said, "Keep going this way."

"I can't. I'm beat!"

"You won't believe what I thought I saw . . . " BJ began. Then he thought he saw something out of the corner of his eye. "I ain't puttin' up with this anymore!" He shakily pulled out the .38. "Show yourself!" He wanted to say, "Dad!" But he didn't. He might be imagining things — his fears and wishes combining.

Both heard the quiet, mocking laughter.

BJ hesitated, unnerved and unsure of where to fire.

Gloating laughter came from several directions.

"That old guy is everywhere!" CJ whispered desperately. "Like a vampire!"

The brothers looked at each other and ran again. Running harder but moving slower, CJ was behind his brother when something suddenly grabbed him, jerking him off his feet.

"Got you!" Chandler cried.

CJ couldn't breathe! Couldn't scream!

"CJ?" BJ called as he skidded to a stop. Where was he? Damn the fog! "What's wrong, bro? BRO! COME ON! THAT VAMPIRE'S COMIN'!"

The white mists whirled and roiled. A cold breeze rippled past as something dark took shape within the fog. Eyes of red flame held BJ frozen for a moment, then he raised his .38 and fired again and again, the blast ripping the night and echoing along the lake.

The .38 finally clicked empty. BJ turned and ran. It wasn't his dad! He was just imagining things! Wishing Dad could save them!

CJ heard his brother flee. He jerked back a bit and managed to gasp, "BJ! Don't. . . ."

"You're going to pay!" Chandler shouted at CJ. The angry moviemaker leaned forward, his pale face twisted with anger and his eyes red and blazing hotly. "And how! You'll wish you'd never come here!"

Panic surged through CJ. He tried to escape, but he couldn't. The fog seemed to thicken, then darkness encroached from all sides.

Chapter Three

KEEPING SECRETS

"I made it," Russell gasped, rushing out of the pitch-black woods.

The fog was lighter along the road and in the empty fields across the street. Moonlight slipped between the clouds to shine upon the mists, causing everything to have an ambient glow and a soft, fuzzy texture.

Russell paused at the rent in the fence and wondered if the others had escaped. With that thought hounding him, Russell quickly crawled through the chain link barrier. He snagged his shirt, then tore free, heading for the abandoned house.

The dilapidated one-story structure had been long deserted, as the broken windows and gaping holes in the wind-ravaged roof attested. The chimney was crumbling. Battered bricks lay scattered on the ground. The walls were skeletal, stripped by weather and neglect; old paint flaked as if sunburned skin peeling away.

Russell laughed nervously, then noticed that Garrett's Trans Am was gone. Would he leave them? Of course, Russell thought. But Racquel . . .

Rushing forward, Russell hoped their bicycles were still there. Surely, out here in the middle of nowhere, nobody would steal them.

Humming to fill the silence and keep his courage up, Russell ran alongside the house, then paused to peer in through the west wall. Enough moonlight was shining through the holes and gaps to reveal that their bicycles were still safely stowed inside.

Russell started to move on, then paused. From out of the corner of his eye he thought he saw something move. Something uncanny about the moon-borne, crisscrossed shadows reminded him of Chandler's eerie house.

With his peripheral vision, Russell imagined he saw the ebony patches shift, but when he stared at them they remained motionless. The shadows seemed tense, as though waiting for him to glance away, so that they could come alive once more. From behind Russell, a low, guttural sound suddenly tore through the silence of the night. It spurred him forward.

As Russell rounded the corner of the house, he glanced over his shoulder. A form darted from one shadow to the next. Something was still chasing him!

Russell paused, glancing right, then left, feeling herded forward. He didn't want to go on, but the soft snarling came again, closer this time. Russell bolted into the house.

The shadows came alive, collapsing upon him. Long black tendrils wrapped around him, dragging him rapidly across the floor toward a window. Held immobile, he was forced to stare outside.

An unnaturally long-limbed man with a white face and dark hair slowly appeared from the shadow of a tree as if he were stepping out of a gate; then he walked through the fence.

His skin, if there was any, was pulled taut, giving Russell the impression of a walking skeleton dressed in a swirling black robe. With finality in his steps and cold flames dancing in his eyes, he slowly approached.

Russell struggled to break free of the black tendrils, but he could hardly breathe, let alone move. He opened his mouth to scream, but the blackness gagged him. Russell could only blink his eyes as the pale man stopped to stand before him. Then the skeletal figure reached out with his taloned hands, his claws clicking toward him.

Somehow Russell managed to scream.

"Russell? Russell? Wake up! You're having a nightmare!" someone said, cutting into his dream.

Russell awoke with a start, his eyes wide and his face ashen. "W . . . W . . . Wh . . . What!"

When he saw Racquel leaning over his bed, Russell relaxed; fright drained from him as quickly as the pale figure had disappeared and his bindings had melted away. The table lamp behind Racquel was on, driving away the darkness and illuminating the rock-and-roll posters — especially those of The Grateful Dead — that covered the walls. "Oh — hi, Racquel."

Racquel's expression changed, concern giving way to disappointment. "I swear, Russell! You need to grow up. Nightmares are for kids, you know," she said coldly, rubbing away her goose bumps. "I didn't know you could scream like that."

Russell didn't say anything about it, but his sister looked barely composed to him. "T . . . tonight s . . . scared me. T . . there was something about that ranch and the w . . . woods. And the dream — it seemed so real!"

"I'm not surprised you have nightmares," Racquel sat on the edge of his bed, flicking her dark locks over her shoulders. "You frighten so easily. How we can be brother and sister, even halfies, I simply don't understand. I mean, you still like playing with models." She waved about the room at the numerous shelves housing models of every kind, but mostly cars.

"I b . . . build them, I don't play with t . . . them. It'll make me a better driver, when I can drive. Hey, Racquel, I'm w . . . worried about Scooter. W . . . what if s . . . something happened to him?" Russell asked.

"He's a big boy now. Remember, he wanted to be a Graveyard Armadillo," she said, as if that explained everything.

"I think . . . we should t . . . tell Father, in case they need to search for him or something."

"Don't you dare!" she almost screeched, then whispered harshly, "You'll betray the Armadillos, you chicken! Don't worry. Everything will be all right. Garrett says so."

"Bu . . . "

There was a knock on Russell's door, then it was pushed open as their father entered. "Russell? Is everything all right?"

Sheriff Knight was a broad man, stout and muscular with massive shoulders. Long ago he'd been an All-American football star at Texas A & M University in College Station. His close-cropped mustache was wheat-colored, matching the hue of his thinning hair. When he wasn't working, his face was kind and expressive.

His concern was obvious as he asked, "Racquel, is Russell okay? He looks pale."

"Just a stupid nightmare," she said. "I heard him scream and came running. He just needs a teddy bear."

"Now, now," Sheriff Knight said. "Don't be so hard on your brother. He's younger than you." Their father came to the bed and sat next to his kids, putting an arm around them.

Racquel wriggled free. "Not that much younger."

Their father shrugged, then looked at Russell. "Want to talk about it?"

Yes, Russell thought, but if he did, Racquel would tell the

Graveyard Armadillos, and he'd get the cold shoulder. But he was really worried about Scooter. In fact, he wanted to phone him right now and make sure he was safe. That, though, would only get them all in trouble. Russell slumped, feeling it was a no-win situation — the story of his life. "Not now. No," he said.

"You don't sound sure. Why don't you try? You might feel better," his father asked patiently.

Russell glanced again at his sister, whose stare was burning holes into him, and then he began to talk about the dream. Russell didn't relate it to anything that happened tonight, so it sounded like another nightmare. When he was done, he felt badly about the entire evening.

"Sounds as if you should cut back on some of that morbid rock-and-roll," Sheriff Knight said.

"The D . . . Dead are not m . . . morbid. They're great musicians!"

"Or stop borrowing Scooter's comics. They're not the same as when I was a kid, especially that Spawn character."

"They're not scary," Russell said boldly, standing up for Scooter without stuttering. "And they're less violent than TV or movies."

"Oh," his father said, taken aback.

"They're for kids," Racquel said with disdain. "Comics! Grow up! Jeez! I'm glad I'm only your half-sister!"

"Racquel!" her father glared. After a moment of silence, he finished more gently, saying, "Y'all are still young enough to be kids."

"Oh, Father, you just don't understand, do you?" Racquel said.

"I think I understand just fine," he replied. "You both feel you're already grown up, but you don't have the experience or wisdom — the things that help you cope. But don't worry — that comes over time, and then you'll wish you could be kids all over again."

Racquel's distaste at the thought twisted her beauty.

"One of these days your . . . face is gonna get s . . . stuck that way. Then nobody, especially G . . . Garrett . . . will want to be seen with you," Russell told her.

Racquel angrily grabbed a pillow.

"Don't be childish," her father chided.

In a huff, Racquel stormed out of the room.

"You going to be okay, sport?" his father asked.

Russell nodded.

"Then I'll see you in the morning." His father hugged him, then kissed him on the forehead.

"I miss Mom."

"I miss her, too, son. She'll be back soon." His father kissed him again.

After his father left, Russell spent a long, long time staring at the ceiling. He felt badly about tonight. Even about what he'd said to his sister — although she had deserved it, especially that crack about being only half related.

Remembering what his mother said about not going to bed mad, Russell slipped out of bed and left his room. He knocked on Racquel's door, then entered when she said, "Who is it? Oh, it's you, again. What do you want?"

"To say I'm sorry."

"Oh." Racquel almost smiled. "That's okay. I wasn't really mad at you, but at Father. I hate being treated like a little girl. I'm not, you know. I'm sixteen. I can legally drive now."

Drive people crazy, Russell thought; but he didn't say anything and just stood quietly by the door.

"I also worried you'd mention tonight. I'd just die if Father grounded me, and I couldn't see Garrett!" Racquel threw herself across the bed. "He is so cool! All the girls would just die to be with him. But he wants me," she said. "I was afraid you'd ruin it by not keeping our secret."

Russell had concluded, especially after tonight, that he didn't care for Garrett. And he didn't like the effect Garrett had on his sister. But all Russell said was, "I can k . . . keep a secret. Remember the birthday p . . . party we threw for you? You never had any idea. I wasn't sure it was worth keeping our secret if Scooter was in trouble. If you were in t . . . trouble and I had to reveal a s . . . secret to help you, I would."

"Oh, Russell, when you get older, you'll understand about these things. Secrets are about sharing and trust," Racquel began. "That's very important between friends. Lots of friendships get destroyed because of a broken secret. Someone confides in you, you spill your guts, and bam, they don't trust you anymore. Do you understand?"

"Sort of. I still think there are mitigating circumstances."

"Where on earth did you hear that word?"

"Scooter. His grandpa is a judge."

Racquel sighed heavily. "With parents like ours, I'm surprised we have any fun. I'm surprised Father lets me go out with boys at all."

"About . . . Garrett," Russell began, but froze when he heard a tapping at Racquel's window. He went white as he said, "S . . . something's out there! It f . . . followed us home!"

"Oh, don't be silly," Racquel said as she walked to the window. "It's Garrett."

As she opened the window Garrett said, "Hey, Chaquita, want to go for a midnight ride? I got some beer!"

"Just a minute, let me get dressed," Racquel said, then looked at Russell. "Do you mind?"

"Uh, w . . . what if Father checks on you?"

"He won't, if you don't say anything. If you do, I'll make sure the girls at school never talk to you again. Ever. Now go."

Russell reluctantly left the room. He stood outside the door until he heard his sister giggle and the window shut.

When she was gone, he wandered back to his room, still thinking that something had gone wrong tonight. As he was lying in bed trying to sleep, he had a sinking feeling that things were going to get much worse before they got better!

Chapter Four

JUDGING

"**O**h, man," Scooter groaned as he slowly sat up. He felt immediately dizzy. His stomach lurched and thrashed as if ready to leap free. Scooter closed his eyes and slumped back to the ground.

Where was he? What time was it? He thought it was night time. Late night time. He listened carefully, trying to hear over the pounding in his head. Something nearby moved. A shuffling movement. "Who's there?"

Another shuffling — closer this time.

"I said, Who's there?"

More shuffling was followed by a chuff, then a wet tongue slurped across his face. "Hi, Flash!" Scooter sighed, relieved. "What happened?" Just hearing his own voice made his head hurt.

Flash whined.

"It's going to be all right, boy." Scooter patted his dog, then rubbed his eyes. Yes, it was dark. Far above, beyond the black silhouette of twisted tree branches, the stars were blurry globs that seemed to swirl about in a large circle.

His head throbbed, and his lower left leg hurt — a sharp burning pain. What had happened? Scooter noticed he was damp, and the air was hot and humid. He'd been sweating. "Did somebody hit me?" He touched his leg. The pain was narrow and across his upper shin. "Maybe I tripped over something."

Flash whined again.

Scooter touched his face. "Ouch." It felt swollen. He gingerly rubbed it, feeling pieces fall from his face into his hands. "Ahh! I'm falling apart!"

He rubbed his fingers together; they felt gritty. "Dirt! Just dirt and pebbles." He sighed, relieved.

Flash woofed.

Scooter smiled. Smiling hurt a lot.

Scooter crawled around, trying to stand and bumped into a wire. He felt along it, around it, and discovered several wires holding up an old tree. "I tripped over this?" he asked Flash.

The Lab woofed.

"I'm lucky I wasn't closer to the tree. It would have taken off my head."

A gentle breeze swept through the woods, rattling leaves. Branches shifted, rubbing against each other, sounding like brittle bones clacking against each other.

Flash suddenly whirled around.

"Easy, boy. Do you hear something?" Scooter whispered.

Flash growled deeply.

Scooter felt the hackles rise on the back of the Lab's neck. Fear raced through him. What would scare Flash?

Scooter suddenly remembered what had happened. He'd

been running! Running away from Chandler! Away from the vampire! Was the vampire still looking for him? Still here? Nearby? Scooter heard another shuffling noise.

"Let's get out of here!"

Scooter screamed and jumped to his feet. The woods spun around him; he could barely stand, his knees threatening to buckle. He swooned, stiffened his stance, then grabbed Flash's collar and held on tightly. "Get me out of here, Flash!"

A heavy thud sounded nearby.

Flash bolted, dragging Scooter with him. They raced through the woods, bounding through the high grass and around trees.

Scooter couldn't make out anything but flashes of dark and light — shadow and moonlight playing back and forth. He stumbled over roots, tufts of weeds and ant mounds. He clung tightly to Flash's collar as the Lab hauled him along, running faster. Light and dark streaked past. Then, they sprinted wildly for a seemingly endless time. Flash huffing. Scooter gasping, his legs pumping to keep up.

His arm ached from Flash pulling on it. My arm will be longer after this, he moaned, but he didn't let go of Flash's collar.

Something grabbed his shirt. "AH!" Scooter screamed. His shirt tore, letting him go as Flash dragged him through the rent in the chain link fence.

Suddenly they were standing before the dilapidated cabin where he'd left his bike. Shadows of skeletal trees were splayed across the abandoned structure, and the windows were slightly illuminated, as though a dim intelligence hid within the dark eyes of its facade.

Scooter was hesitant, but Flash yanked him through the front door. His bicycle was still there, standing in a pool of moonlight that cascaded through a hole in the roof. Fog drifted inside, making everything fuzzy but clearly marking swaths of light and dark. The shadows were thick, velvety and appeared opaque, almost as if solid.

"I don't like this," Scooter mumbled.

Flash woofed and led Scooter to the bicycle. He heard the snap of a breaking stick, and his heart jumped into his throat. Leaves crunched loudly. Fear surged through Scooter; and with that, he hopped onto his bicycle, whirled it around, and raced for the open door.

Despite being dizzy and sometimes seeing double, he shot cleanly through the doorway.

He bounded unsteadily across the dirt, putting down a foot to take a corner, then sprinted toward the road. Like a golden comet, Flash followed.

Leave the monster behind! Leave it behind! Scooter kept telling himself as he pedaled faster and faster, now standing on the pedals and running. He tried to outrace the bicycle's headlight, pushing himself until he could no longer stand. Then he finally sat down on the seat, his legs throbbing painfully.

Scooter looked around, not recognizing anything. "Flash, where are we, boy?"

Flash woofed quietly.

"Can you take me home?" Scooter asked. He touched his forehead. His head was pounding louder than a drum in a marching band.

Flash darted forward, looked back, then when he was sure Scooter was coming, the Lab trotted along the road. Scooter followed, his light barely clipping Flash's tail as his companion led him homeward.

After what seemed like endless time, where minutes stretched into hours, and Scooter never thought they'd make it, they arrived at the gate to Siete Hombres Estates. He wasn't sure what route they'd taken; he was just glad to be home.

Scooter stared dumbly at the gates. They were locked. What was the combination? Something about Columbus. Scooter wanted to curse, but even a single word made his head hurt. He played with the lock, trying different combinations.

He couldn't think straight, and his fingers didn't always follow orders. Finally, Scooter gave up.

He locked his bicycle to the fence, then climbed the gates, the gates shifting and rattling as he struggled over them. Sensing he was going to get sick or fall backwards, Scooter launched himself forward. He landed awkwardly, sprawling on his chest.

Flash woofed and began licking him.

"Lucky dog," Scooter moaned. "You can squeeze between the gates."

After a brief rest, Scooter climbed to his feet and staggered down the road, past a trio of dark houses on each side of the road. Beyond them, the moonlight wavered and glittered off the surface of Lake Tawakoni. The reflections were muted by fog, and he couldn't see much beyond the shore. When he reached the trees lining the gravel road to the end of the peninsula, the fog grew much thicker. He couldn't see even ten feet — not that he could really see anything very well. His vision was unsteady. As though a restless crowd, the trees kept shifting around on him.

Scooter didn't remember reaching the house, but he was there, digging through his pockets for a key. He couldn't find it or the spare hidden — wherever it was hidden.

"It never ends," Scooter moaned, putting his head in his hands.

After a while, he said, "Stay here, Flash. Time to use the secret entrance." He stumbled to the side of the house. Without a second thought, he began climbing the latticework.

He must have blacked out during the climb, because he lost time and found himself clinging unsteadily to the wooden slats with the misty world spinning below. He swore the lattice was shifting under his hands. The wood groaned and squeaked with every movement.

Many times each summer he'd traveled this route, scaling the ivy-covered fencing and crawling across the porch roof to sneak in through the bedroom window. Tonight it seemed harder than ever. He wished he hadn't lost his house key.

Scooter misjudged his next hold, and his fingers slipped off a slat. Unbalanced, Scooter's feet slipped free, leaving him hanging by one hand. The latticework protested under his weight, threatening to give way.

Below, Flash whined.

Scooter foolishly glanced down to find the ground obscured by fog.

The white fencing weaved and writhed, disappearing long before it reached the ground. It wasn't much more than ten feet down, but it felt much farther, almost as if he were climbing in the clouds.

A small, wood-wrenching squeak reminded Scooter that he was in danger. He grabbed hold with both hands and quickly clambered back onto the lattice.

He wasn't worried about getting hurt, but the noise he'd make falling or tearing down the lattice would give him away. He didn't want to face his grandfather after pulling down part of the house. Although Judge Grandpa was a kind man, he didn't tolerate having his rules broken. By sneaking inside, Scooter was violating several right now.

He continued climbing. Ahead, the latticework seemed to lean and twist. The stars beyond the roof whirled, transformed into a dark kaleidoscope. "Come on, Johnny boy, you can make it," Scooter encouraged himself. Reach, grasp, pull and step. Hand over hand. I can do this. Step following reach. Go for the top. Don't stop!

Something suddenly struck Scooter's head, and he saw a flurry of falling stars. He slowly realized he'd climbed past the porch shingles and bumped into the roof overhang. The fog in his head was as dense as the mists far below him.

Scooter carefully worked his way down and stepped on the porch roof. He dropped onto his stomach and hugged the shingles, thankful that he'd finally made it. It was only a few more feet to his bedroom window, but it seemed miles away.

"Time to rest." Scooter rolled onto his back and stared up at the sky. Why was sneaking around always so difficult for him? It seemed as though BJ, CJ, Jo, and Garrett had no trouble being devious.

Scooter suddenly wondered how the others were doing. Had they left him alone to face whatever it was that had scared him witless?

And how were Russell and Kristie? Had they been caught? And did it serve them right? Scooter felt terrible about the situation, enraging a total stranger for no reason other than a stupid prank. And worse, it was a stranger he'd wanted to meet to ask about writing. How stupid could he be? He kept seeing Chandler's pale, monstrously contorted face. One of the few things he remembered clearly.

Could Garrett have been right? Was Chandler a vampire? He had to be addled even to considered it.

Still waiting for the spinning to stop, Scooter breathed deeply and stared out over the lake. He was above the fog and could see the quarter moon shine between the clouds and onto the mist-blanketed waters. The roof of his grandparents' shore-line gazebo stuck up as though a mushroom from the fog. The peninsula appeared to exist in some ghostly shadowland where all shapes were hazy and ill-defined.

After a time, Scooter felt a little better. He crawled to the window and, trying to be quiet, lifted it open. Scooter wriggled inside and somehow managed not to flop onto the floor. But he suddenly had a sickening feeling of dread. He wasn't alone in the darkness!

Something was on his bed! And it was moving! IT — THE VAMPIRE — HAD BEATEN HIM HERE! Scooter froze, his heart jamming into his throat. He tried to scream and failed, managing only a squeak. His eyes were wide open, so the sudden brilliance blinded him.

"Well, hello there," drawled the old man sitting on Scooter's bed.

Scooter jumped a foot and clutched at his eyes. "AHHHHhhh!" he finally managed to scream. He was about to scream again when he recognized the voice. "Grandpa?"

"Who else in tarnation would it be, the Bogeyman?"

"Oh . . . " Scooter breathed a sigh of relief. He squinted through his fingers, finally convinced it really was his grandfather, even if there were two of them.

Judge Grandpa was a white-bearded man who could look both kindly and stern within the same moment. He was dressed in a red pajamas top, black warm-up pants, and dark blue slippers. He held his pipe near his mouth and wore a speculative but slightly amused expression, as though Scooter's fright had lightened his somber mood.

Because of his twinkling blue eyes and large ruddy nose, Scooter was briefly reminded of Santa Claus, then his grandfather's expression became stern.

"Mister Jonathan Melvin Keyshawn, where have you been?"

"Uh." Scooter knew he was in trouble by his grandfather's tone of voice and the use of his full name. His eyes had finally adjusted to the light so he lowered his hands.

"Mercy, Jonathan! Are you all right?" Judge Grandpa was aghast at the lacerations and bruises along Scooter's swelling nose and left cheek. There was only a little blood, but already the skin around his left eye was turning purple. "You appear to have been the loser in some kind of physical contest." His grandfather moved closer to examine Scooter. "SIT."

Scooter slumped into the chair by his desk. Above it were bookshelves filled with comic books and several track trophies. His walls were lined with posters of Spawn, Wildcats and several Marvel superheroes — Spiderman, Silver Surfer, The Uncanny X-Men and more. Some he'd purchased, and some he'd drawn in pen and ink, using watercolor paints for coloring.

"What happened?" His grandfather's touch was light and shaky. "Is this dirt?"

"I tripped over a tree wire and landed on my face," Scooter

moaned. "I'm glad I was wearing jeans." He rubbed his leg, then put his face in his hands. "I wish I'd stayed home."

"I'll get you something for the pain and an ice pack," Judge Grandpa said. "I'll be back in a minute, and then you'll answer some questions, young man."

"Aw, Grandpa . . . "

"Don't aw Grandpa me. I'm not the one coming home late, sneaking in through a second-floor window like a thief in the night and looking like I've been in a scrap."

"Yes, sir," Scooter said meekly. His grandfather left the room.

Minutes later Grandpa returned with an ice bag, pills and a glass of water. Flash followed closely, nearly on his heels. When the Lab saw Scooter, Flash moved to his master's side, nuzzling his legs and licking his hand. Scooter patted Flash, then washed the pills down and put the cold pack against his face.

"Okay, young man. Where have you been?"

"Well, I wa . . . " Scooter began to fib, but one look at Judge Grandpa's expression — his probing gaze — made Scooter change his mind.

Flash whined.

Scooter glanced at his companion, who displayed puppy-dog eyes as if pleading for Scooter to be honest. Scooter sighed, his shoulders slumping as though his balloon had been punctured. Flash laid his head on Scooter's knee to lend support and whimpered.

With a hangdog expression, Scooter said, "I've been to Marcus Chandler's ranch."

"The famous actor?" his grandfather asked.

"I thought he was a director and writer."

"That's true, but he was originally an actor. You didn't know that?"

"Uh-uh."

"A 'no sir' would do just fine. Yes, in the 1950s and 1960s he was an actor before he started directing. Then he directed and acted, and finally took up writing. Is this who we're talking about?"

"Yes, sir."

"I see. Do you know it's after midnight?"

Startled, Scooter shook his head. He wished he hadn't moved; the throbbing increased.

"And what were you doing at the Chandler Pickup Ranch? A social visit?" Judge Keyshawn asked. "I know you've wanted to visit him to ask him about writing."

Scooter was again amazed by his grandfather's perceptiveness.

"Was that it?" his grandfather demanded.

Scooter had been given a way out, but he knew Judge Grandpa could spot a lie. So in one long breath, Scooter told his grandfather what happened. Flash joined in, making a variety of noises as if adding to the tale.

The Judge told Scooter to slow down and go over his story a second time, then said, "Quite a group y'all had there. And if I know Russell's father, Sheriff Knight will provide the same appropriate instruction as I shall soon attempt. Now tell me about your new-found friends."

Scooter told the truth, but he didn't tell everything — nothing about it being an initiation, BJ's gun, the knives, or the drinking.

"I see," Judge Keyshawn said thoughtfully. "I wonder if they're really the type of friends you need if they're going to get you into such trouble. Now listen to me, Jonathan. I don't know about this Garrett fella, but I don't like what I hear. This I do know: BJ and CJ Mochrie have reputations as mischief-makers and problem teenagers."

Flash woofed quietly in agreement.

Judge Grandpa nodded, saying, "Flash agrees with me. A resounding confirmation if I ever heard one. You should listen to him."

Flash barked, then smiled broadly, his grin pushing back

his ears.

"I swear," said Grandpa, "if I believed in reincarnation, I'd think your deceased Aunt June might have come back as Flash."

The Lab appeared wounded and slumped to the floor in disgust.

"Sorry, boy. It's all those facial expressions. A different one for every occasion."

Judge Grandpa seemed confused for a few moments, as though he'd forgotten what he was talking about.

Scooter could only hope.

"You crafty dog, you. Trying to sidetrack me, are you?" Judge Grandpa finally asked.

Only Flash's eyebrows moved.

"You know, Jonathan, you have yourself a real friend right here."

Flash immediately stood proud as though on display at a dog show.

"As I was saying, Jo comes from a bad lot. Most of the Gunns have been in jail at one time or another." As if that were enough for Scooter to digest for a moment, Judge Keyshawn sat back and lit his pipe.

Scooter now knew that this was going to be a long talk. Whenever a pipe was lit, a chamber discussion, as his grandfather called it, was in session. It was time for further education on being a human being — a civilized and just person. Scooter glanced at Flash and mouthed the word, "Brown-noser." Flash huffed and appeared insulted, rolled his eyes, wrinkled his nose, and then held his head high.

"Scooter, who are your best friends?"

"Russell. Flash. You and Dad, I guess," Scooter replied.

"No one else your own age?" Judge Grandpa asked.

Scooter shook his head.

"Scooter, even though you're almost fifteen and beginning to think you know everything, you're still new at friendships." He puffed on his pipe. "Just last year you complained no one except Russell would have anything to do with you because you were short, red-haired and too brainy. Kids were mad at you because you wouldn't help them cheat."

"But I've grown," Scooter protested.

"Yes. But just because you've grown a foot in a year doesn't mean you have to grow stupid too, does it?" Judge Grandpa asked.

Scooter shook his head.

"At your age, you're built a lot like your father, tall and skinny with lots of elbows and knees, except he wasn't red-haired or freckled. That's from your mom. Don't worry, though, you'll eventually fill out like me." He patted his bulging stomach. "But before you do, there's a lot to learn in life, both about people and friendships." He puffed on his pipe, then blew a smoke ring. "Jonathan, sometimes friendships aren't what they seem. Just as people aren't always what they seem. Use good judgment and patience when choosing your friends. Look for friends who remind you of Flash here."

The Labrador woofed, then smiled, panting softly.

"Dad always said you can choose your friends but not your relatives," Scooter said. "And that's what makes friends special."

"Very true," His grandfather nodded solemnly. "You know, I think I had some success in raising your father; and I'm going to assist him in doing the same with you, young man. Trust and friendship should be given with care and earned by being good to each other. Sometimes people will want things out of friendships besides trust and companionship, possibly questionable favors, fun at your expense or something that would get you in trouble — like tonight."

"Yes, sir."

"I know you're a fine, young man. So don't let yourself be led about by the nose like you're a simpleton. You're not. Be alert and be smart. I know you have good judgment, at least most of the time. Don't let peer pressure or your hormones rule your actions. I believe there are some bad apples in this 'gang' you were with tonight. You may believe it, too. I can hear the regret in your voice about what you've done. Do you feel good about this — prank?"

Scooter shook his head, which reminded him that he was a slow learner. His head was pounding again.

"You enjoyed being part of the group, didn't you?" Judge Grandpa asked.

"Yes."

"I can understand that. It's lonely being a young boy in Texas who doesn't play football, but that doesn't mean I condone what you did. Why do you think Garrett Brashear chose to bother this Chandler fella?"

"I don't know. Because he's weird looking?"

"You mean because he's black?"

"No, he's pale, almost colorless, and has red eyes."

"That's right; he's an albino. So he looks different? Or acts different? Isn't that what you complain about? Girls don't like you because you're not handsome enough. The guys tease you because you're not athletic enough? And the 'in' kids ignore you because you don't fit neatly into their groups?"

"Dumb, I know. I wasn't thinking. I'm sorry."

"In the future, Jonathan, think: Might I be ashamed of this later? Would I like this reported on television for all to see?'"

"I will. Thanks, Grandpa." Scooter noticed he didn't get a cold stare for moving away from "sir" and believed that everything would be all right — if his head would only stop pounding.

"So what does Kristie look like?"

Scooter was surprised by his grandfather's question.

"You must think she's cute."

Flash barked, then panted loudly.

"How did you know?" Scooter asked, dumbfounded.

"You talked about everybody else but avoided talking about her."

"Oh," Scooter replied. His grandfather was amazing. He just seemed to know things as if he read people's minds.

His grandfather stood and said, "I believe it's well past our bedtimes."

Flash immediately found a spot and got comfortable.

"Thanks for waiting up to see if I was okay," Scooter told him. "It was a bogus evening."

"What's bogus?" his grandfather asked. Scooter explained. His grandfather shook his head. "Youth. Got to invent new ways of saying the same old thing just to be different. But you're welcome." He walked toward the door, then paused in mid stride as though making a judicial decision. "Jonathan, until further notice, you're grounded."

Scooter groaned.

"Except for church. And I need two cords of wood split when you're feeling better."

Scooter groaned again.

"It's good exercise and gives you time to mull things over." Judge Grandpa stepped out, paused just before he closed the door and said, "You know, I might be willing to compromise, reach a settlement with you."

Scooter's face brightened.

"If you'll personally apologize to Mr. Chandler, face to face, I'll make the grounding for just this weekend; and you only have to split one cord of wood."

Scooter's expression was crestfallen. "But, Grandpa, you don't understand. It's a really strange place. There was something wrong there. Ah — I was scared. I've never been so scared in my life."

"You do have such an active imagination. Must be all those comic books. Ah, well, you can sleep on it, Jonathan, and let me know in the morning." The Judge turned off the light and closed the door behind him.

Flash immediately jumped into Scooter's lap. He held the Lab, just sitting there and wondering if he could return to the ranch after what happened tonight.

Scooter groaned. He had to; otherwise, the summer was history — a total waste!

"Flash, would you go back there with me?" Scooter asked.

The Lab whined and tucked his head under both paws.

"Yeah, I don't want to go back there either. But what else can I do?"

Flash was silent.

Scooter sighed heavily, his mind awhirl. Thinking about the eerie place and facing the pale man with red eyes kept him awake for a long, long time.

Chapter Five

TRUE BUDS

On his way to visit Scooter, Russell climbed the ivy-over-grown fence around Siete Hombre Estates, then dropped onto the grass. Worry had gnawed at Russell all night, and it was worse this morning when nobody answered the phone at the Keyshawn place. Had something terrible happened to Scooter? Russell had to find out! He felt partly at fault, encouraging his best friend to join the Graveyard Armadillos.

Russell quickly walked past the three lakefront homes, their gardens in full bloom, roses and gardenias tiered along the porches and decks. All the houses' windows were shuttered, and the lawns had grown tall, ready to be mowed for the first time this summer. These homes, including the three on the channel side of the peninsula, were summer homes and empty through the winter and most of the fall and spring. Each house had a boat winched high under a covered dock. Two docks were double-decked with flat, carpeted roofs. The neighbors didn't care if he and Scooter fished or stargazed from them, as long as they didn't do any damage or leave any trash.

Russell paused to stare at the lake. The green waters were fairly calm; the waves gentle and rolling. It was still early in the day and almost that time of year when the sweltering heat stifled any breeze, smoothing the water and making it perfect for canoeing.

Russell absolutely loved summer, a time for friends and freedom. He glanced upward, letting the sun bake his face.

Despite the brilliance of the day, Russell still felt uneasy, as if the cool shadows of last night weren't gone but lurking nearby. Last night's nightmare and the news he'd heard this morning only reinforced those feelings. Even the bright sunshine and the smell of mimosas in bloom didn't dispel the dread that had dogged him while he'd ridden from Gunstock to Siete Hombres.

As Russell neared the point of the peninsula where the Keyshawns lived, he heard the sound of wood being chopped. Russell passed a low-lying, partly collapsed and waterlogged dock; the thumps and splashes of surprised turtles clambering back into the water filled the air. Through the tall grass, Russell saw the stragglers scuttle off the edge of the dock and plummet into the channel. Russell laughed; he absolutely loved being near the water.

When the three-story house of pale yellow and orange brick came into sight, Russell heard music mingling with the chopping of wood. Scooter was probably at work.

Russell approached the open garage door. A weed eater and grass-stained lawn mower sat on the concrete walkway next to a coiled hose and a mess of extension cords that might take hours to unknot.

There weren't any cars around, so Russell figured Scooter was alone. Then Russell heard Flash bark and realized Scooter was never alone.

Russell peered through the garage. With the far door also open, Russell could see Scooter splitting wood. He was all right! Russell wanted to whoop and holler with joy. His bad dream was just a nightmare, not a vision after all!

Thrilled, Russell ran around the back, ready to hug his friend, then he suddenly slowed. He had an idea! He would surprise Scooter! After last night, his friend would probably jump a foot!

Russell snuck through the trees and the tall, coarse grass. With the radio on, Scooter would never hear him coming but Flash might. Oh, well! Nothing ventured, nothing gained.

Scooter wiped his brow and rested on the maul handle, letting the soft breeze cool him. He'd pulled off his shirt to keep from overheating, but he was still thoroughly soaked with sweat.

The hollow-rotted oak he was working on had snapped, the upper half having fallen during a spring windstorm. His father and grandfather had cut it apart with a chainsaw, often using a ladder to reach the branches of the fallen colossus. They wouldn't let him use the chainsaw, but they were glad to let him use the maul.

Scooter sighed; it was too nice a day for chopping wood, mowing the lawn, and swinging the Weedeater. But they didn't call it punishment because it was fun.

Flash whined, then woofed.

Scooter looked at him and shrugged.

He hadn't told Judge Grandpa that he would apologize to Mr. Chandler. But what else could he do? Twiddle his thumbs as summer wasted away? He knew apologizing was the right thing to do. He wanted to meet the infamous director, but just thinking about the Pickup Ranch still made Scooter shiver. He shook himself, then knelt and prepared another log for splitting.

Flash barked, and Scooter said, "I know. I want to go play too, but we can't now. Well, at least I can't. You can go, though." Flash chuffed sullenly and sat.

Scooter easily lofted the maul behind his head, then let the weight of the tool do most of the work, cleanly splitting the round. Now he had to split the halves in half so they would fit in the wood-burning stove. Scooter sighed. Then he had to cut kindling. He might split a log sixteen ways or more before he was through with it.

Scooter found a rhythm and lost himself in the music. Set, heft, easy swing and split. Repeat. The music helped him keep pace. He suddenly felt alone no longer. Blurred and murky snatches of last night gripped Scooter; and he whirled, the maul raised and poised to swing.

Flash barked excitedly with the tone and stance of "See, I told you so."

"H . . . H . . . Hey, S . . . Sc . . . Scoot, it's just me. R . . . Russell," Russell stuttered as he backed away, his eyes wide.

The combination of fright and aggressiveness slowly drained from Scooter's face, leaving him flushed. He let out a long breath. "I'm sorry, Russell. You scared the bejeeses out of me."

"T. . .That's what I wanted to do."

"WHAT ARE YOU DOING HERE, YOU DESERTER?" Scooter blurted. "And some watchdog you are!" he told Flash.

The Labrador wrinkled his nose, then plopped down on the ground, grumbling quietly. Flash stared skyward as if wondering how people could be so dense.

"I didn't know you w . . . were an ax . . . axe murderer!" Russell said.

Scooter looked at the maul, then laughed.

"Still friends?" Russell asked, stepping forward with his hand outstretched.

"Of course," Scooter said, and they shook hands. "It'll take a lot more than you being a total chicken to break up our friendship."

"T . . . thanks, I think."

Flash barked, jumping on Scooter and Russell.

"H . . . hey, boy. G . . . glad to see you, too. And I . . . I'm g . . . glad you're all right, Scooter. I w . . . was w . . . worried. I'm sorry about last night. I s . . . see you've been busy." Russell started stacking firewood.

"I'm in trouble," Scooter told him and sat on the stump, ignoring the parade of carpenter ants. "I'm grounded."

"H . . .hey, what h . . . happened to your face?"

Scooter cleared his throat. His grandmother had laughed at first, and now he was embarrassed to talk about it. "I tripped over something," he mumbled, "and knocked myself out."

"W . . . what?"

"I was looking back for you and tripped over one of those stupid wires they use to keep trees from falling over!!"

Obviously, Russell was trying not to laugh. "S . . . So that's w . . . what happened to you."

"Yeah. Thanks a lot for NOT checking on me. I could still be lying out there, unconscious or worse," Scooter told him.

"I'm r . . . really, really sorry. I was really scared."

Scooter thought for a moment, then said, "That's okay. I was scared, too. Let's not do it again. Okay?"

"W . . . want to go for a canoe ride? T . . . talk ab . . . about it? I brought some bottle rockets." Russell pulled them from his pants, holding out the plastic-wrapped packet of sticks.

"I can't. I have lots of things to do," Scooter replied glumly.

"I'll help c . . . chop wood," Russell volunteered.

Scooter looked stunned.

"When will your grandparents be back?"

"They went shopping in Emory. Grandpa said he'd be back soon, but he left me plenty to do." Scooter waved at the entire peninsula. "But Grandma said to fix my own lunch. Why?"

"Together we g . . . got plenty of time. I'll help, but first, let's g . . . go canoeing before the winds come, okay?"

"I don't think we'll have any wind today, it's too hot." Scooter's smile slowly grew. "But okay, no more than an hour." He set down the maul and grabbed his shirt. "Let's go."

Flash jumped all about, barking and spinning around as though chasing his tail.

The threesome walked the short path through the woods to the dock. Next to it was a fiberglass canoe painted beige and brown in a camouflage pattern. They flipped it over and set one end in the water.

"Life j . . . jackets?" Russell asked.

"Under the seats." Scooter handed him an oar. He held the canoe steady as Russell walked to the front and sat. Flash gently climbed in, moved to the center, then lay down. Under the dock, Scooter found their blackened rocket-launching bottle and threw it in the canoe. He pushed off, then hopped into the craft. "Which way?" Scooter asked.

Russell looked left and up the channel. Deserted like this, the channel was a neat place to explore. Docks lined both sides, and some were very elaborate, built for partying and picnicking. Russell enjoyed weaving in and about and sometimes paddling under them. But today he wanted to talk about last night, and what he'd heard this morning. "Open w . . . water." Besides, in the middle of the lake he didn't have to worry about his aim or wild bottle rockets.

"Sounds good." Scooter began paddling, and they moved away from the dock and around the peninsula's point. Across the way was an open field where a house had burned down last year. A charred foundation and blackened trees still remained, a reminder of the devastating power of fire.

"Stay right," Russell suggested. "They've let out some

water, and there are sandbars now."

"Okay. Stroke."

The canoe smoothly cleaved the water as the boys headed toward the middle of the lake. Their strokes were strong and well timed, carrying them quietly toward the center of the lake. Both were silent, enjoying the wonder of being on the lake. Except for some whorls from a gentle but constant breeze, the olive-green waters were still calm. Tawakoni was a good-sized lake, with two major areas to the north and west.

"Does your face hurt?" Russell asked, no longer stuttering. Something about being on the water calmed him, allowing him to speak clearly.

"Yes. And don't say it has always hurt you just by looking at it."

"I hadn't thought of that," Russell laughed, "but it's true!" Both laughed. "What'd you do after you woke up?"

They kept paddling as Scooter responded, telling his tale.

"You told him everything?" Russell asked.

"Not everything. Not about drinking, the gun, the knives, or that it was an initiation."

"And you're really going back?" Russell said without stammering. "Going back to see that weird guy?"

"Yeah. Apologizing is probably the right thing to do. I feel awful about last night."

"Me, too. We were sorta stupid, weren't we?"

"You want to go with me?" Scooter asked.

"Heck, no!" Russell exclaimed. "That place totally froze me. That's why I ran when I heard something, probably you, falling. I thought somebody else was joining the chase. The gunshots almost made me pee in — "

"Gunshots?"

"That's right! You didn't hear 'em?"

"Really? Shooting!" Scooter asked.

Russell nodded.

"Do you think it was BJ?"

"I don't know. I just ran," Russell said.

Flash looked up and stared at him, accusing him of desertion.

"Hey, let it rest, will ya?"

Flash snorted.

"But who else could've been shooting? And why? Geez, I slept through everything cool," Scooter said dejectedly. "How do I miss out on everything?"

"It's a gift you have." Russell laughed.

"Or a curse," Scooter said.

" I wonder how the others are doing? Hope they're okay."

"They'll be mad if they find out you ratted on `em, especially Garrett and BJ."

"I didn't tell your father."

"No, but your grandfather might. Maybe that's why he went into town — to tell . . . " Russell's eyes widened as his face went white, " . . . to tell my dad!"

"Damn! I'm sorry," Scooter said, lightly touching his bruises. "I think I scrambled my brains last night." They canoed in silence for a while.

"It's okay, Scooter. I feel lousy about not telling my dad, but Racquel wanted me to keep her secret. She was afraid Dad would keep her from seeing Garrett," Russell said glumly.

"That would be a good thing," Scooter said.

Russell nodded.

"Judge Grandpa said keeping secrets almost always gets you in trouble. Secrets are usually things that might hurt people, but hiding the truth makes it worse."

"Lots of people keep secrets," Russell shot back.

"Grandpa says there is a difference between keeping someone's confidence and keeping a secret."

"Oh. Let's float," Russell suggested. He spun around and leaned back, facing Scooter. "Ahhh, what a great day."

"It washes all cares away," Scooter laughed. Well, almost, he thought. He still had to go back to the Pickup Ranch. They coasted along, enjoying the sensation and gentle slap of the water against the canoe. "I love the sun. I think I'm solar charged."

"Me too. I'm thirsty. We should have remembered to bring something to drink."

"Schnapps?" Scooter asked.

Russell's expression was one of distaste. "My first drink of liquor was definitely my last."

"You like beer?" Scooter asked.

Russell shrugged but couldn't help smiling as Flash began to gag.

"You didn't even tell me about drinking beer. What's it like?"

"Awful. Smells like sweaty garbage."

The look on Russell's face made Scooter laugh. "Why did you try it?" Scooter asked.

"To get into the Armadillos — just like you did last night."

"I should probably stay away from them," Scooter said "At least for a while, anyway. Maybe they'll forget everything by summer's end. I hope Jo doesn't get teed off at me. Her brothers are huge." Scooter sighed heavily. "I guess I wasn't supposed to be a Graveyard Armadillo. But then, you know, that's okay. The more I've gotten to know Garrett, the less I like him."

"I wish Racquel felt that way," Russell said. "I'm worried about her. She's crazy about him. He's to die for, Racquel says. She'd do anything for him because he's popular and cool. That's all that matters. Either she can't see or doesn't care that he's selfish with an ego the size of this lake."

"Yeah, thinks he can get away with anything `cause he's the principal's son," Scooter said, then asked, "Think Kristie might like me?"

"Not if she's like my sister," Russell responded.

Flash barked once abruptly, a stern expression on his face. Scooter didn't think she was either. Or at least he hoped not. "Well, good riddance to the Armadillos. We'll have fun without them! I'm sure we can go canoeing and bicycling as long as I promise Grandpa I won't hang around Garrett, Jo, or the Mochrie brothers."

"That'd be cool. Friends forever! Hey, did you have any bad dreams last night?"

"Nope. I was out like a light. Slept like a rock," Scooter told him. "Did you?"

"I did, but I don't remember much. Some kind of creature was chasing me through the woods. I have a bad feeling about things."

"Things?" Scooter asked.

"The future. Hey, you think I'm precognitive?"

"What's that? Something psychic?" Scooter grinned.

Russell nodded.

"Heck, no!" Russell was the last person in the world, Scooter figured, that might be able to see into the future.

Then he added, "Did you feel watched last night?"

"Come to think of it, yeah, a little," Russell admitted. "You?"

"Yeah."

"Are you sure you really want to go back to the Pickup Ranch? I'll help you chop as much wood as you want to keep from going back there. I mean the fog and the way the house was glowing." He shivered. "And that guy's face — "

"It'll be okay," Scooter told him. "Judge Grandpa's driving me." Scooter felt a strong gust of wind and watched the water ripple. He looked northward for signs of swelling or waves. Lake weather was mercurial.

"Uh, Scooter, that's not all that's bothering me about that place. Did you hear the news?" Russell asked, suddenly remembering what he'd come to tell Scooter.

Scooter shook his head.

"They found Debbie Harrison dead at the dam."

"Debbie? Dead?" Scooter couldn't believe it. Though not well, he'd known her for years at school. Debbie was quiet and pretty.

Russell nodded. "Yes. She's dead."

"Hasn't she been missing?"

"Yes. For a while, they found her near where Missy Watkins was found last week."

Both boys were quiet, thinking about tomorrow's funeral for the Watkins' girl. Neither of them had known anyone who'd died before Missy, but now they knew two. That was two too many.

"Had Debbie been shot?" Scooter asked, thinking about the proximity of the dam to the ranch and how the sound of gunshots could travel.

"No. They don't know how she died or exactly when, according to my dad, but they think it was last night. And two other kids, Tony and Terri, the Newbaker twins, are missing. Have been for a couple of days."

"Now I'm really scared," Scooter admitted.

"My dad thinks there might be a serial killer in the area. They may call in the FBI. Hey, do you think it might be a vampire?"

"No," Scooter replied without conviction.

Thinking about the fog, the darkness, the strange noises and cold breezes, Russell reached inside the pocket of his cutoffs. "I brought you something."

Scooter watched with surprise as Russell pulled out a crucifix hanging on a silver chain. Russell held it out toward Scooter. "Just in case Garrett's right."

Scooter was speechless.

"I feel better wearing this," Russell replied, showing Scooter his own cross. "And I'd feel better if you would, too. Okay?"

Scooter took the cross and slipped it over his head. "Thanks."

Against his bare sweaty chest the cross glinted in the sunlight. He thought it was sort of silly; but obviously Russell was really frightened, so Scooter humored him. Still, there was a hint of something that nagged him.

"Hey, want to shoot off some rockets?" Russell asked, his mood suddenly changing.

Scooter smiled, feeling more comfortable with this Russell. "Do bees like honey?"

"Okay, dumb question." Russell unwrapped the packet and grabbed the bottle. Flash whined, then hunkered down, crawling as far away from Russell as possible. "Very funny. I'm not that bad a shot." Flash whined again, then began trembling.

They lit a rocket and tried to lose themselves in having fun, trying to forget about the deaths and the funeral they'd be attending tomorrow.

Chapter Six

GRIM GATHERING

"**H**ey, I gotta go. Mom's heading to the funeral for Missy," Russell told Scooter.

For the solemn occasion, the boys dressed in their best Sunday suit and tie. They stood in front of the church, along with most of the congregation, grimly waiting for the service to begin. The sun was bright. The day was beautiful, an odd contrast to the somber mood of the mourners.

"I'm gonna pray for Missy to rest in peace and for these nightmares to go away," Russell said.

"I thought you thought they were visions?" Scooter asked.

"I h . . . hope not. I'll s . . . see you later."

"Okay." Making a face, Scooter fingered his collar. Dress

nooses, which most people called ties, made it hard to breathe. Usually church was the only time he had to wear one, but this was a special occasion, a time to show respect and reverence, Judge Grandpa told him.

No one close to Scooter had ever died, and he wasn't quite sure how to feel. He'd known Debbie, but they weren't friends. That didn't make it any less tragic, just a bit more distant — distant for him anyway. He'd never really thought about dying before. Where did the spirit go when the body died?

Scooter glanced around. Distraught faces were worn by restless people dressed in black and dark clothing. Some wept. Some spoke quietly and tried to console each other — to make sense of things. Scooter was amazed at the size of the crowd and moved by the turnout. Did Missy have that many friends? Touch that many lives?

Scooter recognized most of the kids but didn't see the Mochries or the Gunns, which didn't surprise him. Principal and Mrs. Brashear were attending without Garrett.

Scooter drifted closer to a crowd of adults; and as he did, he heard, "Yeah, it's terrible. They found little Debbie Harrison dead along the lakeshore, north of the dam, not far from where Missy was found. They're to perform an autopsy Monday. Odd how two young ones died so close together. That's three in the last month. One was from south of Emory."

Scooter shivered. Could this somehow be tied to Friday night? If Chandler was angry with them, could he be taking it out on other kids? Were the girls' deaths the fault of the Grave-yard Armadillos? Was Chandler a murderer? Or a vampire? Was Garrett right? First old Mr. and Mrs. Chandler, and now kids? Prey on the elderly and the weak? Scooter's imagination shifted into overdrive.

"Hey, Scooter," a feminine voice drawled. Scooter turned around. To his surprise, Kristie Candel walked toward him. Scooter's morbid thoughts shifted quickly, uplifted by the sight of the minister's daughter.

"Hi, Kristie!"

Kristie's smile was slight, and she looked lovely, dressed in flats and a dark bluebonnet print dress. Her auburn hair was unbound, falling over her left shoulder and glinting as if it were a coppery waterfall. Scooter thought she was the perfect contrast — a balance — to the events of the day.

"Are you okay? You look like you've seen a ghost." Her drawl was silky smooth.

"Oh. I was thinking about Missy and Debbie. I'm really glad to see you survived Friday night."

"I'm glad to see you, too," Kristie shivered. "You know I still have nightmares about Friday night. It might have been one of us. Whatever's going on has the whole town frightened."

"I'm scared, too," Scooter admitted. Scared of dying. Scared of vampires, but he didn't want to say that. "You say you've been having nightmares?" Scooter asked.

She nodded.

"Russell has, too. Bad ones."

"Vampires?" she asked.

Scooter nodded.

"Related to Friday night?" Scooter nodded again.

"And you don't?"

"No. Who needs to dream about nightmares? I'm living one," he groused.

"What do you mean by that?" Kristie asked.

"I came home real late Friday and got in serious trouble."

"What happened?"

She still hadn't mentioned anything about his facial bruises, but the subject kept heading in that direction. Scooter didn't want to tell her the truth, but then again he didn't want to lie while standing on the church steps. "Uh, I tripped over something and fell. I was knocked out, so I got home late, after midnight."

"I'm surprised I didn't fall down and hurt myself. I stumbled all over the place. It was so dark, and I was totally scared." She shivered again, despite the heat.

"Me, too. So," Scooter sighed, "I'm grounded through next weekend. Russell came over and helped me split wood and do chores."

"Russell's very nice," Kristie said.

Scooter tightened up, fighting stupid jealousy. So what if she liked Russell? "Uh, yeah. Well, I would have been grounded longer, but I plea bargained with my grandfather to lighten my sentence — I mean my punishment."

"What is plea bargaining?" Kristie asked.

Scooter was surprised at how expressive Kristie could be.

"My grandpa, he's a retired judge. I'm staying with him and Grandma while my parents are traveling in Europe. They go on a long vacation every summer, so I get to stay with my grandparents."

"That's too bad."

"No! I like staying with my grandparents. My grandpa's pretty cool, and I love the lake." He explained about how they lived at the end of a peninsula, having it all to themselves. "Anyway, he agreed to lighten my punishment if I'd apologize to Mr. Chandler."

"You're going back there? After all that has happened? Is happening?!" She asked, horrified. "Kids are disappearing and dying." She nodded toward the dark red brick church, then touched his forehead as though to ascertain whether he was feverish.

"Yeah. I'm a little nervous about it," Scooter admitted.

"I'm not surprised! I would be too! Is Russell going with you?" Kristie asked as she absently curled a strand of hair around her finger. She hadn't stepped back and was standing very close to him.

"No. He said he wouldn't," Scooter replied. With her so

close he was starting to get warm. Where had the refreshing breeze gone?

"If you want," she hesitated as if unsure, "I'll go with you — "

"Really?" Scooter was surprised and impressed. He was glad she wasn't like Racquel; otherwise, with his looks, she wouldn't give him the time of day. He and the word cool mixed as well as oil and water. "How come?"

"I don't want you to go alone; and to tell the truth, I feel sort of bad about the whole thing. Call it penance, if you like. My father would probably recommend it."

"Yeah, I feel low about Friday night, too. You can come if you really want, but I won't be going alone. My grandpa wants to see how Mr. Chandler feels about the whole thing."

"Oh." Kristie looked both disappointed and relieved.

"But thanks for volunteering. You're pretty — brave," Scooter managed. "Has your father said anything to you about Friday?"

Kristie shook her head.

Scooter breathed a sigh of relief. "I was afraid you might get in trouble because I told my grandpa about everything."

"Don't worry," Kristie told him, "if he does, I'll just have to deal with the consequences. It's not your fault I went along with them. Have you seen any of the others? Wait, there's the Mochrie boys."

Flanking Mrs. Mochrie, the brothers walked toward the church. Both were dressed in ill-fitting dark blue suits and navy ties with white stripes.

"They look like a pair of book ends," Kristie said, "except CJ isn't wearing his hat."

"They certainly don't look happy," Scooter pointed out.

Both brothers wore frowns on furrowed faces, and they obviously tried to avoid looking at each other. As they reached the steps, each went in a different direction.

While their mother spoke with a group of women in a deep and avid discussion, BJ sat on the railing wall away from everyone else and CJ met some other boys Scooter recognized from school.

"Any idea what's going on between them?" Kristie asked.

Scooter shook his head. "I'm supposed to stay away from the Graveyard Armadillos." Scooter glanced at his grandfather who was talking with Russell's father.

Kristie followed his gaze and said, "Bad influences?"

Scooter nodded.

"'Cept for CJ, your grandfather's probably right. For some reason, CJ idolizes and imitates BJ. Although neither looks too brotherly right now. CJ really looks downhearted."

"Hey, listen!" Scooter said as he waved her quiet. They could hear CJ talking to the group of boys.

As he continued his tale, two girls joined in to listen. "No, his favorite color is yellow, as in yellow-bellied and yellow-livered," CJ said loudly. Then he continued his version of what happened Friday night.

BJ stood and slowly sauntered over. He must have heard; he was getting angrier with each stride.

"O . . . oh," Kristie said. "Brotherly love time."

The secret's out, Scooter thought. He wasn't the only one who was interested in the conversation. Several people, including Sheriff Knight, listened to CJ's story. Russell's massive father ambled closer to the gathering. Neither brother noticed him.

CJ talked about how they'd been chased; then when Marcus Chandler grabbed CJ it scared him nearly to death. While he'd been caught, waiting for the Sheriff, BJ had split with his tail between his legs.

"Gonna be trouble." Kristie said, closely watching BJ.

"He's lying," BJ snarled as he pushed through the crowd.

"And what's the truth, boys?" Sheriff Knight was suddenly standing among them.

The brothers looked hatefully at each other, then away as though they had no idea what was going on.

"Boys, I've got a report by Deputy Lewis about Friday night. Is there something you'd like to add to your Saturday morning stories? It sounds as though something's missing. I've heard Mr. Chandler's story. Plus another version from Judge Keyshawn. I'm all ears for your new updated and expanded version."

Scooter turned away. He knew all eyes were suddenly upon him. He was gonna be blackballed!

Kristie touched him to reassure him everything would be all right, to let him know she didn't care.

"We have time before the services begin to hear the truth. Exactly why y'all were on private property stirring up trouble," the sheriff told them. Spying Pearl Mochrie, the sheriff gently took CJ's arm and steered him toward his mother. "Let's set the record straight."

All the boys scattered except BJ who dutifully followed.

"Pearl, I'd like to speak with you about your boys."

As she whirled to face Sheriff Knight, anger flashed across Pearl's face, matching the coloring in her dress. "What is it this time, Sheriff? I'm sure it's more important than the funeral services for a sweet young child."

The sarcasm slapped the sheriff who refused to be baited. His expression grew stony and professional. "If I thought it would help, I'd wait. But right here on the front porch of the Lord's house, it's time your boys told the truth about Friday night."

Even before he finished speaking, Pearl took a step forward and shook a finger at the sheriff. "Sheriff, you should be out looking for the killer of those young girls, not picking on my boys! My boys don't lie!"

"Neither does Cal Lewis nor Judge Keyshawn," the sheriff replied. "If there are any honest men in this town, it's my deputy sheriff and the Judge."

Pearl nodded hesitatingly, still trying to digest it all.

"Your boys are lying, Pearl. Not only did we find their footprints at the Chandler place, but we found others, as well as a Polaroid photo and a bottle of booze. Mr. Chandler says several kids were harassing him and taking pictures. One was carrying a gun."

Pearl faced her boy. "Is what the sheriff's saying true?"

CJ spread his arms and mumbled, but BJ didn't back down, "We were just trying to see him, to get a picture of him! Chandler's famous! Who else in this town has ever been famous!" BJ raced. "And we weren't drinkin'! And about the gun, I swear there was somebody else already there! Chasing us, too! I swear!"

"Probably your friends, whoever they were," Sheriff Knight mused. "I'd like to know more about them. Who was with you?"

"Wait a minute, Sheriff! There was more than one person chasing you?" Pearl asked.

"Yes! Someone with red eyes!" CJ replied. BJ nodded.

"This isn't exactly what you told me Friday," Pearl Mochrie snapped. "Nothing about a camera, a gun or ALCOHOL! You know how I feel about drinking!" Pearl threw her arms up in exasperation. "I don't want to hear anymore. It's time to go into church and pray for guidance. We'll settle this after the service."

Sheriff Knight cleared his throat, "That won't do, Pearl. Your boys need to be punished, taught a lesson about responsibility. Mr. Chandler filed a complaint. I expect your boys to apologize and make amends for what they've done. And I must know who else was with them."

Scooter knew the sheriff already knew who had been there. Why was he doing this? Would he have to pay twice for what happened Friday night? Maybe Judge Grandpa would speak on his behalf.

Kristie squeezed his arm and smiled reassuringly.

"I'll punish them myself, Sheriff. I don't need any help from authorities in disciplining my kids."

"Well, I think you do," Sheriff Knight began, then motioned to all the onlookers, "and I think it's obvious to every-one else that you do. We're tired of it. Your boys have been running roughshod and causing trouble for much too long. With all that's going on, it's time we keep a better eye on our young."

Pearl glanced about and obviously didn't like what she saw in the grim onlookers' faces. With lips tight and a grim expression, she looked ready to explode. Finally she snapped back with, "My sons aren't yours to judge!"

Reverend Candel stepped onto the porch as if to call every-one inside, then quickly descended the steps. Scooter was sur-prised things had flared so rapidly. This was a serene place — a place of sanctity. Maybe this had been brewing for a long time. Or maybe everybody was a little spooked by the recent deaths. He remembered how fear could make you react without think-ing! Irrational was the word.

"Pearl! Sheriff!" The Reverend called out as he ap-proached the two.

Seething and flushed, Pearl turned to face the Reverend.

"May I be of help in sorting this out? If we wait until after the service, I'm sure we'll all be much wiser."

Pearl smiled thankfully, "Why, thank you, Reverend. I think that would be appropriate, don't you agree, Sheriff Knight?"

"Oh, all right," he agreed reluctantly.

"I've got to go," Kristie said, squeezing his arm.

As Scooter watched her ascend the steps, he wondered why he felt she might be next. Maybe it was the close proxim-ity of death. Tonight he and Judge Grandpa might be next. They might meet their end at the vampire's ranch.

Chapter Seven

THE APOLOGY

Staring unseeingly out the windshield, Scooter rode in the front seat of Judge Grandpa's white Buick. Sunday was winding down and, just after sunset, the sky was full of pink and purple clouds imitating shredded cotton candy.

Scooter and Grandpa were on their way to see Marcus Chandler so Scooter could apologize. Just the thought of it made Scooter's mouth drier than west Texas in a dust storm. Scooter wished Kristie was here, too. He needed one of her sunshine smiles right now.

He also wished Judge Grandpa hadn't made him leave Flash at home, but Grandpa said this was something Scooter had to do on his own.

As they turned left, off the road and onto a gravel drive,

Scooter wondered if it was too late to change his mind. At least he knew that Marcus Chandler had called the sheriff instead of killing CJ. That eased his fears a little, though not much.

Scooter glanced at his grandfather. Definitely too late to change his mind. Besides, what would he tell Judge Grandpa? That he was scared to death? That there might be a vampire living on the ranch?

Somehow it seemed fitting that the day started with a funeral and was ending with a visit to one of the undead. Was death in the air?

They drove through the open gate and down the bumpy road. As though they were being pelted, gravel ricocheted off the underside of the car and clattered in the wheel wells.

Scooter placed his hand on his churning stomach. He tried to push away the dread, but he had the sinking feeling neither of them would see civilization again.

With trembling fingers, Scooter stroked the crucifix hidden under his shirt. He hadn't gathered any garlic, but then his grandfather probably wouldn't have let him wear a necklace of the pungent herb anyway.

Scooter cursed himself for forgetting to ask Kristie for holy water. According to comic books and movies, it worked against vampires. Now it was too late. He hoped Chandler helping CJ wasn't just to protect his cover; that Chandler was ill and not a vampire.

"Don't worry, Jonathan. It'll be over soon, and you'll probably find it wasn't so bad," Judge Grandpa said. "It takes a man of strong character to apologize when he's done something wrong. Heck, even to admit he's done something wrong. Not enough of that is done today. Too many people blame others. More people need to take responsibility for their own actions, as you are doing right now."

Scooter didn't respond. He was trying to soak up the sights of the farm — the last sights he expected to see. They passed a small pond on the right, and Scooter wondered if he'd ever go fishing with Russell again.

Accompanied by the random pinball-like sounds of rock on metal, they continued along the wandering driveway and around a corner, driving over a rattling cattle guard and through the line of buried pickups. In the distance, beyond the trucks among a copse of trees, Scooter could see the house, a tool shed and the half-painted barn. The buildings captured the fading light and seemed to glow with a crimson radiance.

As they pulled to a stop in front of the house, Scooter found it hard to breathe, as though his lungs had totally collapsed. His heart was on a rampage, thundering in his ears. He wiped his sweaty palms on his pants.

"Are you ready?" Judge Grandpa asked.

Scooter shook his head. "Well, waiting isn't going to make it any easier, is it?"

Scooter shook his head again.

"Then let's go."

Together, they got out of the car. "And remember. I don't want you to react to how he looks. Vitiligo is a serious disease. It saps the body, then the mind."

Earlier, Scooter had asked about Vitiligo. It was some sort of anemia that led to a skin condition — a loss of pigmentation, even from the eyes in some circumstances. Victims weren't allergic to the sun, as Garrett had implied, but they were highly sensitive to it — burning very easily. If he has Vitiligo he isn't a vampire, Scooter told himself.

The front gate stood between shoulder-high hedges, and it opened just as Scooter reached for it. Violently startled, he barely quelled a scream. Gasping for breath, Scooter knew it was all over, right here and now. He might as well bare his neck and kiss the sunshine goodbye!

Before him in the fading light was Marcus Chandler, the man — or rather, the vampire — Scooter had harassed Friday night. Scooter tried to look away but couldn't, drawn by the strangeness of the figure before him.

Chandler was tall and gaunt, not much more than a wizened skeleton clad in dark clothing, and much older than Scooter recalled — at least fifty and maybe even sixty. Once again, due to the contrast of light and dark in the twilight, Scooter had the impression of a free-floating head and ghostly hands. Even in the pale light, Chandler's lily-white skin appeared to effuse a faint glow as would a dying flashlight. His eyes did not; they were red — like fire deep down in a fathomless pit.

Scooter found it hard to believe the man was African-American. He was so white and, frankly, strange-looking to boot. Why didn't Garrett think he was an alien instead?

"Can I help you?" Marcus Chandler asked. The old man's expression wasn't menacing, just openly curious.

Scooter couldn't find any words. If he had, they would have been squeaks or dry whispers. He tried not to, but he couldn't help but stare.

"Hello, sir. Are you Mr. Marcus Chandler?" Scooter's grandfather asked.

"I am. And you are, sir?"

"I'm Judge Oliver Keyshawn. I have a young man with me who wants to apologize for his involvement in last Friday night's prank — bad humor at your expense. Do you have a moment?" Judge Keyshawn asked.

Chandler nodded.

"Jonathan?"

For a moment, Scooter just shook — too scared to speak. He tried to meet Chandler's eyes, then looked away, afraid he would get lost or be mesmerized — the first step in becoming one of the legion of undead.

"Jonathan," Judge Keyshawn repeated.

Scooter mustered his courage and forced the words out. The first squeaked, then as though the dam had burst, the rest came in a torrent. "Mr. Chandler, I'm sorry that I and some others bothered you and made you angry. I can't speak for them but please accept my sincerest apology. I really am sorry. I wasn't thinking. I was just trying to have fun and be one of the guys. I dunno . . . stupid, I know. I'm sorry. I won't come back ever or bother you again. Cross my heart and hope to die." That word seemed to hang in the twilight air.

"No need to go to that extreme," Chandler said "You could enlighten me by telling me what happened Friday night."

Scooter gave a relieved sigh. Chandler wasn't going to kill him or his grandfather after all! Maybe he wasn't as terrible as he appeared.

"Uh . . . okay," Scooter haltingly told the elderly moviemaker what he knew, including tripping over the tree wire and knocking himself unconscious. The longer Scooter spoke, the more fluid his speech became. Scooter noticed that Chandler stared closely at his bruises but didn't smile or laugh.

"What about the drinking?" Chandler asked. His gaze was penetrating, and Scooter thought he could see right through him. No! Right into him. He knew! That's right, Scooter remembered. Some vampires knew you — your entire history — just by looking into your eyes.

"Uh . . . " he glanced at Judge Grandpa. "I only had one sip of Schnapps. It was awful stuff."

Before his grandpa could say anything, Chandler coolly asked, "And the gunshots?"

"I don't know about them! I was out, you know, the tree wire thing. Russell mentioned them; he heard them." Scooter knew — just knew — he was going to get spanked when he got home. It was called capital punishment. His grandmother might even wash out his mouth with soap.

After a silence, Chandler asked, "Scooter, do you read?"

"I read okay. Mostly comic books, though. I'd like to draw or write them one day, but my imagination is sorta weak. I'm only good at math and running track. You know, normal stuff." Scooter was now very willing to talk. Caught between a rock and a hard place, he didn't want to go home. The longer the delay, the better.

"Comic books, eh? You want to draw and write them?" Chandler asked.

Scooter nodded, wondering if he was also going to ridicule him. "I wanted to write and act my own plays when I was your age." He sighed. "Well, I can't help you with the drawing, but, Scooter," Chandler began, leaning closer, "I write screenplays. If I give you a couple to read, will you promise to read them, pay attention to the style and formula, then come back here and discuss them with me? We can talk about the art of writing. Comics are written using the screenplay style. The screenplay structure, if you will."

"Really?" Scooter asked in disbelief.

Marcus smiled and nodded.

Scooter seemed to forget he was talking to a would-be vampire. Chandler didn't smile, exactly, but he came close. It almost touched his troubled red eyes.

"Maybe they'll keep you occupied reading and thinking about writing so you won't get into any more trouble," Chandler told him.

Behind Scooter, Judge Keyshawn smiled.

"Wait here a minute." Chandler disappeared inside the house, then returned shortly with a pair of loose-leaf bound books. "Here are two. *Hellions* and *Darkness Walks the Day*."

Scooter accepted them.

"Come back and tell me what you think from a future writer's perspective. Okay?"

"Okay!" Scooter said as Chandler smiled, making him appear less frightening. Maybe he wasn't so bad after all.

"Thank you, Mr. Chandler," the Judge said. "You're kinder than I would've been."

"I was young once, too. A long, long time ago," he replied sadly.

"Ah, yes, youth. Well, he'll come up the driveway and ring the doorbell as normal folks do next time."

"I would appreciate that. Scooter, please call first." The elderly moviemaker scribbled his number in the front of one of the bound manuscripts.

"Well, we've taken up enough of your creative time," Judge Keyshawn said. "Say thanks again and let's be off, Jonathan."

"Thanks," Scooter said and boldly stepped forward to shake Chandler's hand. It wasn't cold like Scooter thought it would be but warm and firm. Maybe, Scooter thought, Chandler wasn't a vampire. Unless, Scooter's mind briefly twisted, he was being nice, hoping he'd return without his grandpa next time. Then he'd have him for dinner.

Scooter looked at Mr. Chandler again. No, this vampire stuff had to be a product of his imagination. Maybe his imagination was better than he thought. Maybe he should put it to good use. Harness it! Why not?

As they drove away, Scooter couldn't wait to start reading, and tell Russell and Kristie about his adventure. Mr. Chandler was going to teach him how to write comics! For the moment, all thoughts of the vampire were long gone.

82

Chapter Eight

LIKE ATTRACTS

Scooter set down Chandler's bound manuscript, *Hellions*, atop his three-ring binder of sketches, and leaned back against the storage chest on the boat dock. Warm and relaxed, he was tempted to imitate Flash. The Lab was on his back, eyes closed and legs limply pointed skyward.

Smiling, Scooter closed his eyes. The day was beautiful, warm and sunny. A breeze whispered off the channel waters, ruffling his t-shirt and the stringy fringes of his cutoffs. The soft lapping of the water against the dock's pilings added to the summer lullaby. Yesterday evening's terrifying trip to the Pickup Ranch seemed a long time ago. Funny how dire expectations could be worse than the actual event, Scooter mused.

He had spent most of the morning consuming *Hellions*. Many of his drawings were from the story. From the moment Scooter started the script, he'd been unable to stop, except to draw, and most of the sketches were of characters or scenes in the story. Scooter had never known reading — or studying — to be so much fun! It was like discovering a whole new world. Somehow, Marcus Chandler had transported him to San Francisco, a city of fog, bay breezes, steep, winding streets, and a veritable — a word he had to looked up — melting pot of races. Scooter had been able to see, smell, touch and even feel the Bay Area. When he wasn't caught up in the story, he examined the format and structure.

Reading Chandler's manuscript gave him a glimpse at a new way to write and expanded his vocabulary. He'd written down the words *ennui, sarcophagi, circumvent*, and *extol*, so he could look them up in the dictionary. Scooter planned to read Chandler's second script, then visit him.

Reading a story and asking the author questions was great. Scooter felt special, as if the writer wrote the story just for him.

"Hey, Flash," Scooter began, interrupting the dog's snooze, "do you think Mr. Chandler can really teach me to write?" Flash barely opened his glazed eyes, then yawned mightily. "Yeah, he doesn't exactly owe me any favors." With fanciful thoughts of writing his own comics, Scooter began to drift off.

As he was about to fall asleep, he felt soft footfalls on the dock. It was probably Russell trying to surprise him again. Cracking one eye open, Scooter peeked, then both eyes popped open, and he abruptly straightened up. Kristie's presence was a wonderful surprise.

Kristie was clad in bicycling apparel — black biking pants, a lime-green tank top, rolled socks, sweatbands, and white sneakers. She carried a helmet under her arm and a pastel rainbow-colored backpack over her shoulder. A large, crooked smile brightened her face. "Aw shoot, you've spotted me!"

Scooter managed to scramble to his feet without knocking the binders into the water or stumbling over Flash. He tried to think of something witty, but failed, and said, "Hi. Nice day for a ride." Flash opened his eyes, stretched, then stood to greet Kristie with a lazily wagging tail.

"And to sleep in the sun."

She kneeled and hugged the Lab, as if she truly liked the dog in a special way.

"I was reading." Scooter held up the bound script. He kept his sketch binder hidden.

"I could tell. Was Flash reading, too?" She laughed and playfully roughed Flash's ears. The Lab huffed and grinned.

Russell said that pressure made his stuttering worse, and that pretty girls were big-time pressure. Scooter found himself agreeing. "It's by Marcus Chandler."

"Oh." Now Kristie appeared embarrassed.

Her blush was pretty, he thought. An earlier statement from Judge Grandpa, about letting his hormones rule him, swept across him. Scooter now had some inkling of what that meant.

Kristie was very pretty, outdoorsy and attractive, with her auburn tresses tied in a pony tail. What a difference a year made! Scooter thought. He was glad she'd remained nice, easier to speak with — be with — than he'd ever imagined. "When I went to apologize, he gave me some movie scripts to read," Scooter told her.

"That was nice of him. So he wasn't mad?" she asked as she sat on the storage chest. Flash moved to her side and nudged her hand, so that she would start petting him again. The dog wore a satisfied grin that stretched from ear to ear.

"He didn't seem to be. He was very nice — strange looking but friendly. After talking with him, I didn't feel threatened at all. Maybe he really is sick and not a vampire, after all."

"But he looked so terrifying Friday night — "

"Maybe that's 'cause he was furious. People look different when they're mad," Scooter said.

"My father said something similar. Well, that's a relief. I was worried about you. I almost called last night, but . . . Anyway," she said quickly, "I was out riding so I thought I'd check to make sure you're okay. And you are!" she smiled. "Would you and Flash care to join me for a ride?"

Flash woofed and sat back as though ready to go, right now.

Kristie laughed and added, "You get ready fast. I'm heading out to Don's Port, where there's some great wild blackberries waiting to be picked. I brought some sacks."

"Sure!" Scooter said, agreeing to any excuse to spend time with Kristie. "I just have to tell my grandparents," he said, heading for the house. "Be back in a minute." Kristie stayed on the dock petting Flash.

His grandma was cutting vegetables at the kitchen sink. Judge Grandpa was sitting at the table reading the *Wall Street Journal*. Scooter ran upstairs to his room and grabbed a clean shirt, the one with the Silver Surfer soaring on it, and then carefully combed his hair.

"Grandpa, I'm going for a bicycle ride," he said, as he came back downstairs and into the kitchen.

"You are?" He didn't even look up from his paper.

"Dear, it's almost lunch time," his grandma told him.

"Oh, I'm not hungry."

"Not hungry? You?" Judge Grandpa glanced up. "And where are you headed?"

"Near Don's Port to pick blackberries."

"Changed shirts for that?"

"Uh-huh." Scooter leaned against the open door now.

"Don't uh-huh me," Grandpa corrected.

"Yes, sir."

"Jonathan, who's the young lady in the yard with Flash?" Grandma Keyshawn asked.

"Kristie," Scooter said, trying to sound casual.

"Ms. Candel?" Judge Grandpa asked with a slight smile.

"Uh, yes sir."

"Going berry picking, are you?"

"Dear, are you sure he's old enough?" Grandma asked with a smile.

"Emily, don't tease the boy; he'll regress. He already looks nervous enough as it is. Go put on the shirt you just took off."

"What! Why?" Scooter asked, a pained expression on his face.

"Just do it. We don't want you developing bad habits."

"Dear!" Grandma Keyshawn said sternly to her husband.

"Aw, heck, go ahead." Judge Grandpa waved him outside.

Scooter opened the screen door and sailed into the outdoors to enter the garage. In a rush now, he rolled his black and gold Schwinn ten-speed out to meet Kristie, who was softly singing, *Somewhere over the Rainbow.*

As she stared off into the distance, she looked almost grown up to Scooter. "Sorry. My grandparents were discussing my clothing."

She stopped singing and said, "You look fine to me. Is that the Silver Surfer?"

Scooter nodded and smiled broadly; she knew comics!

"I thought so. He is so cool." With that, she climbed onto her pink and turquoise Sears model bicycle. "You ready?"

"Uh-huh," Scooter said, watching her stretch. His imagination was working overtime.

"Catch me — if you can!" Kristie yelled, taking off down the packed grass and dirt pathway through the woods toward the driveway gate of Siete Hombres Estate.

Almost falling over in haste, Scooter climbed onto his bicycle and followed. Flash caught her in no time and began boasting about it.

A short time later they were cruising along the oil-covered back roads of dirt and gravel. They rode at a casual pace, avoiding the potholes and the spots that were sticky from the heat. Scooter impressed her by calmly riding no-handed through several rough stretches, while warily watching out of the corner of his eye. Flash wore a skeptical expression.

Kristie tried to imitate Scooter, but when she hit something, her bicycle swerved. "How do you do that?"

"Steer with your knees," he said with masterful authority.

"Really?"

"I wouldn't lie to you."

"Really?" she repeated, but this time with a smile.

"Cross my heart and hope to die."

"So why did you want to join the Graveyard Armadillos?" she asked.

"Uh, I thought it was cool. That I'd be accepted. I don't have . . . I don't know many kids that I like. So were you looking for new friends?"

"Yeah — and adventure. Life is so dull."

"Me, too!" Scooter replied. "But Judge Grandpa thinks some of them are the wrong type of friends, so no more Armadillos for me."

"Yeah, it did go badly."

"Oh, well, it worked out okay. I mean, better than okay. I got to meet you, know you, sort of," Scooter stammered, suddenly feeling frustrated. "I mean, I knew you at church, but that's not the same."

"No, it's not," she said with a smile.

"After Friday, I was afraid this summer was going to be the pits. But now I think it might be okay. The entire summer is ahead of us."

Kristie suddenly said, "Shoot!" and slowed. "I have a flat tire."

They pulled off the road where they weren't in danger of getting run over.

"Got a spare tube?" Scooter asked.

She nodded and unzipped the little bag under her bicycle seat.

"No problem. I'm fairly good at it. I changed one Friday night on my way to the initiation. It happened in front of the Pilot Point graveyard."

"At least there's no graveyard here," Kristie said. There was a moment of uneasy silence. "Scooter? Russell said you like running even more than bicycling. Why?"

"Uh, I don't know. A sense of freedom, I guess. And the runner's high takes you away, makes you feel invincible." He didn't feel there should be secrets between friends — but Russell had never asked him why he loved to run — so he had told her the truth. "Actually, I started running because of a bully in first grade. He used to steal my lunch money. He was a big dude. If I could outrun or out think him, I got to eat and keep my skin. Fear makes you fast."

"Friday night it did!"

They laughed and Scooter felt that his secret was safe.

"Didn't you say your parents were in Europe?" Kristie asked.

Moving Flash's sniffing nose a time or two, Scooter began to remove the wheel. "Yeah, they take a vacation every year, so I'm staying with my grandparents. My second parents, Mom says. Judge Grandpa and Grandma are very cool, especially for old folks. Judge Grandpa claims he's trying to mold me into a decent human being." Scooter grinned. "After Friday, he thought I'd slipped."

"That's neat. I wish I had cool grandparents, but they're even more straightlaced and stifling than my parents. I'd trade almost anything not to be a minister's daughter. Sometimes I can barely breathe! You think they'd at least understand that we're in the twentieth century."

"Sometimes Judge Grandpa is like that, too; but he claims he gives me enough rope to hang, but not kill, myself." Scooter suddenly yelped, having somehow nicked himself.

"You okay?" Kristie asked.

Looking solemn, Flash came over to inspect the injury, then made pitying whines.

"Yeah," Scooter mumbled as he sucked on his finger. "Just a scratch."

She checked it, then said, "I have a Band-Aid in my pack." She dug through the pack, then pulled out several things. After applying first aid cream, she put on the bandage. Flash woofed softly in approval, then sat back smiling.

"You did that like a professional."

"I want to be a nurse. Being the oldest of seven kids gives you plenty of practice," she laughed.

"You really want to be a nurse?"

"Not really. How could you tell?" she asked.

Scooter shrugged. "Something in your voice."

"What I really want to be is a singer."

"You have a great voice," Scooter said. Flash woofed then began panting. "What would you sing?"

Kristie laughed. "Anything but gospel. I mean, I like it, but I'm tired of the same old thing."

"If you could sing anything, what would you sing?"

Kristie looked embarrassed, then said, "Promise you won't tell anyone else?"

Scooter nodded solemnly, knowing that he was being entrusted with something special. He noticed that Flash also nodded.

"I want to sing in a Disney animated movie! I love those movies, plus the *Wizard of Oz* and other musicals. But if I had first choice, I'd do a voice for Disney, be a princess or a mermaid, anything but a minister's daughter."

If Scooter remembered correctly, the girls in those movies were often wishing they were someone else, too.

"I know that sounds silly," Kristie continued, "but it's true. Russell claims I should do rock and roll, the Dead, you know. He even gave me some lyrics. It's okay because you can really let loose and even experiment some. What about you?"

Having heard her confession, it was hard not to do the same. "What I really, really want to do is write and draw my own comics — you know, my version of the *Avengers*, *Spawn* or the *Silver Surfer*. Mr. Chandler said he'd help me get started, with the writing part anyway. He says screenplay form is used in writing comics."

"That sounds cool. I didn't know you could draw. Can I see some of your drawings sometime?"

"Well . . . " Scooter hesitated, as he finished changing the tire.

"Look, if you want to be an artist, you have to let people see your work. Be proud of it! And listen to constructive criticism instead of being all defensive — like I used to be, thinking they were just picking on me." She blushed. "Eek. I sound like my mother!"

Scooter's head was swimming, and he was stammering and rambling. "Sure, you can see the drawings, I guess. When we get back to the house — if you really want." Flash nudged him, almost knocking him over. "Hey! You're ready to go, aren't you?" he asked, and Flash woofed, the need to run obvious in his face.

"Thanks for changing my tire," Kristie said. "Well, we'd better get moving. Someone else might be picking our berries!"

They continued riding along the deserted roadway. The conversation quieted as they picked up the pace, then they turned right at a big sign proclaiming, Don's Port, ahead.

Kristie sang some, doing "Under the Sea" from *The Little Mermaid*.

Tall grass fields surrounded the road, with several mobile homes scattered about. Real houses were usually reserved for lakeside plots. Ahead, the road seemed to disappear, but actually made a 90 degree turn. Inside the curve was a large mobile home. With a loud snarl, a black dog suddenly scrambled out from underneath the trailer and raced toward them.

"Hey!" Kristie yelled and pointed at the Rottweiler.

Flash growled, the hair standing up on his neck and his ears twitching.

"Flash! NO! Heel!" Scooter cried. "Come on, Kristie! HAUL!"

Standing on the pedals, the redheads put on a burst of speed, leaving the dog behind. They had to slow down as they navigated the sharp turn, putting one foot out to keep from falling over.

But instead of chasing them down the road, the Rottweiler raced across the front yard, cutting the corner. Before they could gain speed again, the beast was at Kristie's heels, snapping and gnashing.

"Scooter, I can't outride it!"

Flash had seen enough. Growling, the Lab attacked, a flash of gold barreling into the big, black beast. The two became entangled, tumbling along the pavement like a scene snipped from a cartoon.

"Oh, no!" Kristie yelled as she watched, fearing they might crash into her and send her sprawling. They rolled together in time, side by side, bicycle wheels and dogs. Then the dogs slowed, and Kristie coasted away.

With his metal bicycle pump in hand, Scooter stopped and quickly jumped off his bike. "Don't hurt my dog!" he yelled as he joined the fray, solidly striking the Rottweiler several times. The dog ignored Flash and leaped at Scooter, bowling him over. Scooter's head hit the pavement, and he saw stars.

Barking ferociously, Flash rammed into the black dog as it bit Scooter on the arm.

Kristie joined the fracas, wielding her bicycle pump and yelling, "Go away!" She smacked the beast hard, bending her pump and eliciting a yelp from the dog. It quickly turned and fled.

"Thanks for saving me, Flash!" Scooter hugged his dog.

Wearing a quizzical expression as if to say "what did you expect?", the Lab cocked his head, woofed, then licked Scooter all over the face with sloppy kisses.

"And you too, Kristie."

"Are you all right? I was worried . . . " Kristie began.

"It's just a scratch," Scooter protested. They looked at his arm. The skin was torn by two shallow but bloody grooves.

"I can't believe it!" Kristie said, incensed and cursing as though she'd never been to church. "I'm going to report that — that beast to the sheriff! They'll put it to sleep!" Then she calmed a little and said, "Your arm doesn't look too bad. Time to play nurse again."

"You can whistle while you work or sing if you prefer," Scooter said with a smile. He received one in return.

Kristie went through the same process as before. "First a tree, now a dog." She sighed. "I didn't know you were acc . . . I mean, led such an exciting life." She laughed.

"Not until recently," Scooter said. Flash woofed, as if saying things had gotten more exciting since they'd met.

Kristie laughed again, then kissed Scooter on the cheek, leaving him dazed. "I like you and your companion." Just as quickly, Kristie kissed Flash, too. "Well . . . we head home and wash you in antiseptic, or go on to pick berries."

"Are you kidding? That's a choice? Boldly onward!" he proclaimed and climbed on his bike. As they continued riding, Scooter couldn't keep his eyes off Kristie. He couldn't believe he was alone with her. Had she heard his thoughts — wishing he could spend more time with her?

She caught him looking, smiled and said, "You know, this is fun. Seems something exciting always happens to you."

Scooter wasn't offended in the slightest, despite the fact she meant his accidents. He was looking forward to the rest of the day. Maybe she'd like to go canoeing or come with him when he visited Marcus Chandler again. Well, he could only hope!

Chapter Nine

BLANKS

"I can't wait until I can drr . . . drive," Russell said, leaning his bicycle against a tree, "then I wouldn't have to ride. I could cruise."

He and Racquel had traveled several blocks from their home to the park next to the church, where the Mochrie brothers were cleaning and grooming the grounds as part of their punishment. It was a small place with a central fountain and a statue of the town's founder. Several benches, a swing set and a jungle gym spread out across a bed of pebbles.

"It's not far enough to bother driving," Racquel said, skating in slow circles along the sidewalk. She preferred rollerblading to riding. "And what makes you think Dad is ever going to let you drive? Just because you build car models doesn't mean you know anything about the real thing?" Her stare was dark and icy, but her face was flushed.

Russell knew his sister was in one of those moods. She hadn't seen Garrett recently, and when that happened, she became unbearably short-tempered. She'd argue about anything just to vent her frustration. Besides, Russell knew he'd drive one day; then he'd show them what racing and rock-and-roll were all about with the Deadmobile.

"I don't see Garrett, just the brothers," Racquel muttered.

BJ hauled bags of grass clippings, while CJ trimmed under the trees. A lawn mower and a variety of other lawn tools were scattered about. The park looked better than it had in a long time, all neat and tidy; and it was only Monday. They would be doing this all week; they were even supposed to clean and polish the statue.

"Here c . . . comes Garrett," Russell stammered, pointing down the street at the oncoming black Trans Am. It pulled to the curb and stopped.

Her raven-colored locks trailing behind her, Racquel raced toward the car. She almost knocked Garrett over as they hugged. Garrett responded by sticking a cigarette between her lips.

Russell almost said something, but Racquel silenced him with one look. She thought she was so mature.

"How you doing, Russ?" Garrett asked.

"F . . . fine."

"You seen Scooter?"

"Before the funeral yes . . . yes . . . yesterday."

"Well, when you see him, tell him I overheard my old man and the sheriff talking. I know he spilled his guts to the judge, who passed the story onto your dad. You ought to be p.o.'ed, too, man. Anyway, tell him he's on my list; and if I see him, he's history! When I'm through with him, nobody in this town, nobody in school, will talk to him. He'll be an outcast! He might as well move away! You tell him all that, okay?"

"O . . . okay."

"Then you have a decision to make. Racquel said you didn't breathe a word about us to your dad. That's good. I respect you for that; I like a man who can keep a secret. But now you have to decide, do you want to hang with us or Scooter? I'll give you a day or two to think on it."

Russell felt sick. What should he do? Scooter was his best friend. But if he got booted from the Graveyard Armadillos, he couldn't keep an eye on Racquel, and he worried about her. As long as she was infatuated with Garrett, trouble was brewing big time. He didn't need to be a genius to see that.

"Hey, you seen Kristie?" Garrett asked.

Russell shook his head.

"I got the feeling she's flown the coop, too. Oh, well, there's more wanting to join the Armadillos. That should be lots of fun." Garrett chuckled. "Hey, either of you seen or talked to Jo?"

Russell and Racquel shook their heads.

"I tried to phone her, but nobody answered. Oh, well, she'll just miss out."

Still arm in arm with Racquel, Garrett moved toward the Mochrie brothers who hadn't noticed them and were still hard at work. "Speaking of fun, aren't they having a ball?"

"Th . . . they spilled the beans, too, ddd . . . didn't th . . . they?" Russell stammered, wondering why Garrett wasn't mad at the Mochries. Everyone heard them at the funeral. Two people chasing them? Who believed that? Besides, the sheriff hadn't found another set of adult footprints.

"Yeah, they did, but that was stupidity and circumstance. And they didn't finger us. Besides, they were pressured by your dad, who as we all know, can be damn intimidating. Scooter, on the other hand, was just plain scared," Garrett said. "Hey, BJ, CJ, come on over here! Take a break!"

The brothers ambled over. "This sucks!" BJ complained. The pair was dirty and sweaty with grass clippings stuck all over them. "And what do you want, Garrett? You got us into this!

Did you come to help out?"

"Heck, no. If the principal can't do yard work, then neither can his son." Garrett laughed, patting BJ on the shoulder. "But I did bring the Polaroids from Friday night. You aren't going to believe them!"

"Well, let's see 'em!" BJ cried.

Russell watched BJ's face as he leafed through the photos. At first he was confused, then disappointed, and finally angry.

"What's the meaning of this?" BJ demanded, handing them to CJ. "They're blank!"

"Yeah, very interesting, aren't they?" Garrett said. "They tell us what we need to know. Marcus Chandler is definitely a vampire! He couldn't be photographed."

"What makes you say that?" CJ asked, wiping the sweat off his glasses. "I expected some background in the pictures, the barn door or the front of the barn. Something, not just fuzzy grayness. Besides, if he is a vampire, why didn't he kill me when he had the chance? Instead, he called the sheriff."

"He was covering up," Garrett replied. "Too many witnesses. He'd already killed Debbie. He probably wasn't hungry. Come on, CJ, don't you see? No, I can see you don't. Chandler did something to the camera," Garrett told them.

Russell could see the light dawn on BJ. "H . . . how do you know the film was ggg . . . good?" Russell asked. He didn't believe Garrett and didn't like where this was heading.

"It was almost brand new, and the other photos I took of Racquel were fine. See." He showed them pictures of Racquel standing on the lakeshore. They looked normal.

"Maybe . . . Scooter's just a lousy p . . . photographer," Russell said.

"Nobody's that bad." Garrett said. "Nope, pale-faced Marcus Chandler did something to the camera so we wouldn't see the barnyard without him in it! Otherwise, it'd be obvious to everybody he's a vampire. This way, people think the same way you do," Garrett explained. "That there was something wrong with the film and not Chandler. It looks like we're gonna have to try something else. We gotta do something!"

"Count me out," CJ said. "I don't want anything to do with him!" He jerked a thumb at his brother. "Besides, I don't think it was just Chandler chasing us. Like I said yesterday, there was somebody — something else out there. Something," he swallowed, "strange."

"Doesn't matter what you think," BJ said, obviously downhearted. "Whether or not Chandler's a vampire doesn't mean anything to us. Mom's watching us so closely, we can't even go to the bathroom without being questioned. Maybe next week."

"Next week, boys, may be too late," Garrett said. "Haven't you noticed kids are dying near the Chandler Ranch? What about Missy and Debbie? That could have been us! Chandler is trying to lull us into a false sense of security. And, remember, BJ, you shot him and nothing happened! Right?"

BJ nodded. "I'm sure I hit `em. Maybe I need silver bullets."

"You're thinking about werewolves, stupid," CJ snapped.

"Guys! Guys! Listen to me! People need to know that Chandler is dangerous! That he's at fault. Hey, I have an idea! Racquel, can you get your father's video camera?"

She nodded.

Inwardly, Russell groaned. He didn't want to go back there. Maybe if they stayed away, nothing would happen. Why couldn't they leave well enough alone? So what if Chandler was different. What did Garrett have against him?

Russell had an awful feeling about the direction things were heading. It made him sick to his stomach. Images from his nightmares briefly returned to him. Was he precognitive? Could he see the future?

Garrett looked thoughtful, then said, "And you know what, that may not be enough. If Chandler truly is a vampire, and we can't prove that he's a killer, we may have to destroy him ourselves."

Chapter Ten

RUNNING AWAY TO TROUBLE

Although exhausted from their day's work at the park, the Mochrie boys weren't done yet. It was early evening; the summer sun was still up. As extra punishment, they were cleaning the garage, sweeping and picking up trash and mislaid items.

"I don't care what you say, BJ," CJ drawled and leaned against the wall, so tired he could barely stand. "You let me down big-time. It opened my eyes. Maybe what people say about you is true!" He tossed some cans into a box.

"And what's that!" BJ yelled, slamming the broom against the garage floor.

"You're selfish and conceited! And in case those words are too big for your teeny-tiny brain, it means you don't care about anything or anybody but yourself!" CJ replied hotly.

"What?"

"Listen, BJ, no matter what you say, you ran off and left me with whatever that — that thing was — that was chasing us. And I'm not talking about Chandler. If he hadn't shown up . . ." CJ shuddered. "I'm your brother! I'd help you no matter what! But you! Did you care? I thought I was a goner for sure. Was gonna die!" CJ was almost in tears. He took off his new glasses and wiped his face on his sleeve.

"At least tell me what happened after I — left?" BJ asked.

CJ's smiled sadly. "You — I never thought you'd desert me. What an idiot I was! You were long gone! You turned tail and ran! You're just like Dad!"

"WHAT?! Don't you dar — "

"Some brother you are! You're chicken! After all your big man, tough guy kind of talk and walk, you're just a wimp."

"I don't take that from nobody!" BJ shouted. Fists raised and ready, he walked slowly toward his brother. "And you, you were so scared, you passed out! Did you pee in your pants?"

"Come on, tough guy!" CJ yelled. "Let's see if you can beat up somebody smaller than you! I dare you!" CJ launched himself at his brother.

Although surprised, BJ still landed a blow to his brother's gut just before CJ slammed into him, driving BJ into the rickety metal shelves behind him. The shelves rocked back and forth, threatening to dump their contents. Then BJ surged forward, and the shelves started to fall. CJ jumped back, but the tumbling shelves briefly stunned BJ. Bottles, boxes, cans and jars pelted them, making a tremendous racket. The shattering glass echoed in the garage and carried out the door into the night.

CJ jumped on top of his brother. Flailing and rolling around, the boys struck at each other as they wrestled, each trying to get on top. CJ got in several good blows, rupturing BJ's lower lip, but eventually the older brother ended on top.

With blow after blow, he pummeled CJ, who despite the onslaught of blows, was still yelling, "Chicken! Wimp! Sissy!"

With a resounding smack, the door to the house flew open. Their mother stormed out. "Byron Jefferson! Calvin Jefferson! What in tarnation is going on here?" Wielding a belt, Pearl Mochrie stalked toward the brothers. Each froze. "I said, what's going on here!"

Neither boy spoke.

Resembling a dragon, her face was bright red with flaring nostrils; her eyes were wild and wide open. "You know you're not allowed to fight! Get off him, BJ!"

BJ stood slowly, then pulled his brother to his feet. Both bled slightly from several cuts. CJ's nose was bleeding freely, blood running down his chin.

"I swear! You two never listen to me! Well, I'll speak a language you'll understand." Pearl Mochrie walked behind BJ and lashed out with her belt.

The belt slapped across the back of his legs; and despite the jeans, BJ cried out.

"Now — are you listening?" She lashed him again.

"Yes!" BJ tried to move away.

"Stop that!" She struck him again with the belt. "There'll be no more fighting between you or with anybody else. Hear?"

"Yes!"

"There'll be no staying out after dark, either. And if you get in trouble and embarrass me one more time, especially in front of the whole town, I'll send you to stay with your Uncle Bart and Aunt Ethel."

"No, not that!" Both boys cried at once.

"Now, I know this isn't just your fault, BJ. It takes two. Now — ten lashes for each of you, then it's off to bed without supper."

"But, Ma, you already hit me three times!" BJ cried

"Well, I figure you're older and should know better. Don't ya?" She stared him down.

Finally, he nodded.

"Now drop those jeans and grab your ankles."

Trembling, BJ did so.

Silently but ferociously, Mrs. Mochrie gave him the ten lashes.

BJ refused to cry, but his face got very red.

As CJ steeled himself for similar punishment, he heard BJ groan, "I ought to take the car and run away." That was all CJ heard before he felt the stinging slap of leather on tender flesh.

Later, after everyone was in bed, the click of a door closing awakened CJ. He rubbed his eyes and looked over at BJ's bed. The moonlight cascading through the window highlighted the empty bed. CJ noticed his brother's clothes and shoes, the ones that had been piled next to the bed, were gone.

With a sudden flash of insight, he knew where BJ was headed.

CJ quickly climbed out of bed and quietly dressed. Not knowing how long he might be gone, CJ grabbed his gym bag and stuffed it full of clothes. As he reached the door, he remembered and returned to grab his robotic money bank off his desk. He jammed it into the bag, then quietly opened the door. The hall was dark and silent. BJ had snuck out without waking Ma.

CJ sneaked down the hall, through the family room and then the kitchen. He looked at the peg on the wall where extra keys were hung. A set was gone!

BJ was really going to do it! Well, he wasn't going to leave him behind again! He'd be damned if he'd take the heat for BJ's departure; Ma would surely blame him. Lash him when he didn't know where BJ had gone. She'd think he was lying. No matter what, he wasn't going to live with Uncle Bart. He had huge, meaty fists — fists he liked to use on them even when they weren't misbehaving.

CJ slipped through the laundry room and opened the door to the garage. He felt a draft. The garage door was open! Looking out and expecting to find BJ, CJ was startled by what wasn't there.

The car was gone!

Stunned, CJ stepped into the garage and peered down the driveway.

Grunting and groaning, BJ was pushing the car down the driveway. He reached the beginning of a slight decline, and the rusted Pinto started to roll by itself. The driveway was straight, so curves weren't a problem; but as the car gained speed, it drifted a little, heading for the mailbox.

BJ frantically ran around and tried to jump inside the Pinto to steer, but he was too late. It was too close to the mail-box. If he opened the door, it would strike the post. He watched helplessly as the Pinto rolled away, narrowly missing the mailbox, then coasting out of the driveway and across the street. The car gently hopped the curb and finally stopped with two wheels off the road.

Both brothers breathed a sigh of relief. CJ quietly closed the door, then ran over to his brother. "You ain't leaving without me! Not again!" he whispered harshly.

"I thought you were mad at me," BJ said, "and wouldn't want to come with me."

"That's what you get for thinking," CJ said. "Don't you think Ma would take this out on me?"

"Uh . . ." BJ cocked his head.

"So I'm going with you."

"Okay, what'd you bring?" BJ asked quietly.

"Clothes and money," said CJ.

"Me, too, but I also got some food."

"Where you wanna go?" CJ asked.

"Anywhere but here. Let's roll it down the street a bit more," BJ suggested.

This proved to be hard work, but they were still driven

by the fear of discovery. That gave them extra strength. Straining, they succeeded in moving the Pinto another 100 feet.

"Let's get outta here!" BJ whispered as he opened the door to the driver's side and hopped onto the seat. He jammed the key into the ignition and fired up the engine. Before the car had a chance to warm up, they raced off. The Pinto sputtered and jerked for a time, then rattled down the road.

They drove in silence awhile, navigating the back roads along the lake. In spite of the late hour, they stayed off the main roads where suspicious sheriffs and highway patrol cars might be waiting. The farther they got away from Gunstock and home, the more they relaxed. BJ even began to hum. The Pinto's radio had quit working long ago.

"Where we heading?" CJ asked.

"Dallas, I'm hoping Aunt Regina will take us in for a while. We can make it there easily before daybreak, long before Ma will call the sheriff. I suspect there'll be an APB out for us. If so, we'll have to sell the car or trade it or something. Heck, we may even have to thumb rides. I've always wanted to go to California; that's where Dad went when he disappeared."

"You always have Dad on the mind! Wake up! He left us! I don't understand why you want to see Dad. I don't. Not ever again! Besides," CJ finished more quietly, "California's a long way away."

"Doesn't look too far on the map," BJ replied.

"You never did study."

"So what. I know all I need to know," BJ replied defensively. "Like there's lots of beautiful girls in California. Babes. Lots of babes."

CJ suddenly shivered.

"You okay?" BJ asked.

"We just passed the entrance to the Pickup Ranch," CJ replied. "Feels like someone walked over my grave."

"Don't worry, we're in a car! We can outrun him this

time, even in this hunk of junk!" BJ laughed. Shortly, they passed the gated fence blocking off the road leading to the dam.

"Hey, did you hear that?" CJ asked. "I never heard the car make that noise before!"

"Don't worry, this car makes all kinds of noises," BJ said. Before he finished the sentence, the car began to vibrate wildly as though caught in an earthquake. It shook so badly, it rattled their fillings; and they couldn't see straight. BJ slowed down, but the reverberations continued — longer and slower, but just as bad.

"S . . . s . . . stop!" CJ tried to say. They thrashed about as if they rode a wounded bull elephant.

BJ pulled over onto the shoulder, stopping in front of the Pilot Point graveyard. "Man-o-man! I thought the car was coming apart!"

"Damnation and double damn!" BJ began, warming up for a string of curses that continued as he got out of the Pinto. "Just our luck!" He slammed the door. An orange cloud of rust arose. "It's only Monday, and everything that could go wrong has! Why me? WHY ME?!" He started pounding his fists on the car's hood, adding to the dents and knocking off more rust.

"Hey, BJ, graveyards give me the creeps."

"Don't be a sissy," BJ said, slumping to his knees, his head resting on the hood. "We're in deep dung now. Mom'll really kill us. We wrecked the car, and I didn't even do anything! Heap!" He struck the car again.

"Hey! Hey! BJ, there's somebody in the graveyard!" CJ whispered.

"What?!" BJ asked, looking up. He stared past the low stone wall and into the graveyard, which was on a gentle knoll. The moon was silhouetting the lithe figure and the headstones all around her. BJ blinked. He couldn't see her face, but her shapely curves seized his attention.

The very tan woman with the long, curly blond hair was dressed in a formal gown, cut low and boldly revealing. When the gentle breeze blew, her cape billowed behind her, and the slit in her dress parted, displaying most of her tan thigh.

BJ swore he heard the whisper of silk and her breathy sigh. "Maybe she's in trouble," BJ said aloud, licking his lips, "and needs help. At least I hope she is."

"What's she doing out here at this time of night?"

"Who cares?! She's a total babe!" BJ's eyes were wide and round, his attention riveted. "I ain't never seen anyone like that except in a magazine or on TV!" Somehow, his vision seemed telescopic and, despite the darkness and the distance, he could see the woman clearly.

She was flawlessly beautiful. Her eyes were blue, the color of tropical waters reflecting the dappled moonlight. She smiled, cupid red lips parting to reveal perfect, pearly white teeth.

BJ's breathing accelerated, and he started to perspire. "Just like I'm always dreamin' about."

"Wow," CJ whispered. His eyes were as large as saucers. His glasses fogged, so he quickly took them off to rub them dry.

"Is that incredible or what?" BJ asked. "Who needs to go to California?" He wiped his sweaty palms on his jeans. His tongue was thick and his mouth dry. He licked his lips.

The woman glided down the slope toward them, gracefully moving between the headstones. The brothers were so enthralled they didn't notice the fog trailing her.

She opened the gate and approached them, her gaze steadily holding theirs. She didn't appear to strut or sashay, but something about the way she walked — the movement of her hips — spoke to them in some primeval way.

Finally, BJ managed to whisper dryly, "Can we help you, Miss?"

She smiled even more broadly.

He tried again, louder this time: "Can we help you, Ma'am?"

"Ah, I am such a lucky lady to find two gallant gentlemen to come to my aid. And here I thought I'd have to search for something to slake my thirst," she chuckled quietly.

"Then, you do need help?" CJ asked, surprised. At first he'd been afraid of the woman, but no longer. In fact, he couldn't think about anything except how gorgeously sexy she was, as if she'd walked right out of one of those girlie magazines BJ smuggled into the house.

"Yes, I am very, very thirsty," she said as she reached them.

Enthralled, neither of them moved; they simply stared at her.

The stranger reached out and caressed their faces, long red nails leaving slight marks along their cheeks.

"You do want to help me, don't you?"

Both nodded.

"Good." She chuckled and slipped her arms under her cape. With a dramatic flare, she lifted it, surrounding and swallowing them within the dark cape.

The brothers saw black, felt something hot, then very cold. Then — they were gone.

The darkness around the woman suddenly writhed as though alive, then the fog engulfed her. Moments later, a pale man dressed all in black stood there.

His elderly frame appeared renewed, standing straight-backed and shifting restlessly. He laughed, then pulled his cloak around him.

It seemed to shrink, then widen, bulging in odd places. The cloak suddenly flapped as though a mighty gust of wind tugged at it. Then, a large bat appeared, flying rapidly toward the lake.

Chapter Eleven

MISSING PERSONS

"**O**hhh," Garrett Brashear groaned and rolled over in bed, clamping the pillow to his head. The ringing in his head wouldn't stop.

Last night he convinced Racquel to sneak out, and they'd done several nights worth of partying. He'd tried to get her drunk enough so they could have some fun besides just kissing. But although he'd gotten her jeans off, she'd turned him away at the last moment. Garrett hoped she felt as bad as he did this morning; even the tiniest movement hurt.

The ringing was louder, and Garrett realized it wasn't in his head. He reached over and pounded on his clock radio, but the sound continued. Then he heard the front door open, and his mother talking with someone. Garrett sat up and wished that he hadn't. The room spun, whirling around as though caught in a tornado.

"I hate mornings," he muttered and collapsed back onto the bed. Again Garrett heard voices, more distinctly this time. Who was Mother talking with? Who cared?

"Water," he breathed. His mouth felt like he'd swallowed a desert. Somehow he managed to stand and stagger to the door. He almost blundered outside when he realized his mother was talking with Rains County's largest sheriff. Garrett didn't think it would be wise to talk with Racquel's dad this morning, especially if Racquel looked as he felt right now.

What if Racquel had told him about their making out? Or the sheriff had guessed? Garrett grabbed his clothes and began dressing. A quick exit out the window would be the better part of valor.

"Don't apologize again," Mrs. Brashear said. "I can guess why you're here. It's to talk about Garrett and Racquel."

"And some other things." Sheriff Knight spoke in a deep, baritone voice that reminded Garrett of someone speaking from the bottom of a well. "I also want to talk to him about that incident Friday night at the Chandler place."

Not sure which subject was worse, Garrett silently groaned.

"I've talked with everyone except your son," the sheriff continued. "After speaking with Judge Keyshawn's grandson, Reverend Candel's daughter, and my kids, I know Garrett's involved. I'd like to get everyone's story. Be thorough, you know."

"How about from the Mochrie's?" Garrett's mother asked. "Weren't they involved?"

"I didn't get much from the Mochries," the sheriff began, "and nothing about Garrett, just enough to confirm their own guilt."

Garrett's smile was sickly. Except for Scooter, he could really pick them: loyal pawns and playthings. But when Garrett heard Sheriff Knight recount what happened, his smile disappeared, and he grew angrier and angrier.

THE SHERIFF KNEW EVERYTHING! TOTALLY BETRAYED! Garrett fumed.

Quickly he forgot about his hangover, as though it had been boiled away by his rage. He would definitely boot Russell out of the Graveyard Armadillos. And both weasels would pay for this! Cutting out their tongues would be too good for them. He'd have to think of something. Nobody crossed Garrett Brashear. NOBODY!

"Can you go easy on Garrett?" Mrs. Brashear finally asked. "It's his first offense, unlike the Mochrie boys."

"First time he's been caught, Thelma. According to everyone involved, he's the ringleader of a gang called the Graveyard Armadillos."

"Oh, no! Joseph will be very upset."

Garrett covered his mouth to keep from swearing out loud.

"Yes, I understand being disappointed by your kids. It sets a bad example, and some people lose faith in us." The sheriff sighed. "And the news gets worse. From everything I've heard, Friday night was your son's idea."

His mother gasped.

"I'm sorry, but I can't turn a blind eye to his involvement."

"That's not what I'm asking. I promise we'll keep him so busy he won't have time to see the others. Teenagers cause so much trouble when they're together. And idle hands — well, you know."

"Tell you what: as punishment, Russell and Racquel are cleaning up around the administrative offices. If Garrett joins them for the rest of the week and apologizes to Marcus Chandler, I think that'd be punishment enough."

"That sounds fair to me," Mrs. Brashear replied.

But not to me, Garrett thought; I'm outta here. He wished the hammering in his head would stop. Everything seemed painfully loud.

"But we have more serious problems than pranksters. We've called a volunteer meeting for this afternoon to organize a search for the missing kids."

"To look for Jo Gunn?" Mrs. Brashear asked.

Garrett stopped in his tracks. Jo was missing? He couldn't believe it.

"Yep, and now the Mochrie boys are missing, too. Some say good riddance, but we must find out what's going on around here. I have a bad feeling about all of this," the sheriff said.

"What happened to them?"

"It seems the Mochrie boys took Pearl's car for a joy ride, or more likely, to run away. But the car broke down near the Pilot Point graveyard. The U-joint broke."

"That's near where Missy Watkins and Debbie Harrison were found dead," Garrett's mother gasped. "Not far from the Pickup Ranch!"

"We found the car, but no sign of the boys. Strange thing is — they left everything behind. We found clothing, food, money and even BJ's gun still in the car."

So the Mochries were missing, too, Garrett mused as he put on his sneakers. Was this connected to Friday's adventure?

Chandler's Pickup Ranch was the last place Garrett had seen Jo. If Chandler was a vampire — and he wasn't positive of that despite what he'd told the Armadillos — Chandler might have done something to Jo. Maybe he should personally search the area.

It was daylight, so he wasn't worried about Chandler bothering him. Vampires couldn't stand the sunlight, so they didn't venture out during the daytime.

As Garrett opened the window, he heard Sheriff Knight say, "The meeting is at the VFW hall at one o'clock. It's going to take at least that long to put up fliers, make calls, and pass the word. We're even trying to get the farmers to come, offering them rides; but we can't wait any longer. Clues might disappear. The town is already real shaken, and I'm afraid it's going to get worse unless we do something fast."

"I'm pretty shaken, too," Garrett muttered.

"Now, let's go talk with your son," the sheriff said.

Garrett heard those infamous words as he quickly slipped out the window.

Garrett ran around the house and jumped into his Trans Am. Without looking back, he fired it up and drove off, heading for Jo's house. If he didn't find anything there, he was going to the Pickup Ranch.

An hour later, he parked at the abandoned house near the Chandler Ranch — the same place they'd all parked Friday night. He'd been to Jo's house and talked to her elderly mother. She hadn't seen Jo since Friday dinner, and she was sick with worry. Her boys, Jack, Jake and Tom were out looking for her. Garrett felt Jo had never left the ranch.

Garrett climbed out of his car and locked it. Just for grins, he peeked into the dilapidated building. It was empty. He'd hoped he might find Jo's motorcycle; no such luck. Curious more than concerned, Garrett headed toward the hole in the fence, intent on searching the ranch.

At the break in the rusty chain link fence, he found a piece of torn black cloth. Maybe a shirt, Garrett thought. Making sure he didn't tear his clothing on the sharp, rusty barbs, Garrett carefully moved through the gap and headed onto Chandler's property. The woods were hot and sticky, despite the thick growth that draped everything in shadows.

Garrett wasn't sure where to begin searching. He thought for a minute, then decided to head to the '74 Ford pickup and start from there, backtracking.

After ten minutes or so tramping through the forest, Garrett was sweating like a galloping horse in summer and his head was pounding as though it had a stampede running through it. He paused and took a deep breath while he looked around.

Garrett could see the line of nose-down pickups and the ranch beyond them. Against the green of the field, the house beyond the row of trucks looked very clean and white — the menace of last Friday evening disappearing in daylight. He noticed cows and horses in the pasture near the shore of Lake Tawakoni.

Garrett cursed. He knew he hadn't imagined things Friday night! Maybe vampire's didn't feed off animal blood, just that of humans. It didn't matter, Garrett decided. Chandler was dangerous, vampire or not! At the very least, an abomination! They didn't need someone spreading AIDS or any other diseases. Whatever Chandler had was certainly dangerous. You could tell that by looking at him.

Garrett continued walking. As he neared the barn, he glanced frequently at the house. He wondered if Chandler might be keeping Jo hostage, keeping her cold so the vampire could drain her blood slowly. Garrett shivered. Shaking off that thought, he forged ahead, reaching the row of pickups.

Garrett glanced at the barn. His curiosity getting the better of him, he skirted along the edge of the woods, through the row of trucks, and around behind the barn, so he couldn't be seen from the house. He passed the occupied pigpen and stopped at the side door, listening for a minute. Did vampires make noise? They didn't have living bodies or flesh.

After hearing only silence, Garrett opened the door. A blast of hot air and the heavy aromas of hay and manure escaped the barn and briefly stunned him. He wiped the beaded sweat from his forehead, took a deep breath and peeked inside.

The place looked to be a typical barn with several stalls leading to the back pasture. Farming tools and utensils hung on one wall. Shelves crammed with jars, boxes, and cans lined another. Bags and barrels of grain were scattered about. Corn dust lingered in the air and glittered in thin shafts of sunlight streaming between the planks of the walls.

Garrett opened several closets, finding nothing of interest. He shivered. He felt watched. Eyes followed his every move.

He passed the ladder to the hayloft, then a set of empty stalls. Beyond them, Garrett saw what he was looking for — a padlocked closet. Garrett heard a soft thump and a scratching noise. He turned and looked around but saw nothing amiss. He still felt watched. He waited a moment, carefully searching for an observer, then headed to the closet.

Garrett was disappointed to find it double padlocked. He cursed, having left his tools at home. He'd have to return tomorrow before discovering what was inside. A morbid thought suddenly assailed Garrett: What if Jo was locked inside? "Jo?" he asked, his voice quivering. Garrett put his ear against the door and listened. Was that breathing? He strained, urging himself to hear something, but he wasn't sure.

Garrett glanced around. He still felt watched. But he had to do something.

He rapped lightly on the door. No response. No sound. Dead quiet.

As Garrett turned around, he spotted movement. Something black darted from rafter to rafter. He craned his neck. What was that? It moved again, claws scrapping along wood. Garrett looked for something to throw.

A loud, angry caterwauling suddenly pierced the air. It was so loud and so awful, Garrett's ears hurt. A second, then third beast joined the first, and the sound grew louder, almost driving Garrett to his knees. He staggered toward the door.

Seized by his imagination, he wondered if vampires had cats for pets. He burst from the barn, sprinting as though chased by ghosts. Finally he slowed down by the metal row of trucks, chiding himself and promising to return tomorrow.

Still intent on finding signs of Jo, Garrett backtracked along Friday night's path of flight. Occasionally he found a foot print or two, but no signs of Jo. He thought the red and white flashlight was BJ's, and the black wire-framed glasses were certainly CJ's.

Garrett almost gave up, then a strong wind gusted. Dirt, twigs, and leaves ripped past him. He covered his face, protecting it and waiting for the debris storm to subside.

When it did, Garrett lowered his hands. The blowing leaves had moved enough to expose a knife — an ivory-handled switchblade!

Garrett ran to it and snatched it up. It was Jo's all right! She never would have left it! It was her lucky charm!

Garrett searched the area and found a black and white bandanna. It was Jo's, too! Now he raced back to the car. He had to tell someone! Then he remembered the meeting this afternoon.

They would know what to do!

Chapter Twelve

THE TOWN MEETING

Scooter attended the meeting for volunteer searchers with Grandma and Judge Grandpa. Surprised by the turnout, Scooter's gaze wandered over the crowded room.

He'd been to the VFW meeting hall before for cakewalks, sockhops and other fundraisers, and as today, the place was overflowing with restlessly expectant people. Unlike the times of a celebration, the crowd was grimly concerned, as if debating a crucial community issue.

No banners or party decorations enhanced the Spartan hall. The air reminded Scooter of the church during the funeral. People were obviously steeling themselves for bad news. With tight lips, grim expressions, and flat gazes, the deaths and disappearances were weighing heavily upon the people of

Gunstock.

Were they readying themselves for war? Scooter wondered. After all, they were in the hall of the Veterans of For-
eign Wars; and every chair was occupied, leaving many folks
sitting on tables, squatting in the aisles, or leaning against the
walls. Scooter recognized lots of people: teachers, volunteer
firefighters, ranchers from outlying plots, and people who
worked with his grandfather at the courthouse. The forces had
been marshaled. Unrelenting smokers had to wait outside, getting their news second hand from the man standing in the doorway.

Scooter spotted Garrett Brashear in the back corner of
the room. He appeared disturbed, a frown on his face, his
eyes darting from side to side as if he were being hunted. Scooter
wondered what was going on. He didn't see Racquel. Had they
broken up? For her and Russell's sake, Scooter hoped so.

Mayor Jones, several town council members, Mrs. Mochrie, Reverend Candel, and the three Gunn brothers sat impatiently along the front row. Mrs. Mochrie was leaning against
Kristie's dad. Still wearing their hats, Jack, Jake, and oddly
slim Tom Gunn shifted about restlessly, chewing tobacco and
spitting into cups. Russell and Kristie sat a few seats away next
to the sheriff.

Sheriff Knight stood and climbed the stairs to the stage.
After getting the nod from Judge Grandpa, Scooter moved
to his friends and sat in the sheriff's seat next to Kristie.

Sheriff Knight started explaining the situation, but sitting so close to Kristie caused Scooter's mind to wander to
yesterday and their berry-picking adventure.

"Ow!" Scooter felt thorns jab him in several places, and
he stopped moving. Somehow, he'd backed too deeply into
the bushes and was held prisoner by the thorny brush. Several briars clung to his socks, cutoffs, and shirt; but worse,
more of the thorns dug into his back, arms, and legs, effec-

tively holding him captive.

He would have to ask for help. How embarrassing. "Uh, Kristie?"

"Yes?"

"Could you give me a hand?" Scooter asked, then took a deep breath and closed his eyes. "I'm stuck."

"You're stuck?" she asked incredulously. She tried not to laugh but wasn't too successful. "Boy, you really are in a mess," she said, looking at him.

She leaned back and looked thoughtful. "What's it worth to you?"

"Kristie! That's mercenary!"

She made a face. "That's a terrible word. Anyway, what's it worth?"

"A quarter of my berries?" Scooter tried.

"Three-quarters.

"Three-quarters?" Scooter blustered. He started to move, felt the thorns rip and tear at him and stopped. "Half!"

"Done." Kristie laughed and moved to help. "Plus, you have to do a drawing of me!"

"No way!" Scooter didn't feel like embarrassing himself further.

"Okay, a quarter and a portrait of me," Kristie countered.

"But — "

"Or I let you rot right here. It's that simple."

"Okay," Scooter finally agreed.

Kristie slowly untangled him, pulling the thorn branches away from his socks, then his legs, flinching as she extracted thorns from his skin. She stuck herself once or twice, even through her gloves. She yelped but continued, "I wish I had Mom's garden shears."

Kristie suddenly seemed much too close for Scooter's comfort. She brushed him, then eased against him, reaching around behind him to remove several entangled branches. When she straightened some, her face was just below his.

It seemed very warm and very still. For a moment, she quit working to free him.

Scooter had the impression, or at least thought he did, that Kristie wanted to be kissed. But he'd never kissed a girl before! He'd thought about it several times, especially since Friday. But what if he missed? Or he was sloppy? This wasn't one of his better days — first the bicycle, then the dog, and now the thorns. Scooter sighed. Was he a klutz?

Kristie smiled, then pulled the last few thorns from his shirt. Her touch was surprisingly gentle. Wherever she touched him, Scooter tingled.

"Thanks," he said, not knowing what else to say. "I'll draw you looking like an angel or something. Maybe a singer — "

"That'd be cool," Kristie said.

Next time, Scooter thought, I will kiss her. I will!

Scooter received a jarring elbow to his ribs.

"Pay attention," Kristie whispered with a smile.

Scooter wondered if she knew what he was thinking.

On the short stage and dwarfing the speaker's stand, Sheriff Knight was finishing his well-phrased explanation, "And that is the extent of our knowledge. Deputy Sheriff Lewis is passing around copies of photographs of BJ and CJ provided by Pearl Mochrie. They were last seen at home and believed to have abandoned the car near the old Pilot Point graveyard."

Scooter shivered. He remembered the eerie feelings, the cold fingers running along his spine as he fixed his flat tire last Friday night. With the sun setting, the shadows of the tombstones had grown long, reaching for him. Flash had acted like a sentinel guarding him against the oncoming darkness. Scooter had never changed a tire so fast. Those moments were still so vivid in his mind, he wouldn't have any trouble describing it or drawing a picture.

"We aren't sure when Jo disappeared," the sheriff continued. "It might have been as early as Friday night. She was last seen at the Chandler Ranch."

A murmur suddenly swelled within the crowd. "Now, now. Let's not jump to conclusions."

"Have you searched the place yet?" Mayor Jones' assistant, Merl Cauthon, asked.

Scooter had met the short, rotund man more than once and always came away with an unfavorable opinion that he couldn't quite explain. He just didn't like the man.

"No cause to. Motorcycle tracks leave the abandoned house where she'd parked near the Chandler Ranch. We think something happened to her while she was riding. We've asked at stores and gas stations in the area, but no one saw her that night or any time since."

Ramon Hernandez, the owner of a landscape development company, asked what she looked like.

"We don't have any photographs of Jo," Sheriff Knight responded, "but all you have to do is look at her brothers to get a good idea of what Jo looks like. Stand up, boys."

Jake and Jack, the two stout brothers, got to their feet, followed by the whipish brother, Tom. The threesome turned around for all to see.

With the news Jo was missing, possibly since Friday night, Russell felt very low. If he hadn't kept the secret, if he'd told his dad about Friday night right away, then maybe Jo wouldn't be missing. Maybe what Scooter's grandfather had said about secrecy was right, and that Racquel was full of it. It wouldn't be the first time that 'Miss Know-It-All' had been wrong.

"I want to thank y'all for your support. I'm mighty pleased by the turnout. I can't stress how important it is to have as many eyes searching as possible. Let's leave no stone unturned. Pay particular attention to the areas around the lake. Unfortunately, at this time, we don't have any concrete leads, especially on the Newbaker twins."

"Yes we do!" Garrett Brashear announced as he jumped

to his feet.

Everyone was stunned for a moment, then a wave of murmuring and muttering filled the place. Without a trace of nervousness, Garrett walked to the stage with switchblade knife and a bandanna in hand.

A low jabbering of speculation began. A man in back stepped outside to pass on the latest turn of events to the smokers. The tension in the room rippled with anticipation, a harp string ready to be strummed.

As Garrett walked past the front row to the stage, Jack Gunn gasped loudly, "That's Jo's knife! I gave it to her!"

"I'll be damned!" Jake said. All the brothers' expressions were the same, gaping and wide-eyed as though they'd been slapped. "That's her lucky charm!"

"Where'd you get that?" Tom jumped to his feet, moving toward Garrett.

"Garrett, what is the meaning of this!" the principal asked his son as he rose from his chair.

"Just what the Gunn brothers said. I found Jo's knife and her bandanna." Garrett flipped the switchblade over and showed him, saying, "And the knife is even engraved with her name."

The hall was tensely silent once again.

"Where'd you find them?" Jake Gunn shouted.

"At the Pickup Ranch, in the woods," Garrett said. "Chandler's Ranch."

The silence was long gone, destroyed by the astounding revelation. Chaos ensued as voices erupted, everyone asking questions at once. Many stood to get a better view of what was going on. Wanting to hear more, some folks from outside crammed into the room.

"Order! Order!" Sheriff Knight yelled. No one listened to him. He pounded futilely on the podium. "This doesn't tell us anything new!" His words didn't seem to have any impact.

"Exactly where'd ya find it?" Jack yelled, grabbing Garrett by the sleeve and spinning him around.

"Unhand my son!" Principal Brashear yelled.

Pearl Mochrie was moving closer, trying to hear the conversation. Others crowded forward, too.

"I want to know where! NOW!" Jake grabbed Garrett with both hairy paws and shook him. Jake's sneer was threatening, his fingers tightening on Garrett's jacket lapels.

"About halfway in, not far from a creek," Garrett said. "Head due north from the abandoned house next to his property on Tawakoni Dam Road."

"I knew that Chandler was twisted!" someone behind Scooter shouted. "Now we know what he's really like."

Scooter turned. It was Herb Carlson, the man who owned the local gas station. He was a cynic — never believing the best in people or that good things might happen.

"Yeah, he's a real weirdo all right!" a woman with a high voice shouted.

Jeremy Evan from the water company agreed. "Looks weird! Writes weird! Acts weird! I don't want him around anymore. Send him back to Hollywood. Plenty of weirdos there!" Mr. Evans had such a large birthmark on his face it appeared to be a tattoo.

He should talk, Scooter thought.

"PEOPLE! ORDER!"

The crowd was slowly creeping forward.

Scooter noticed the mood in the room had changed from uncertainty and anticipation to a mixture of hate and excitement. He was reminded of something from his history class. This was how mobs and riots got started. Everyone was ready and willing to blame somebody else — somebody different. Emotions were doing the thinking, just as they had for him Friday night.

Sheriff Knight jumped off the stage and landed next to the crowd around Garrett. "What do you think you're doing?" the sheriff said hotly as he pulled Jake's hands away from Garrett. As the sheriff moved in, the Gunn boy stepped back. Like an umpire in an argument with a manager, the sheriff confronted Garrett nose-to-nose. "I said, what do you think you're doing?"

"Trying to help my friend," Garrett said.

Jack and Tom crowded close behind Jake. "We demand to talk with this Chandler fella!" Jake hollered.

"I just wanna kick his butt," Jack yelled.

"String him up!" Jake snapped. "Hang 'em high, like in the Old West!"

"Listen here," the Sheriff began, "nobody — "

Pearl Mochrie pushed her way to demand of Garrett, "What about my boys? Any sign? Any clues?" Her expression was hopeful and her eyes aglow.

"Pearl!" Reverend Candel called to her, afraid she'd get her hopes up only to have them crushed.

"It's probably revenge for Friday night," someone in the back yelled.

Scooter thought it sounded like Mr. Ringly, the nice owner of the Tawakoni General Store.

"Yeah, we all know Chandler was embarrassed Friday night. Now he's avenging himself on our young. I've always said his movies were the product of a psycho," a tall lanky man Scooter didn't recognize called out. A few others nearby agreed with him.

Much of the mob seemed to need to grab onto something tangible, to condemn somebody right away, as if that would solve the problem and drive away their fear and uncertainties. Scooter wondered if any of them had seen one of Chandler's movies. Did they believe that the movies reflected the man? It was fiction! Just fiction! Wild creations! What was wrong with that?

The crowd shuffled forward, wanting to hear something. A few were bumped a little hard and grew angry. Several chairs were knocked over. A table was shoved aside. Somewhere a glass broke, shattering loudly.

An elderly woman grew outraged and yelled, "STOP THIS! Don't speak about Marcus that way! I've known him since he was a kid! I went to high school with him! He's a fine man! He's just ill, that's all."

Scooter thought it was Ms. Emmitt, the librarian.

"We don't want to catch it," a stout red-bearded man muttered.

"You just don't like him cause he isn't white!" Washington Thomas was a neighbor of the Chandler's. "Even if he looks white!"

Ms. Emmitt ignored them both and said, "You may not like his movies, but that doesn't make him a bad man!"

"But he never comes into town!" a young woman pointed out. It was Mrs. Short. Her husband worked for the power company and had been to Judge Grandpa's place more than once.

"That could be because he doesn't enjoy the company of people who won't accept his appearance. That doesn't make him weird! It makes him normal!" Ms. Emmitt admonished them. "You all should be ashamed of yourselves!"

Pearl Mochrie appeared to snap, lunging wildly past the Reverend Candel and knocking him aside as she grabbed Ms. Emmitt by the shirt. "YOU'RE A FRIEND OF HIS? WHAT HAS HE DONE TO MY BOYS?"

The abrupt act of aggression seemed to surprise everyone. The people stopped dead still and simply stared. No one said anything or moved to help.

Ms. Emmitt tried to pull away from Pearl. "Get ahold of yourself, woman! He hasn't done anything to anyone! He's a good man, I'm telling you! He has taken my grandchildren horseback riding!"

"Stop this!" the sheriff shouted as he grabbed Pearl.

Angry, distraught and weeping, Pearl began to curse.

Scooter thought he should say something. This wasn't

right! But what could he say?

Kristie suddenly sang out loudly. Her voice was thunderous at first, then slowly receded as if a tidal wave were wash-
ing back out to sea.

Everyone stared at her; many looked as though she might
be possessed or something. She took a moment to look
around.

The silence was deafening. Scooter could hear breathing
and the soft, gritty sounds of restless feet shuffling.

"Honey?" Reverend Candel asked.

She touched him on the arm to reassure him. "I'm fine,
Father. I just wanted everyone's attention. I wanted everyone
to hear — to know — that we all whipped ourselves into a
frenzy Friday night, not much different than now. In fact,
very much like now." She sighed.

"Go on, dear," the Reverend told her.

"We had convinced ourselves that Mr. Chandler might
be a vampire — childish, I know — and when he reacted angrily to us, we ran scared, thinking a vampire was chasing us.
I dropped my flashlight. CJ lost his glasses. I don't know what
else was dropped, but I'm not surprised you found something
of Jo's at the ranch. I was scared. We were all scared. We'd
scared ourselves."

Scooter was so proud of her. He took her hand and
squeezed it.

"But it was her lucky charm!" Jake emphasized. "She
wouldn't leave it. No way! No how!"

"We were so scared, none of us ever wanted to go back
there again," Kristie replied.

"Peace!" Reverend Candel called out. "Please, think, and
let cooler heads prevail. We're not animals, so let's not act as
such!"

After Kristie's admission, his words seemed to embarrass the crowd. He gently took Pearl Mochrie into his arms
and comforted her.

"Pearl has a reason to be fraught with worry, but we mustn't succumb to reckless emotions. As my daughter said so well, fear can devour us if we let it rule our lives. Instead, we should move with love to help Pearl, not jump to judgments. That will not help the missing children. It is the children who are important. We can help them best by doing what we came here to do."

"Go forth and scour the lands; see what you can find. The Lord be with you."

The crowd milled about, disconcerted and uncertain for a few moments before shuffling toward the exits.

"There'll be an investigation, I promise! We will discover the truth!" Sheriff Knight announced to everyone. Then he moved close to the Judge Keyshawn and whispered, "Judge, I need to talk to you about a search warrant."

Chapter Thirteen

THE UNWELCOME VISITOR

*J*ust after sunset, Scooter leaned his bicycle against the front hedges of the Chandler place. He yanked open the gate, ran up the front walk, then ascended the steps to the darkly enshrouded front porch. Flash lagged behind, huffing and puffing and looking wilted from running alongside Scooter all the way.

The house still felt odd and foreboding; but Scooter wasn't scared this time. Maybe it was loneliness or alienation — a word he'd just learned by reading Chandler's scripts — that he felt from the house. Or maybe, Scooter thought, he just feared for Marcus Chandler, and his imagination was racing wildly again. Mr. Chandler was being picked on — persecuted, his grandfather might say — because he directed bizarre movies, and looked and acted differently.

To some, just leaving Texas made him different. Odd. Who would want to leave the Lone Star state?

Scooter boldly stepped into the shadows and knocked on the front door. A minute or two passed before he heard the sounds of someone coming down the stairs. Neither an inside nor a porch light was turned on before the front door slowly opened.

Scooter stifled a gasp. Mr. Chandler seemed to have instantly appeared in the dark doorway. With his shirt off and white skin gleaming, Chandler looked like half a man, his black slacks blended with the darkness.

Fighting his instinctive urge to run, Scooter stood his ground, his knees slightly knocking. "Hello, Mr. Chandler," Scooter said breathlessly.

"Well, this is certainly a surprise," Marcus Chandler said in a rough voice as if he'd just awakened. "Finished reading the scripts already?"

"No, sir. I'm not here to talk about writing. I have something important to tell you," Scooter breathed, still a bit winded.

"Oh, really?" he asked with raised eyebrows. "Then come on in." Mr. Chandler pushed the door open; it reminded Scooter of a dark mouth, a hungry maw waiting to be fed. "Here, let me turn on a few lights."

"Flash, you wait . . . "

"No, bring him in. He looks to be a fine dog. I'm sure he won't hurt anything," Chandler said, looking down at the Lab.

Flash barked happily, then went into his "I'm being watched, I'll pretend I'm show-walking" routine. Scooter wasn't sure, but there seemed to be a certain self-satisfied smugness in the Lab's expression.

"Seems intelligent, too."

Flash held his head high and moved past Scooter to enter the house.

"And he's a sucker for a compliment," Scooter said, smiling.

Flash raised his nose higher, huffed, and kept going. If the house felt okay to Flash, Scooter thought, then it was all right. Flash didn't judge a book by its cover; he read it using his uncanny instincts.

Pushing aside the shivers, Scooter entered the foyer. There was a stairway ahead and entrances into a formal living room to the left and a less formal room on the right. Beyond the stairs was a hallway to the kitchen. The house was a bit rundown and dusty as if rarely used, and more cluttered than Scooter's room at his house. But then, Chandler was reclusive, probably not caring what visitors thought.

"You look as though you raced over here. Would you like something to drink?" Chandler asked.

"No, thank you."

"How about you?" Chandler asked Flash.

The Lab cocked his head and whined, then panted loudly. He appeared to wilt before their very eyes, as if he'd been walking in a desert for days.

"Water it is for your golden companion. Come on into the kitchen."

Chandler headed down a hallway full of enlarged photographs of the lake during storms, sunsets and sunrises. Flash followed, his tail thumping both walls.

"Did you say his name was Flash?"

"I named him after the DC character because he's fast. I thought about naming him Quicksilver, but his fur is golden," Scooter replied as he followed Chandler into the kitchen. Even though painted and decorated in yellow and orange, the kitchen and dining area seemed dim and dingy.

"Seems to be appropriate." Chandler grabbed a plastic bowl from a cabinet, filled it with water, then set it down on the floor for Flash. "Are you sure you don't want something?" Chandler asked.

Scooter nodded. "I'm sure, but thanks for asking. I have a water bottle on my bicycle."

"Well, have a seat then and tell me what you're in such a hurry to tell me."

Scooter joined him at the kitchen table, but then immediately stood back up as though he had a spring attached to his tailbone. "Did you hear about the meeting in town today, Mr. Chandler?"

"Call me Marcus," Chandler said.

Scooter liked him more already.

"Which meeting was that?"

"The one to organize a search for the missing kids," Scooter said. "The Newbakers, Jo Gunn and the Mochrie brothers are all missing. Did you know that two girls, Debbie and Missy, have been found dead not far from here?"

"Yes, I've heard the tragic news," Chandler replied, appearing a bit distracted.

Either that or he wasn't fully awake, Scooter thought.

"Weren't they found near the dam and the old Pilot Point cemetery?"

Scooter nodded. "I — I thought you didn't keep up with town news — "

"Ophelia — Ms. Emmitt — calls and keeps me current on the town gossip and happenings. She called earlier today, all upset about the meeting.

I must admit, I wasn't fully alert when she told me what happened, but then she did ramble some. She's always been excitable, especially for a librarian." He chuckled, then grew serious, the many lines in his face deepening.

With the shadows, the lines in his face could have been cracks instead of folds in the pale flesh, Scooter decided.

"Ever had bad news hang over your head like a thunder cloud for months, raining on you all the time?"

Scooter thought for a moment, then replied, "Sometimes it seems like that."

"People are blaming me for this. Convicting me already, aren't they?"

Scooter nodded. "A couple of people," he understated, "accused you of being a murderer."

"Well, at least I won't be surprised when the sheriff and his deputies show up." He sighed. "Why don't you tell me about it in more detail while I brew a batch of coffee?" he asked with soft grimness. "Do you drink coffee?"

Scooter said no, but it was nice to be treated as an adult. He started the story by mentioning the surprising number of people at the crowded meeting and went on from there.

As Chandler puttered around the kitchen, he said very little and asked no questions.

He only spoke once, saying, "It seems everybody loves a spectacle and easy answers."

Scooter was just about finished when Flash quickly jumped to his feet and stiffened from snout to tail. The growl was low, deep and foreboding. The Lab's tail stood straight out.

"Is something wrong, boy?" Scooter asked.

Flash's ears were perked, and his eyes were alert, staring down the hall expectantly.

Scooter patted his companion and noticed how stiff the hair was to the touch. Meanwhile, he felt a cold breeze, just as he heard a knock at the door.

Flash barked, then growled menacingly.

"I'll get it," Chandler said. "From what you've said, it might be the sheriff with a warrant. Had more visitors in the last week than all the previous year," he grumbled. "Two weeks ago, before you kids came, someone broke into the place and vandalized it."

That explained his angry reaction Friday, Scooter thought, and the messy house, too. He glanced at Flash, whose stare hadn't wavered. Both watched as the gaunt and pallid author walked down the hall, disappearing from sight.

Again, a low grumble started deep in Flash's throat, then grew to a growl as the front door opened. As though winter had arrived early, a chilling breeze filled the kitchen, followed by voices.

Scooter stood up, curious about the visitor and intending to peek down the hallway. As he passed Flash, his companion latched onto his shorts.

"Let go!" Scooter whispered. He could hear Chandler and a man talking. The stranger's voice was charismatic and compelling, totally gripping Scooter's attention. He wondered what the stranger looked like.

Drawn forward by curiosity, Scooter dragged Flash with him. The Lab stubbornly refused to let go. "I mean it, let go!" Scooter demanded quietly.

Flash whined through clinched teeth.

"What's wrong?" Scooter whispered, trying to pry open Flash's jaws. "Are you opposed to eavesdropping?"

Chandler's and the man's voices were growing louder now.

Were they arguing? It seemed so. Scooter listened, keying into the voices and drawing impressions from them. He looked to Flash and noticed his pleading expression, the one usually reserved for begging for popcorn or table scraps. Flash only acted like that around danger. "I promise not to leave the kitchen," Scooter said.

Flash's jaws relaxed some.

"I promise," Scooter said, patting the dog's head.

Flash whined, but followed Scooter to the hallway.

"And you, Mr. Shade, are a crackpot, which doesn't surprise me," Chandler retorted to some comment. "There are plenty like you in Hollywood. That's one reason I left to come home again."

"I am unique, even in Hollywood," the man replied coolly, even softly, though it echoed through the house.

The voice chilled Scooter. He tried to imagine the man,

draw his appearance in his mind.

"Listen, Mr. Shade. Even if I believed you, which I don't — because I know Micah isn't a vampire — I wouldn't help you." Chandler sighed, sounding distracted as though thinking back.

"Micah's always gotten too involved with his roles, a reason his personal life is in shambles. I'm not surprised he wondered why I was able to film him, the Prince of Darkness, when the undead can't be filmed. Simply put, Mr. Shade, even if I was crazy enough to believe you, I don't work in the business anymore. I don't make movies anymore. I'm retired. And I don't want to write and produce the Life and Undead Times of Joe B. Shade. Even if it is a sure fire hit! Death is not a popular subject with me right now!"

"Ah, yes, my condolences on your parents."

"All I want is to get healthier and to have some peace and quiet! Time to mourn," he finished quietly.

"As for retirement, Mr. Chandler, many people unretire. Micah is not playing a role, as you suggest, that I guarantee you," Mr. Shade responded.

I'll bet he's wearing black, Scooter thought. A nice formal suit and a hat. Both expensive.

"Micah a vampire? Ha! That's ridiculous!" Mr. Chandler laughed.

Scooter thought the laughter sounded a bit strained.

"He'd rather die. He's a camera hound!" Mr. Chandler ended.

"That's why he enjoyed working in your last two movies — all filmed at night, if I recall correctly."

Mr. Shade would be pale and wearing sunglasses; it was a celebrity thing, Scooter thought. His eyes were probably dark and hypnotic.

"And technology has changed much in the last few years," Mr. Shade continued. "Hollywood and special effects are capable of miraculous things now. If they can capture spirits and one who no longer truly lives on film, as Kirlian photography and you have done, then one day they might even create life. Computers have life, and life can both create and destroy."

Scooter imagined Mr. Shade — his smile cool, his lips white and bloodless.

"Ease my curiosity, Mr. Shade. How are you so sure Micah's a vampire?"

"I turned him into one myself."

"I've heard enough! HAD ENOUGH! I'M UP TO HERE! I've been patient, Mr. Shade or whoever you are; but now, just go away and leave me alone! I'm going to get very rude in a moment," Chandler finished, his voice tightly controlled.

Shade was tall, thin and rock solid, Scooter thought — and elusively compelling, a mystery waiting to be revealed. He appeared to be there, but was he really? What would happen if you surprised him and tried to grab him?

To see if he were right, Scooter started to peek around the corner again.

Flash grabbed him by the shorts, nipping him as he pulled him back.

"Ouch!" Scooter shook his head to clear away the fog. Then, he muttered, "Thanks," and patted Flash, his ear still cocked to the conversation on which he was eavesdropping.

"Mr. Chandler, you owe me. The least you could do is invite me inside. Hear me out?"

"OWE YOU? OWE YOU!" Chandler cried.

They probably could hear him several ranches over, maybe even in town, Scooter thought.

"Yes. Owe. For Friday night. I did you a favor."

"You were there!"

HE WAS THERE! Scooter thought. Flash had sensed him before at the dilapidated house. Scooter had felt him before!

"Yes. Three of those children will no longer be bothering you."

"Y . . . you've been terrorizing the kids?" Chandler sounded incredulous.

"Terrorizing? No. They have all died happy in comfortable arms," Mr. Shade replied. "What I give is a gift. A gift of freedom. Few are blessed to walk the night. Most are not worthy. Those who are, such as myself, require . . . sustenance."

"You really believe you're a vampire, don't you?" Chandler asked in dismay.

Scooter was stunned, rooted to the spot. A vampire? Sustenance! A favor, Friday night. Had Mr. Shade fed upon Jo, BJ and CJ? What about Missy and Debbie? Could he really be a vampire? Impossible, except Scooter could feel the evil. It crawled over him.

Flash had evidently sensed the evil, too. Smelled it, Scooter thought. Couldn't Mr. Chandler?

"You know, if I hadn't seen this type of behavior before, I'd call the police on you." Chandler sounded tired. There was a long silence. "On second thought, I am going to call the police."

"HEY! WHAT ARE YOU . . . "

A brief scuffle ensued, then Scooter heard:

"Listen to me, Marcus Chandler. I am real. Deadly real. A vampire in the flesh." Shade chuckled. "So to speak. Come back to Hollywood quickly — or many more in Gunstock will die. I'd enjoy spending more time in this quaint town convincing you to see things my way. Come back to Hollywood. And remember," he finished even more quietly, his low voice full of venomous menace, "I have infinite patience."

Terrified, Scooter and Flash snuck out the back. Vampires in Gunstock! Who could he tell? Judge Grandpa? What would he say? It didn't matter; no one would believe him. Maybe Russell or Kristie? He'd have to try.

With trembling hands, Scooter grabbed his bicycle and rode frantically through the darkness toward home.

Chapter Fourteen

HUNTIN'
KIN

Kristie bicycled along the glistening oil road toward the Keyshawn's place, oblivious to both the heat and her surroundings. The flat, green countryside was sprinkled with cows and horses, and seemed endless in every direction. She absently brushed away a bug and vaguely noticed a battered white pickup passing her. The stink that it left behind made her gag and cough, interrupting her singing.

Kristie thought about Scooter while singing, "Kiss the Girl," from *The Little Mermaid.* She looked forward to seeing Scooter again and going canoeing. There was something special about the tall, lean, redheaded boy with freckles and bright eyes. He made her feel special. They related to each other, as if they were twins. With their looks, they could pass for siblings, but she didn't think of him that way.

Scooter was shy — another thing she liked about him. He wasn't arrogant or selfish, and he didn't try to be cool. He was just naturally friendly. Kristie smiled as she thought of Scooter knocking himself out in the woods, injuring his finger fixing her tire, then getting thoroughly stuck in the thorns. He was a bit of a klutz, but in her eyes that made Scooter even more endearing.

In a frightening instant, Kristie realized she was no longer alone. "Yo, Jack, look what's coming down the road," came a voice from just ahead of her. Kristie glanced up to see two stout cowboys, arms crossed and legs spread wide, in front of the battered pickup blocking the road.

Kristie wished she'd been paying more attention; she might be in trouble.

Both men were unshaven, rough-looking and leering at her. Their builds were similar — barrel-chested with thick arms and legs, wide necks, and jowled, scruffy faces. A third cowboy, resembling the other two but much slimmer, sat inside the truck, impatiently watching it all. They were obviously brothers.

Hey, hadn't she seen them recently? They reminded her of Jo. It was the Gunn boys! Jo's brothers. Kristie shuddered. She'd heard about them. Hadn't they recently gotten out of prison?

"Hey, Jake, she looks ripe enough to pluck," Jack said; then he spat tobacco juice. His left eye appeared to have a life of its own, wandering every which way. A thick pillar of a man, from his black cowboy hat to his snake-hide boots, he was dressed in jeans that hung below his hips and a tan shirt that was too small for him, bulging across his belly and leaving some of his stomach exposed below the tattered hemline.

"Wonder if she wants to play?" Jake said, leering even more broadly. His few remaining teeth were yellowed and stained, reminding her of wickets. A bright red scar marred his right cheek, and his black hat was tilted far back on his head.

Kristie braked, the pads squealing, then she quickly attempted to turn around.

"Hey, where ya goin', skirt?"

Kristie's heart skipped a beat as the bicycle wobbled through the turn. The back tire slid, and Kristie stuck out a foot to steady herself. She quickly recovered and began pedaling furiously. She heard their boots thudding against road as they pursued, growing closer — and closer.

She couldn't breathe — the air was too thick. What would they do to her? She shuddered, then focused on going faster.

The bicycle slowly began to gain speed. Just a little longer, she prayed. Please!

Kristie heard the pickup start, and her hopes plummeted. The running footsteps grew louder and louder, closer and closer. She heard wheezing close behind her and felt breathing down her neck. She felt them right behind her.

"Comin', sweet cheeks," Jake called out.

Claw-like hands reached for her. She tried to pedal faster, but panicked.

Suddenly, Jake plucked her off her bicycle. It wobbled off the road and into the tall weeds.

Kristie kicked and fought to slip free of his wet grip, but he was too strong. "RAPE!" Kristie screamed.

Jake's hand shifted, clamping over her mouth and immediately cutting off her scream. She bit him, but he only laughed.

"We can't have any of that," Jake said with a leer, his eyes wild as he moved his face closer, his scarred cheek twitching as he stared at her. "We don't want no trouble. We just wanna ask some questions." He held her off the ground as easily as he would a baby.

Jack moved closer, the sordid smile igniting his eyes. One eye looked at her while the other drifted about, looking at nothing in particular.

Kristie was terrified. She considered kicking one of the Gunns in the crotch, but didn't know what to do about the other one. He could easily manhandle her and throw her into the truck. Then she didn't want to think about it. She felt like throwing up. If she did, then she might not be so attractive to them.

"Ask questions and have some fun, ya mean?" Jack added.

The white pickup slowly pulled up next to the trio. "We don't want no trouble," the reed slim brother told the other two. "We can't do Jo no good if we're on the lam from the law. Right, Jack? Ya just got out."

"Don't rub it in, Tom, or I'll smack ya," Jake said.

Tom Gunn leaned out the window. He wore glasses, as did Jo. His hair was lighter, and his face much leaner than the other two brothers. He didn't leer when he asked, "Are you Kristie Candel?"

Kristie tried to say something, but couldn't even manage a squeak, so she just nodded. She hoped there was at least one reasonable brother in the bunch.

"I thought I recognized you. We want to ask you some questions about Friday night. When's the last time you saw Jo?"

Kristie eyes were pleading. She could barely breathe through Jake's hairy paw.

"Let her talk, Jake," Tom said.

"Why? She'll only lie. She can't help it. She's a girl. Let me do it. I know how to question them."

Tom's stare was piercing, forcing Jake to look away from him when he said, "Last time ya 'questioned' a woman ya spent five years in jail. Now let her speak."

"That's Knight and Keyshawn's fault!"

"It's your own stupid fault, ya moron. Now listen. Ma's worried about Jo. We promised we'd find Jo, and we can't do that from jail. Now let the girl speak. When was the last time you saw Jo?"

"Friday, just after sunset, right before we were chased. We all split up. I haven't seen her since." Kristie's words were rapid and breathless.

"Lying!" Jack drew a hand back.

Kristie shrank away. "It's the truth. I swear!" Kristie pleaded. "Why don't you talk to Garrett Brashear? They're good friends."

Jake roughly handed Kristie over to Jack, who stuck his face in hers. "We plan to talk to Brashear. But I was looking forward to questioning the Keyshawn brat, first. I owe Judge Keyshawn and Sheriff Knight, and a Gunn always pays his debts."

"Seeing you in the road was just plain good luck," Jake said as he rubbed his sweaty palms on his pants. "Been a long time since I frolicked with a redhead."

"Jake, put it on hold, ya hose bag," Tom said sharply.

"I think she's lying," Jack contended. "This'll make her talk." He wrapped his massive hand around her mouth, then carried her to the truck bed.

"Dang it, Jack!" Tom yelled, climbing out with a pistol in his hand. "Think about Jo! Don't make me wing ya."

"You ain't got the guts!" Jack shouted.

Kristie squirmed, futilely fighting.

A gun roared and the road near Jack's left boot exploded. He jumped back, letting Kristie go. "Hey!" he yelled.

"Leave her alone!" Tom said, waving the gun.

Jack reluctantly released her.

"Thank you," Kristie sighed with relief as she held back the tears and pulled her shirt into place.

"I'll get you for this," Jack yelled, his stare menacing.

"After we find Jo," Tom snapped. "We promised Ma. Okay?"

Jack said nothing.

"Okay?"

Jack finally nodded slowly.

"Now go get her bicycle! Sorry, ma'am. Were you going to see Scooter Keyshawn?"

Kristie wanted to lie, but she thought better of it and nodded.

"We'll take you there. Don't worry, I wouldn't let them harm ya. Ya see, we think somebody's hiding something, keeping secrets. And having you with us, Scooter might be more helpful. He's been visiting that Chandler fella. Right? Right?"

She nodded.

"You just climb in here with me," he began. When she hesitated, he added, "Or I'll let you ride with Jack in the back."

She was thinking of escape, running away, but she saw any such action as futile. Jake firmly escorted her to the door of the truck and jerked it open. She climbed in, and he followed, running a hand up her leg.

Jack tossed her bicycle in the truck bed and hopped in back. Then, Tom shifted the pickup into gear, and with a jerky start, they were off to question Scooter.

Chapter Fifteen

IN SHINING ARMOR

The ebony waters slapped softly against the canoe as the two boys whispered so they wouldn't scare the fish. The night sky was clear, the half-moon blotting out most of the stars and highlighting the lake with dappled reflections of white-gold. A warm, gentle breeze rippled the shimmering surface. The lantern gently rocked, creating a shifting globe of brightness around the canoe.

Russell put a worm on his hook, then sent it sailing into the water with a loud plop. "I'm about ready to give up. I've hardly had a nibble. And when I do, they just steal my bait. Hey, did you hear that?"

"What?" Scooter asked, waving off a pesky mosquito that was taking advantage of the darkness.

"Someone is cruising the lake."

They could barely hear the dull hum of a boat's engine roll across the waters, but it was growing louder.

"Think there's any danger?" Scooter asked.

Flash woofed softly.

The once distant noise was no longer muffled but a crisp whine, quickly getting closer and louder — moving fast.

Russell looked about but didn't see anything. If the on-coming boat was close, he'd see their navigation lights. "Naw, don't sweat it. They'll see our lantern." The words barely out of his mouth, he froze.

Russell stared south across the water. Something was heading straight toward them at a dangerously fast speed. The roaring grew louder and louder, a hungry beast growling at full speed.

"I . . . I don't like this."

"Where is it? I can't see anything, but it sounds close." Scooter said as his head swiveled every which way.

Flash was barking and pointing southward.

"That way." Russell pointed south.

"LET'S GET OUTTA HERE!" Scooter cried.

Russell began to reel in his line.

"Drop it and ROW!" Scooter said.

Russell dropped his rod and reel and grabbed a paddle.

The deafening motor noise was almost on top of them.

"Oh, n . . . no . . . NO! STOP! STOP!" Russell yelled, jumping to his feet and waving his arms.

A large V-hulled boat charged them; white waves churning in their lantern light.

"WE'RE HERE!" Scooter yelled, jumping up and waving.

The canoe rocked dangerously. The boys grabbed the gunwales to keep from falling overboard. Flash's nails scraped across the boat bottom as he struggled to stay on his feet.

The approaching boat's green and red lights suddenly flashed on, but instead of slowing, the craft picked up speed

— preparing to ram them.

"STOP! P . . . PLEASE ST . . . STOP!" Russell screamed, waving his arms frantically.

The boat's bow grew larger, a green and red-hued sea monster frothing at the mouth. The roar of the engine was deafening, a massive swarm of angry hornets converging upon an intruder.

"LET'S GET OUT OF HERE!" Scooter cried.

Russell froze.

"DIVE! DIVE NOW!" Scooter tackled Russell, sending them overboard.

Flash jumped, too, following them into the dark churning water.

Hearing the roar near his head, Russell stroked with all his might into the deep water.

Above, the abandoned canoe squealed a twisted, wrenching cry, exploding into thousands of fiberglass shards. The lantern sailed into the air, the flame dying as it hit the water. A shower of plastic debris slowly fell upon the lake.

The water churned and thrashed about, pulling Russell upward. He resisted, fighting to stay down. Nearby, the water was ripped, the propeller blades spinning and dragging him closer. He was being sucked in!

Russell struggled, feeling the sharp propeller near his hands. The pull was too strong!

Suddenly, the blades of death were gone, passing overhead, leaving a dull, diminishing sound. Like a leaf in a hurricane, Russell was tossed about in the aftermath. On the verge of blacking out, Russell stroked upward for air.

Exploding to the surface, Russell's first thought was to give thanks for the sweet-tasting air; then he yelled, "SCOOTER!" Russell looked around. Pieces of the canoe floated everywhere, bobbing in the moon-sparkled water, but there was no sign of Scooter.

Russell spotted a life jacket bobbing in the surf and swam

for it. "Scooter! There you are! Thank God!" Russell snatched it, holding it in a death grip, only to discover nothing attached to it. Where was Scooter? He wanted to cry; they should have worn life vests. They knew better. But if they had, then he wouldn't have been able to dive under the surface to escape the propeller blades.

"Scooter!" Scooter couldn't be dead. He'd saved his life!

Russell noticed the whine of the engine was growing louder once more. Maybe the boat was coming back to help. Russell looked around and saw the craft returning. "HEY! HELP!" The boat slowed, then angled away from Russell, circling as though investigating the collection of flotsam. "I'm over here!"

The cruiser continued to circle slowly. A pale face with greasy dark hair appeared over the side, its eyes alight with pleasure. "Did you lose something?" Garrett Brashear asked, then laughed. "Where's your boat? Looks like you've fallen to pieces, Russ ole boy. Hey, where's the Scoot man?"

Russell felt something heavy bump against his leg; he was afraid to look. When he finally did, Russell found part of the boat's ravaged bow nudging him.

"Well, I hate to hit and run, so I think I'll stay awhile," Garrett yelled. He disappeared for a moment, the boat's speed increasing. The waves roughened, growing taller and thrashing about, slamming into each other.

Garrett turned the boat around. Russell thought Garrett didn't look right; his pallor looked sickly, the pale flesh giving off a dim crimson radiance. Was it the reflection of lights off the water or something else?

"Hey, I'll bet you can't guess who I brought with me."

"G . . . Garrett, don't."

"You brought it on yourself, Russell. Y'all betrayed me. I don't get even, I get ahead. Way ahead. Anyway — give up? She wants you dead as much as I do, not just for betraying me, but for being a baby."

"Hi, Russell," Racquel said as she leaned over the edge.

She was pale. Her eyes were cold, with a far away alienness that made Russell shiver.

"Garrett! Racquel, p . . . please!" The thrashing swells threw Russell about, reaching five feet or more in height. A wave slapped him in the face; he swallowed water, choking and sputtering. Another wave buried him.

"There's no place for the weak at night," Racquel said as Russell broke the surface and gasped for air. "Thanks to the kiss of the vampire, I'll stay beautiful forever."

"Say goodbye, Russ," said Garrett.

"But . . . "

"Bye," Racquel said.

"Ditto," Garrett said. He and Racquel waved to each other, then they disappeared.

The boat lurched forward into overdrive. The circling craft grew closer, the circle tighter. The waves higher. Russell wildly bobbed up and down, floundering like a wounded gull. Several times he lost a grip on the life jacket, only to clutch at it and pull it back to him. Finally the boat pulled away, and Russell breathed a sigh of relief.

But the boat suddenly swung around, bearing down on Russell once more. He started to swim away when he bumped into something heavy.

Russell glanced down and saw Scooter's bloody face, mouth open and vacant eyes wide and staring up at him. "NO!" he screamed. He looked back to the onrushing juggernaut that was almost atop him, the bow spanning nearly all his vision. He tried to dive, but he'd gotten entangled with Scooter and couldn't.

Russell wrestled himself free, then dove. The boat slammed into him, stunning him and pushing him aside for a moment, only to draw him steadily toward the propellers.

Water slapped Russell in the face and he sputtered. "H . . . hey, what'd you do that for?" he asked Scooter.

They were sitting on the dock, fishing poles in hand. Unfazed by the commotion, Flash was asleep on his back with his feet in the air, soaking up the sun.

Scooter held an empty plastic cup. "I'm sorry, Russell, but you'd gone bonkers! I know we promised to talk about last night's nightmares," Scooter said, "but you were really into it. You seemed to be reliving it."

Russell nodded. "I . . . I was." Inwardly he shivered, remembering his dream.

Scooter understood how his friend felt. Today, he wasn't sure whether he'd actually heard the conversation at Mr. Chandler's ranch last night or if he'd dreamed about it. Now he wasn't so sure he wanted to share his 'nightmare' with Russell. It was real, and yet seemed too impossible to be real.

"I asked a couple of questions," Scooter continued, "but you didn't answer them. You just kept talking. When I turned around, you looked scared to death." Scooter remembered Russell's expression, his face pallid, quivering lips and eyes staring unseen past him. "I grabbed your leg and shook you; but you kept on talking, looking more frightened with each word. It was either slap you or drench you. Sorry, I thought the splash would be more gentle."

"It's okay," Russell said as he wrung the water out of his Grateful Dead shirt.

The silence hung between the boys as the tension slowly subsided.

Nearby, a group of ducks waddled into the water, then swam away. Two pale blue dragonflies patrolled the area around the dock in geometric patterns. All about, birds were chirping, adding beautiful notes to the lazy summer morning. The boys had risen early to do some daybreak fishing off the Jaystone's dock.

"I think you scared the fish away with that story," Scooter finally said with a laugh.

Russell seemed to relax. "They weren't b . . . biting anyway, just like in the dream. You know Scooter, I've had b . . . bad dreams every night since last Friday. Sometimes I even get them during the day! Almost like visions."

"Come see the Russell the Great, Master of Future Seeings," Scooter teased.

Russell threw a bobber at Scooter, then said, "If I believed in premonions — "

"I think you mean premonitions."

"I'd s . . . say something b . . . bad is going to happen. Think I might be pre . . . precognitive?"

"Sounds far fetched, but I guess anything is possible," Scooter said, thinking back to last night. Was there a vampire in Gunstock? Or just a crazy man?

Scooter studied his friend. Obviously Russell hadn't been sleeping well. He had major travel bags under both eyes, and the dark circles appeared to bore into his sockets. After last night's fitful sleep, Scooter wouldn't be surprised if he also looked haggard.

"Hey, you still wearing that c . . . cross I gave you?"

Scooter had almost forgotten about it. He reached inside his shirt and removed the crucifix, wondering if it had protected him, shielding him from discovery last night.

"It's not everyday someone gives me a lucky charm. Except," Scooter said with a smile,

"It doesn't draw fish."

"Did you know t . . . that Dad talked with the principal?"

Scooter shook his head. "I think we should avoid Garrett for the next century." He scratched again, then grabbed his Coca-Cola.

"Or enlist," Russell said, chewing on a fingernail. "What time is Kristie c . . . coming out?"

"About nine-thirty." Scooter checked his watch. "Soon."

"You said you t . . . two went bicycling Monday?" Russell asked.

Scooter nodded.

"How d . . . did you get poison ivy?" he asked with a smile and pointed to Scooter's arm. "Isn't t . . . that what that rash is?"

"Poison ivy!" Scooter exclaimed, awakening Flash.

"Yeah, you usually don't get it by riding your bicycle on the roads. It's usually found near bushes and trees. Uh, you two going s . . . st . . . steady?" Russell asked with a slowly spreading smile.

Scooter choked on his cola.

Russell's smile grew broader as Flash woofed, then pranced about. "Ah, the truth comes out. How's it g . . . go? Scooter and Kristie sitting in a canoe, k.i.s.s.i.n.g. First c . . . comes love, then comes marriage, then comes Scooter junior with a b . . . baby carriage."

Red-faced, Scooter finally managed, "You're about to get very wet, sopping wet in fact."

Flash yawned excessively loud, appearing bored by the threat.

"Actually, I'm h . . . happy for you, bud." Russell set down his pole and suddenly grabbed the front of his shirt with both hands. "Scooter, help. I don't know what's happening t . . . to me?" He shook himself.

Flash jumped up and started barking excitedly, dancing around Russell.

"Scooter! I think my evil t . . . twin has taken control of me? Help!" He clamped a hand over his mouth, then appeared to jerk himself to his feet. His hand slipped away from his mouth, and he said, "He's forcing me to walk off the dock! Help me, Scooter! H . . . "

Scooter didn't move as Russell teetered on the edge, apparently struggling to keep from falling. "Good riddance."

Russell immediately stopped acting and looked stunned. "You wouldn't help me?" he asked.

Scooter shook his head.

"You'd let me walk off the edge? What if I was possessed or sleepwalking?"

Scooter smiled. "I'd shove you in."

Flash huffed, sounding disgusted.

"S . . . some friend you are."

"Then I'd either throw you a life vest, a rope, or jump in after you and save the day. Be a hero."

"A hero? I've got news for you, Scooter. Heroes don't get poison ivy."

"Modern day ones do."

"What if both Kristie and I were drowning?" Russell proposed. "Who would you save?"

"I'd save you both, of course. I'd throw you the life vest, and jump in and save her," Scooter said grandly. "Besides, Flash would help. Now as far as mouth to mouth, there's no question there at all."

Both boys laughed so hard they collapsed on the deck. Flash appeared totally confused, either that or he was too sophisticated to roll around and make a fool of himself.

A noisy truck squeaked to a stop. Flash's ears perked and his nose twitched.

Scooter turned to see a battered white pickup in front of the closed gates of *Siete Hombres.*

"Who is it?" Russell asked.

Scooter shrugged. It couldn't be Kristie, and he didn't think it would be friends of his grandparents.

Scooter set down his pole and pulled cheap, snap-folding binoculars from his tackle box. He watched as a hefty cowboy jumped from the bed of the truck. Getting out of the cab, a second followed the first to the gate. Scooter could hear chains rattle when they shook the gates.

The two men reminded Scooter of somebody — but who? The shorter one turned around to yell something back to the truck, and Scooter got a look at his face. It was one of the Gunn boys!

Why were they here? Did they blame him for Jo's disappearance?

Scooter immediately went into a panic, his heart jack-hammering as though he'd just sprinted five miles. He tried to say something to Russell, but his throat was squeezed tight.

Flash whined and cocked his head, asking what was wrong.

"Scooter, are you okay?" Russell asked,

"Get down! Lie flat! Both of you!" Scooter finally snapped, pulling his friend down with him.

Flash flattened on his belly.

"We don't want the Gunn boys to see us?"

Russell instantly looked ill.

Scooter peered through his binoculars again. "Kristie's with them," Scooter said grimly.

Russell gasped.

Looking frightened and chewing her nails, Kristie was sitting in the front seat. "She seems to be in trouble," Scooter surmised. He couldn't let anything bad happen to her; she was special, making him feel good about himself.

"Why w . . . would they want Kristie?" Russell chewed his upper lip.

"We gotta help her," Scooter said.

Flash woofed agreement.

"We g . . . gotta what? You like being handed your h . . . h . . . head?" Russell was immediately ashamed of himself. "What're we gonna d . . . do? Call my dad?" Russell asked. "The Gunn boys will be long g . . . gone by the time he arrives. And we aren't sure they've done anything wrong. Uh, maybe Kristie just h . . . hitched a r . . . ride."

Flushed with anger, Scooter gave him a sharp look. "Are you stupid or just acting that way?! We've both heard stories about the Gunn brothers."

Flash bared his teeth and growled quietly.

"A g . . . g . . . good reason to r . . . run like hell."

"Well," Scooter said, "I'm gonna do something."

"What are you g . . . g . . . gonna do? Be a hero?"

"See what they want." Scooter began to rise.

"Now who's being stupid?" Russell spat out. "They'll b . . . b . . . beat your brains out." With shaking hands he pulled Scooter back down onto the dock. "Think of something else, Hero Man."

"Uh, right." Nothing else was coming to Scooter's mind. Where was the cavalry, even the local community watch patrol car with the yellow star and the old guy, when you needed him? All he could think of was calling Russell's dad. If he tried to reach his house, he'd be seen by the Gunns; two of them were climbing the rattling gate now.

Scooter felt desperate as he watched Jack and Jake drop to the gravel road. He was tempted to run to the Jaystone's house, break in and use their phone, but that would probably set off their alarm. Scooter thought, then smiled. "I have an idea," he said, "but I'll need help." Then, he whispered in his friend's ear.

"Oh, no," Russell gasped.

Flash woofed and smiled, his gaze darting back and forth from the boys to the pickup.

"Don't worry," Tom told Kristie. "This won't take long." He watched as his brothers walked along the road toward the houses.

Kristie bit her fingernails and wondered if she should jump out and run.

Tom watched his brothers intently.

She was shaking so much she was afraid she'd fumble with the door handle. Her bicycle was in the back, but she didn't care about it right now. All she wanted was to get away — as far away as possible.

Kristie started to shift, slowly edging along the front seat toward the door. She saw something moving in her side mirror and stopped.

"Where you goin'?" Tom asked.

What to do? "I'm just so scared!" Kristie cried, the tears

coming in a torrential outpouring.

"Don't worry, Missy, I won't let them bother you as long as the Keyshawn kid's straight with us. I ain't a lawbreaker like my brothers. I just gotta find out what happened to Jo, understand?"

Kristie continued to sob, as if she might never stop.

"Jo's family, you know, and us Gunns stick together." Tom sighed, then slumped back onto the seat and watched his brothers pass the second house on the left. They were nearing the narrow part of the peninsula and had moved closer to the road.

I can't believe he talked me into this, Russell thought as he lay under the Gunns' pickup truck. You're a hero, Scooter had told him. Be a hero. Russell's hands and knees burned; he'd crawled the last fifty feet down the road and along the gravel drive leading to the gate. If I hadn't deserted him Friday night, Scooter never would have made me feel guilty enough to do this, Russell moaned silently.

With that Russell jammed another handful of thick mud into the tailpipe of the truck. Russell waited to see if anyone noticed. Nothing like red Texas clay to clog the pipes. Now, let's see you start this bucket of bolts.

Seconds passed as though running steeply uphill. Could they hear his heart? Russell heard Kristie crying and silently thanked her. He was amazed no one had seen him crossing the street, hiding in the tall grass, or crawling as he approached the pickup.

As he moved away, Russell couldn't shake the feeling that someone was walking alongside him, just waiting to step on him — squash him like a bug. He glanced back, saw nothing and kept heading for the cover of the tall grasses.

Scooter watched as the Gunn boys disappeared, blocked by the A-frame house. With a leap, he cleared the fence surrounding *Siete Hombres* and ran to the Jaystone's back porch, hoping he hadn't been seen.

Flash somehow appeared to fly instead of leap, like Underdog in the cartoons, and he joined him near the short set of steps.

Time to break the law, Scooter thought, looking around the garden. He picked up a softball-sized rock, hefted it, then moved to a window lined with alarm tape. If he remembered correctly, the Jaystone's alarm was ear-piercing.

Scooter heaved the rock through the window. As the glass shattered, the klaxons sounded an ear-piercing wail. Scooter and Flash sprinted to the next house, rounding it, and hid behind a bush. There they could see the front gate and the pickup through the fence. While Scooter waited, he nervously scratched his poison ivy rashes.

In mere moments, both Jack and Jake were hanging onto their hats and running along the road toward the front gate. Scooter could hear them curse as they passed him.

"Ain't my fault!" one of them whined, as they ponderously clawed their way to the top of the sagging and shaking chain link gate.

Scooter heard the pickup start. The engine turned over, ran for a moment, then coughed and grew silent. A squeaking of brakes followed, then a soft clinking as the white pickup rolled forward, the bumper tapping the gates to *Siete Hombres.*

They tried to start the pickup again, but this time the battered truck engine whirred and clicked.

One of the boys jumped out of the truck bed. He pounded on the hood, then flung it open.

Scooter hoped they'd panic. They were cussing and yelling at each other, using language he'd never heard before. Meanwhile, the driver was banging on the dash in frustration. As for Kristie, she looked frightened beyond words.

Mustering as much courage as he could, Scooter scooped up a stick and walked toward the gate. Flash was at his side, looking tense and ready to spring to his defense.

When they were about twenty feet away from the gate, the Gunns noticed him. "It's the Keyshawn brat and his mutt," one spat.

"Who cares! Just get us out of here!" the other heavy one yelled. The alarm was persistent, demanding attention and adding an air of urgency.

"Is that Kristie with you?" Scooter tried not to choke on her name. He could tell she'd been crying. Scooter mustered an image of Judge Grandpa's expression, then tried to imitate it. Remember, be a hero, he encouraged himself; in the end, everything worked out for heroes. Or so he hoped. As if things weren't bad enough, Scooter had an awful need to scratch, but he knew it would ruin the image.

Girding himself for what he must do, Scooter called out to Kristie, "Do you still want to go canoeing?"

Kristie tried to speak, couldn't and simply nodded.

All this time, Tom Gunn was frantically trying again and again to start the pickup.

"Are you having some trouble?" Scooter said, trying to sound forceful. "First, you set off the Jaystone's alarm, then you can't start your truck. I'll bet Sheriff Knight shows up soon." His mouth was dry but he continued. "If I were you, I wouldn't want to be detaining Kristie."

Jack jumped against the fence, ready to climb it. "Before the sheriff comes, I'm gonna kick your butt!"

Flash snarled in a way Scooter hadn't seen or heard before.

"Fine," Scooter somehow managed to get out through his dry mouth. "Get yourself thrown in jail again. You break and enter, then you kidnap, and finally commit assault and battery. That should get you twenty or more with your record."

"I'm gonna kill you!" Jack started to climb the fence.

Jake jumped to join him.

Flash began to bark wildly, as if to say they'd have to deal with him first.

Scooter was trembling but stood fast. "You . . . you know I'm pretty good with trucks. I'll bet I can help you fix it so you'll be long gone before the sheriff arrives."

"WHAT?" Both brothers exclaimed as they reached the top of the fence.

"Let Kristie go, and I'll fix your truck. Plus, I'll tell the sheriff I didn't see anybody."

"JACK! JAKE! HOLD IT! He's right!" Tom cried. "If you two get caught you'll be locked up for good. That won't do Jo no good. Now get back here!"

Tom moved to the bed of the truck. Grabbing Kristie's bicycle, he tossed it into the grass. "Get out!" he yelled at Kristie, then looked back to Scooter. "You'd better be telling the truth."

Kristie grabbed her bicycle, then looked at Scooter.

"Go that way." Scooter pointed down the road. "I'll see you soon."

Kristie hopped onto her bicycle and with one last quick glance, took off down the road at top speed.

Jack and Jake had gotten down from the gate but were still leaning against the fence, breathing heavily, imitating caged animals waiting to break free. "What do we do to start this thing?" the slim Gunn asked.

"Clear your tail pipe. It's clogged." He tossed them the stick.

"YOU GOTTA BE KIDDING!" Jack screamed.

Tom walked quickly to the back of the truck and then crawled underneath. "My, my, who'd have guessed." After some poking, the pipe was clear. "Give it a try!"

Jack hopped inside and turned the key. The white pickup's engine coughed, turned over and then started.

Two of the Gunn boys quickly piled into the truck. But before Tom climbed inside, he asked, "When was the last time you saw Jo?"

"Friday, before I snuck off to take pictures of Mr. Chandler. I didn't see her when I was running."

Tom nodded, then climbed inside.

"We'll be back!" Jack yelled.

Before the pickup pulled away, Flash darted to the fence, raised his leg and peed on the bumper. Then, the truck backed up jerkily, tires screeching, as it roared off.

"I guess we showed them," Scooter said to Flash. Scooter wished he really was so bold and brave. He stood there a minute, wondering about all that was going on — nightmares, vampires and lawbreakers.

When he saw Kristie riding toward him, he unlocked the gate.

"My knight in shining armor," she cried as she jumped off her bicycle.

And then she leapt into Scooter's arms, kissing him all over his face and laughing while tears streamed down her face.

Flash barked joyously, nudging and nuzzling both of them. For the moment, Scooter was a hero — not a klutz. And everything was better than the best.

Chapter Sixteen

ENTHRALLED

Being grounded wasn't going to keep Garrett from avenging a friend. He parked his Trans Am at the abandoned house and climbed out. Just after sunset, the sky was still alight with clouds that were no longer afire, but slowly fading to the color of ashes.

Not much for sunsets, except for their romantic utility, Garrett headed for the hole in the chain link fence and beyond toward the Pickup Ranch. Something strange was going on here, and he intended to find out what.

The authorities might have to wait for a search warrant — and that was moving slowly — but not him; he hadn't felt like waiting. A wait could be deadly.

If he ran into the twisted moviemaker, Garrett patted the

.22 stuffed in his waistband; he would do whatever was necessary. He owed Jo. Whether Chandler was a vampire or not, they didn't need an 'Afro-American' around spreading diseases — vampirism or otherwise. Either way, Garrett was prepared. He wore a cross, and carried a mallet and stake in his bag, along with his other tools.

Garrett hiked through the forest, waving away gnats and slapping at mosquitoes. He'd been too hurried to put on bug repellent, wanting to escape the house before his parents returned from a meeting at church.

They didn't understand that sometimes a man had to do what a man had to do. Unlike Scooter and Russell, Garrett was loyal to the Graveyard Armadillos. If something happened to one of them, they should pay back in kind — an eye for an eye, a tooth for a tooth — or even better —more.

To not do so would destroy the togetherness of the group, and they had to stay together through good and bad, right or wrong. If someone had killed Jo, specifically Marcus Chandler, then Garrett owed it to Jo to be the hand of retribution and justice. After all, he'd gotten her into this mess.

As Garrett moved through the woods, he noticed how oddly quiet the forest was. All the country noises were missing: chirping crickets, baritone-croaking frogs, and nighttime scavengers moving through the brush. It was as if they'd all gone on vacation, leaving the woods with an eerie feeling of emptiness. He resisted the urge to turn on his flashlight and drive away the lurking shadows, which made him wonder again: Was Chandler a vampire?

He finally reached the woods' edge and stared past the line of buried trucks to the barn. Garrett was surprised to find he was cold. The night was hot and stifling. But his sweat and an unseasonably cool wind chilled him to the bone. Rubbing his arms, he stared at the barn.

The barn emanated a dim radiance that set it apart from the shadowy land around it. Was it his imagination or did it waver in the fading light — a ghostly image ready to disappear at a moment's notice? It didn't matter as long as it didn't disappear before he checked that padlocked closet. Garrett had to know what was in that closet! He couldn't shake the feeling that Jo was inside. This time he was prepared, bringing lock-picking tools and his Polaroid camera. He needed enough proof to ensure Chandler would get the electric chair . . .

Zap! A wonderful sound.

Garrett spotted movement near the barn — two figures coming from around back. Strangely enough, they seemed familiar.

Garrett carefully snuck closer, darting from truck to truck. The figures didn't move, as if waiting for him.

Garrett couldn't shake the feeling he knew them. Suddenly he knew who they were: BJ and CJ Mochrie!

Overwhelmed by curiosity and excitement, Garrett ran toward them. When he was near, he called to them. "BJ! CJ! Hey, guys!"

Where had they been? What had they been up to? Was their disappearance a hoax — a way to get sympathy for skipping out of their punishment? That was a great idea. But what were they doing here?

"Hey, guys, what's shaking?" Garrett asked as he reached them.

They didn't respond.

Before he could say anything else, his throat constricted, his tongue paralyzed by the sight of them. It was CJ and BJ, all right, but they looked bizarre.

They were gaunt and bony as though they hadn't eaten for days. Their eyes were deeply set; bony ridges prominently defined their skeletal forms. Their flesh was pale with an unhealthy glow as though they'd been retrieved from the ocean depths. Their eyes, from what Garrett could see of them, were shiny and feverish. Both smiled, but it wasn't friendly, more as if ravenous and their meal had just arrived.

"Good to see you, Garrett," BJ said, his smile plastic. "We were told — we thought — you might be coming here."

"Yes, it's nice to be joined by friends," CJ agreed.

This certainly wasn't them, Garrett thought, wondering if he should run and get help. BJ had never greeted him so cordially; it was usually something like "How's it hanging, scumwad?"

Garrett began to turn away. As though set in molasses, time crawled, and Garrett felt he was moving in slow motion.

"Do not be in such a hurry to leave," a female voice said melodiously, but with an underlying chill, an iron chime ringing in the winter winds.

With a life all their own, Garrett's eyes were pulled back to BJ and CJ. Tall and dark with eyes burning like portals to a furnace, a woman stood in the shadows behind the brothers. "Please stay with us," the woman said.

Garrett stopped moving — stopped trying to leave. He wanted to see this woman! He felt he knew her, too!

The woman slipped from the shadows and gracefully flowed toward Garrett. He was surprised and enthralled by her exotic beauty; her finely crafted features bespoke of blue blood or royalty from some far distant country. Her hair was long and dark, two strands braided in front. Her eyes were even darker, reminding him of a moonless night. They even glinted as though distant stars twinkled within them. "Hey, aren't you Tai Candace? The model?"

"If you wish it so," she replied. "Mmm. Another fine specimen of a young man, full of life and energy," Tai said as she raised her hands to caress his face.

Cool butterflies seemed to swarm about Garrett, and he smiled, enraptured. Who would ever believe he'd met Tai Candace out here in the middle of nowhere? Nobody, except BJ and CJ were witnesses.

The beautiful woman stared into his eyes, and Garrett's gaze slowly glazed over as though he were drugged.

"You will make a fine addition to my murder of crows. You shall be my eyes and ears during the daylight. Won't you?"

Smiling, Garrett nodded.

The woman smiled back, then kissed him lightly.

Garrett was bewitched; he didn't move.

"Perfect. You want me." She looked thoughtful, then added, "If I have enough crows, then Marcus Chandler will have to see things my way — or I will have a great feast! Yes, and I believe I know of one in particular who will turn the tide — change his mind. Marcus is very fond of Scooter Keyshawn. Yes, very fond." She laughed lightly like wind in the willows, then proceeded to make Garrett her thrall.

162

Chapter Seventeen

ANOTHER TOWN MEETING

Here we go again, Scooter thought with a sense of *deja vu.* He was back at the VFW hall sitting with Kristie, Racquel and Russell. As Scooter listened, he held Kristie's hand tightly. A search of the Chandler place had been conducted yesterday by the sheriff and his deputies — some deputized just for the event — and the town awaited the results.

Once again, the meeting hall was jammed, reminding Scooter of a can of sardines. The air was heavy. The mood was one of dread and restlessness, as though they were afraid to hear the news.

As Sheriff Knight began, Scooter scratched and wondered again about keeping his word to the Gunn boys. Was it similar to keeping a secret? Secrets almost always led to trouble.

But he had given his word, and Judge Grandpa often said a man was nothing without his word and his honor.

Scooter surveyed the room thoroughly; the three Gunn brothers were nowhere to be found. They didn't care about the investigation; they were the type to shoot first and ask questions later, if at all. And from what Kristie said, they thought everybody lied, especially sheriffs and judges.

Maybe, Scooter thought for the umpteenth time, he should tell Russell's dad about the Gunns. But Kristie had said, "No!" resoundingly, afraid it would cause more trouble. Even Russell had argued with her, but she'd been stubborn, saying only she could press charges. She was right; so when Deputy Lewis arrived to check on the alarm, Scooter just mentioned seeing an old white pickup truck drive away.

He had kept his word, but gave the law something to work with. Even so, Scooter felt bad about breaking the window. The three friends had left enough money in the Jaystone's mailbox to cover the cost of repair. Meanwhile, since the incident, he and Kristie had grown closer. She spent as much time as possible with him, holding hands and smiling. She also hugged Russell and Flash often. Scooter wondered when it might wear off; he'd be sorry when it did.

Unnoticed by the foursome, Garrett managed to sneak into the meeting hall. As if invisible, Garrett glided across the back of the room. People didn't even glance at him. He settled into a corner, blending in with the shadows and listening, all ears and eyes for Tai.

At the front of the room, Sheriff Knight cleared his throat and said, "As some of you may have heard, we found Jo Gunn's body on the Chandler Ranch, not far from where Garrett Brashear found her knife and bandanna." A murmur rippled through the crowd, along with several "I told you so's."

Scooter slumped in his chair, heartbroken. Kristie

squeezed his hand.

Sheriff Knight raised his hand for quiet. "We found her in a creek ravine. It appears she fell, cracking her head open and bleeding to death. Not only does a search of this area indicate this — due to the lack of other footprints — but so does the autopsy. The death appears to have been accidental."

"Then you won't be charging Marcus Chandler?" Pearl Mochrie asked.

"No, ma'am, we won't," the sheriff replied.

A couple of people applauded. Many others grumbled.

An older man in overalls, Scooter recognized him as a rancher named Mr. Peters, stood up and asked, "Any connection to Missy's or Debbie's deaths?"

"Not that we've discovered so far."

"Then Chandler could be connected?" Mr. Evans asked. His face was flushed, somewhat hiding his birthmark.

"I didn't say that." The sheriff sighed.

"Let it go, Jeremy!" somebody in back yelled.

As more questions were fired, Scooter thought back to Tuesday night and wondered if he should say something about the crazy man who had visited Marcus Chandler. But he didn't want to sound like a flake.

Back in the corner, Garrett stewed as his mind worked feverishly. He didn't appreciate the idea of Chandler as a murderer being shot down. Thinking about Tai's intoxicating beauty, a sudden wave of jealously overwhelmed Garrett. If Tai wanted Chandler for some reason, that was enough reason for Garrett to want him dead. Once Tai had Chandler, Garrett realized, she would drop him stone cold dead. He would no longer be useful. But if Chandler were out of the way, then . . .

Garrett smiled, noticing he was sitting next to Aaron Nathans, the postmaster. Nathans was a rumor-monger and a paranoid alcoholic who believed his place was haunted and that aliens had landed in his backyard, demanding — of all things — beer and Twinkies. He was the perfect man to jumpstart this mob against Chandler. "Chandler's not only a murderer, but a vampire," Garrett said softly.

With wide eyes, Nathans turned to look at Garrett.

Garrett nodded slowly, as if they might be sharing a secret. "Debbie and Missy were drained of blood, which is why their deaths were bloodless," Garrett said in a whisper. "He just partly drained Jo to disguise the true cause of death, then pushed her down the ravine. Looks like she bled to death."

As if the light of truth had gone off in his head, Nathans nodded, believing every word.

Mr. Nathans abruptly jumped to his feet and asked, "Have the autopsies been completed on Missy Watkins and Debbie Harrison?"

Sheriff Knight nodded.

"Had they been drained of blood?" Nathans demanded.

The question sparked murmurs, and several stunned and disgusted looks.

"For now, that's restricted information."

"I heard they were!" Mr. Nathans charged.

Garrett loved weak-minded people.

Mr. Ringly from the general store agreed. Soon everybody seemed to have heard it. Finally, Sheriff Knight admitted that was the case. And Garrett smiled.

"Then maybe," Mr. Nathans rushed on, "Marcus Chandler's a vampire. He's allergic to the sunlight, isn't he? Living by night and shunning the day! Don't know about the rest of you, but he sounds like a vampire to me. All the deaths have been on or near his property. It started with his return from Hollywood. First his poor parents, now — "

"That's utterly ridiculous," Sheriff Knight replied.

"You're just covering up because he's a celebrity!" Mr. Carlson snapped. He was still wearing his oily mechanic overalls.

The place literally erupted, responding to Mr. Nathans' and Mr. Carlson's accusations.

Scooter was appalled. Some people wanted to believe, since they were desperate to find a cause and end their fear. He hoped he would never be that overcome by fear — that desperate and angry.

"He's evil! Look at the movies he's made!" Mr. Short yelled. "His brain is rotted!"

"Always has been. As a child, he tortured animals! I knew he was a devil child!" someone yelled from the back.

"I've been fishing along his shores before, but I don't anymore. I've seen stuff, horrible stuff, climb from the waters and walk on shore!" Mr. Evans told everyone.

The accusations continued, linking his strange movies to an evil mind. More people claimed to have seen strange things on the ranch. Others conjured further stories from when Chandler was an odd youth — the second coming of Freddie Kruger. They sounded as if they might be reading the headlines from some tabloid newspaper.

But it was the hushed whispers that worried Scooter even more.

"Martin, we should go out to the ranch. Conduct our own investigation."

"Yeah, Ramon, we'll ask the questions," Mr. Short replied.

"And in a none too gentle way," Mr. Hernandez agreed.

"We'll find out how allergic Marcus Chandler is to sunlight," someone whispered across the row to the other men.

"Listen to y'all," Ms. Emmitt, the librarian, began. Mr. Thomas, Chandler's neighbor, joined in to defend him.

"This is horrible," Scooter whispered to Kristie. "Mr. Chandler isn't bad. He just has a wild imagination."

"And he's ill," Kristie pointed out.

"He's d . . . different," Russell added, summarizing the main problem people had with the moviemaker. Once again, Russell wondered if all this would have happened if he'd told his father the truth; Jo might not be missing. But he had put his trust in his sister, who trusted Garrett — a bad decision.

Garrett suddenly leaned between Scooter and Kristie, and said, "Isn't this quaint?"

Garrett's abrupt appearance surprised the foursome. He seemed to have been conjured from thin air.

Scooter thought Garrett looked peaked — his eyes bright, shiny, and feverish. He was also perspiring, a fine sheen of sweat covered him.

Scooter thought of Russell's description of Garrett in his latest nightmare; it seemed uncannily accurate. From Russell's reaction, he agreed. Was Russell clairvoyant?

"Garrett!" Racquel said breathlessly. "Where have you been? I've been looking all over for you!"

Garrett ignored her and stared at Scooter. "I know what happened to BJ and CJ. The same thing is going to happen to you for betraying the Graveyard Armadillos. Then you'll never tattle again. I promise it. 'Bye, Chaquita!"

Without another word, Garrett departed, moving soundlessly as though on cat's feet. He left before they could say anything. He'd heard what Tai wanted to know and had accomplished his own desire — turning the town against Chandler.

Racquel called his name, but was barely audible in the din of the chaos. Accusations were thrown about. Cooler heads argued with hot ones, but the crazy accusations continued unabated like a rapidly infectious disease.

"I'm telling you, he's a vampire," Mr. Nathans continued. "Got sick in Hollywood! Now he's back for revenge!"

"That's why he makes the movies he does!" Mr. Carlson agreed.

"Let's hang 'em, just to be safe!" a man in back yelled.

"Hanging doesn't work for a vampire. Stake him through the heart!" Mr. Nathans told everyone.

"For the sake of the children," Pearl Mochrie agreed.

Crying, Racquel ran after Garrett, pushing her way

through the angry mob. Russell followed, fighting his way to the door.

As Scooter struggled through the unruly crowd, he wondered how Garrett had gotten out so easily. Along with the accusations, the number of people seemed to have expanded.

Just as they escaped outside, the threesome saw Garrett's Trans Am roar away.

Weeping, Racquel pursued, racing down the street on her Rollerblades. Kristie, Russell and Scooter ran for their bicycles, intent on following. Flash joined them.

The chase was on!

Chapter Eighteen

THRALL TRAIL

Late into the day, Russell, Kristie, and Racquel still trailed Garrett's Trans Am. Garret was driving slowly.

They tried to stay out of view, just in case Garrett glanced in the mirrors. Sunset passed to twilight. The car now had its lights on, making it easier to stay near but out of sight.

Earlier, after racing out of the meeting, they had caught up with Racquel. They eventually convinced her it was better to follow Garrett and discover what was wrong than to openly confront him.

Garrett had been obliging, slowly cruising Gunstock, as though getting intimately reacquainted with the town. Or, as Scooter mentioned, perhaps Garrett wanted them to tag along. Finally, though, just before sunset, Scooter and Flash headed home; they had to or be grounded for all eternity. Scooter had looked worried about something.

"H . . . hey!" Russell exclaimed.

The Trans Am headed toward the highway. It wasn't moving slowly anymore, but it wasn't racing away, either.

"Hurry or we're g . . . going to lose it!" Russell pedaled as fast as he could, sprinting down the street.

Garrett paused at a stop sign, crossed the highway onto Tawakoni Dam Road, and drove toward the lake.

Russell shot across the highway in pursuit, relieved there wasn't any oncoming traffic. Kristie was close behind, pedaling as if her life depended on it. Both were afraid they'd lose sight of the black Trans Am, then they'd never know what was wrong with Garrett.

The Trans Am picked up speed, and the tail lights dwindled in the distance. Just before completely blending with the darkness, the car turned right, its high beams rippling across the trees along the road. Without the headlights they might have lost him completely.

"That's the only . . . way in and out of the Lakeview neighborhood," Russell gasped, as he slowed to a stop. He was an expert on the back roads. Over the last year, he and Scooter had ridden all around the lake. "He's t . . . trapped, so to speak."

Kristie stopped next to him and huffed, "I was afraid he was long gone."

Russell nodded, then leaned on his handlebars.

"Let's wait," she puffed, "for Racquel."

Russell nodded again, saving his breath. They had their breath back by the time Racquel finally arrived.

Red-faced and screeching, she was in true form. "DAMMIT RUSSELL! YOU'VE LOST HIM!" She coasted by on her Rollerblades, then circled back around.

"Racquel, he . . . "

"YOU'RE WORTHLESS!"

" . . . just t . . . turned on Lakeview," Russell finished.

"There's no other road out of that subdivision," Kristie finished. "We can sneak up on him, no problem."

"Oh," Racquel said.

"Now c . . . come on," Russell said, riding ahead. As they turned down Lakeview Lane, he and Kristie flicked on their headlights to illuminate the way.

"I hope the moon comes up soon," Kristie said.

Racquel hit a pothole and cursed as she almost fell forward.

"Want to s . . . stop? Go home?" Russell turned around and asked.

"NO."

"Okay," he breathed, "then f . . . follow right behind me. I'll d . . . dodge the potholes. You follow my path."

"Okay."

After what seemed like miles, a neighborhood came into view. Most of the homes were along the shore, facing northward. Smaller, less expensive houses were across the road. Lights were on in about a third of them.

"He's probably meeting another woman," Racquel said tersely.

Before either of her companions could respond, Kristie's headlight illuminated Garrett's Trans Am parked in front of a darkened cabin. The tiny, shuttered dwelling was set apart from the others, as if exiled or abandoned long before the others were built. In the quiet of the night, they heard voices coming from behind the cabin.

"I don't understand," Racquel whispered as she circled to stop. She hit another chuckhole, then leapt toward the car, using it to keep her upright.

Russell motioned to Kristie, and they leaned their bikes against a pair of trees. Racquel followed, walking carefully across the grass.

"I wish Scooter and Flash were here," Kristie whispered.

"Me t . . . too," Russell agreed.

"Come on, let's sneak a look," Racquel said; then she paused to remove her Rollerblades. "We'll walk along the woods," she added, then took the lead.

They crept along the edge of the lawn, next to the forest where there were plenty of hiding places among the shadows, high weeds and thick foliage. Moving carefully and in spurts, the trio darted from tree to tree. Racquel quietly complained about the things she stepped on or those that bit into her feet. Every now and then, when a stick snapped or they made noise, they paused to listen. The voices ahead didn't seem to notice.

When the trio neared the lake, Russell pointed out a small boat that had pulled ashore. By the dim, amber light of the rising moon, they saw Garrett talking with two figures.

"I wonder what's going on?" Kristie whispered.

"I d . . . don't know if this will help, but . . . " Russell pulled a cheap pair of collapsible binoculars from his back pocket and looked through them. "Wha . . . I . . . I don't believe it!" Russell hissed.

"What!" Racquel whispered.

"He's with the Mochrie brother, B . . . BJ and C . . . CJ," Russell whispered.

They were wearing their hats, shadows hiding their faces. Their builds and stances seemed right, but their movements were jerky, almost mechanical.

"At least I . . .I th . . . think it's them," Russell finished.

Kristie and Racquel were stunned and silent.

Despite poor visibility, Russell thought he saw two large shapes lying in the boat. At first, he figured they were bundles of supplies, but with a chill he suddenly wondered if it might be two kids bound and gagged. The Newbakers, maybe? He couldn't tell.

"What's going on?" Racquel asked.

Russell didn't say anything; he just handed her the binoculars.

She looked in them, then whispered, "You're right! It's them!"

"D . . . do you s . . . see anything in the boat?" Russell stammered quietly.

"Is that — two bodies?"

"What did you say? What's going on?" Kristie whispered.

"A k . . . kidnaping," Russell replied.

Along the shore, the Mochries climbed into the boat. Garrett pushed it into the water, then hopped inside as the boat coasted away from shore.

"What're we going to do?" Kristie asked.

"I . . . I don't know," Russell stammered. "Tell our father?"

"But they could go anywhere from here," Kristie groaned.

"We've got to follow somehow," Racquel said determinedly.

"T . . . they'd know it," Russell replied. "They could hear us." He didn't want to follow. This reminded him too much of his recurring nightmare.

One brother yanked on the outboard motor which coughed and rattled. Garrett turned back to shore and yelled, "Bye, guys. It's been fun leading y'all around by your noses. Scooter was smart; he gave up and went home to tell on me." Garrett laughed, his voice easily carrying across the water.

"Garrett! What's going on?!" Racquel yelled. "Is that BJ and CJ with you?"

"Ah, Racquel, Chaquita, you're such a fox!" he told her.

The motor caught and roared.

"Hasta la vista, babe."

"Never should have trusted him," Russell muttered.

"Garrett, wait!" Racquel screamed.

BJ waved his hat, then they headed slowly toward the center of the lake.

With a scream of frustration, Racquel took off in a dead sprint, heading for the house on the other side of the cabin. The darkness around it seemed brooding.

"R . . . Racquel! W . . . wait! Where are you going?! W . . . what are you doing?" Russell yelled as he ran after her.

"Crazy girl!" Kristie gasped, running alongside him. "Racquel! STOP!"

Racquel darted toward the shore, then ran onto the dock. Without slowing, she jumped into a boat, causing it to rock wildly and take on water.

"What are you doing?!" Kristie demanded, racing down the dock toward her.

"I'm following!" She yanked on the outboard's pull cord. The motor coughed. She yanked again. "He's not leaving me! There's something wrong with him! He needs me!" The motor coughed, then sputtered.

"Wait!" Russell cried. He and Kristie scrambled down the ladder and climbed into the boat just as the motor roared to life.

"Untie and push off!" Racquel told him.

"I . . . "

"Come with me or get out! Which is it?" Her stare was piercing.

Russell untied the boat, then pushed off.

"I can't believe I'm doing this," Kristie said. "I wish Scooter were here. I really do."

"He'd just rock the boat," Racquel said. She throttled up the engine and raced after Garrett.

"You don't even know where they're going," Russell said as he turned around from the bow. The wind pulled at his words, and the motor's roar muffled them. "And I can't hear them any more!"

"We'll stop if we need to! Right now I'm following their wake!" Racquel replied over the moan of the outboard motor.

"Look," Kristie pointed ahead, "you can see their wake in the moonlight."

Far ahead at the head of the fading wake, the moonlight reflected on the churning froth behind the engine. Once in a while, the aluminum boat gleamed or flashed. The figures in the boat were dark and mostly seen by imagination.

Russell felt uneasy. This was too close to his nightmare. He began to sweat.

"I wish I had a cellular phone," Racquel sighed.

"They're heading toward the middle of the lake. Think they're crossing?" Kristie asked.

"Or going to the islands," Russell pointed out. "Maybe Fisherman's Island?"

"We'll follow," Racquel maintained.

They traveled a few minutes in dark silence, then Russell couldn't handle it anymore. He told them about his recurring nightmare.

Kristie shivered, but Racquel just laughed. "You've been hanging around Scooter too much. What an imagination you have."

The motor suddenly coughed. It coughed again, then sputtered.

"Oh, no," Russell whispered.

The motor sputtered once more, then died.

The threesome looked at each other. Russell groaned.

"Are we out of gas?" Kristie asked. She shook herself, trying to escape the chill. She hadn't felt cold until Russell explained his nightmare.

Racquel shook one of the gas tanks; it sloshed.

"See if it's hooked up," Russell suggested.

Racquel lifted a tube. "It is."

Russell moved to the back to check the other tank. It was almost full, and he switched to it. The outboard still wouldn't start.

"I think it's clogged," Russell said. He pulled off the cover to examine the inner workings in the dim light. "Anyone have a flashlight?"

"Do you hear that?" Kristie asked, her voice cracking.

Racquel nodded. The whine of a motor grew louder. "They're coming back!"

Chapter Nineteen

DOUBLE VISION

Scooter and Flash stopped at the gates of Siete Hombres, "I'm probably in trouble again," Scooter moaned.

Flash woofed softly. The golden Lab's expression was down-trodden as though his last bone had been stolen.

Scooter was extremely late for dinner. He'd totally missed it, probably by a couple of hours. The sun had already set, leaving the peninsula gray and the shadows murky. The puffy clouds stretched along the western horizon retained a little color — some indigo and magenta — but it would be fully dark soon.

Scooter glanced between a pair of lakeshore houses at Lake Tawakoni. The moon was just peaking over the eastern horizon, shining underneath the dark clouds, making them appear to have a silver lining.

He leaned his bicycle against the chain link fence and grabbed the security chain, reeling it toward him as though it had an anchor on the end. After yesterday and the Gunns, he was glad they always kept this locked.

Ever since being at Mr. Chandler's place and hearing that crazy man claim he was a vampire, Scooter had been wracked with feelings of dread — that something horrible was going to happen.

Today, Garrett's actions added to the strangeness, especially when combined with Russell's nightmare. Garrett looked as Scooter imagined him in Russell's dream. Scooter tried to shake his dread, but with the sun setting, his dire and morbid feelings increased. They fed his overactive imagination. He was already jumping at birds taking flight and squirrels leaping from branch to branch. Were shadows next?

Scooter peeked through the gate, looking for anything strange. His headlight beam stretched ahead along the road, illuminating the hard-packed ruts and tufts of grass in the middle of the long, natural driveway. A soft breeze from the lake gently rustled the trees, then rippled the calm lavender surface of the channel.

All around, the symphony of bullfrogs croaking slowly arose. A new baritone was added to the bass choir every few seconds or so. The concerted effort gradually grew into a throbbing drone. Insects buzzed around him, pestering and biting him. It seemed peaceful enough. Normal enough. Flash seemed to think so, too.

Scooter slapped at a mosquito near his ear. "Remind me to put on bug spray."

The Lab responded with a woof.

Scooter set the numbers in the correct sequence, and the lock sprang open.

He felt bad leaving the others to follow Garrett, but he was late and felt something was wrong at home. He still had that feeling. Scooter couldn't explain it, but he knew Grandma and

Judge Grandpa were in trouble. Maybe he was just thinking about the Gunn boys, but that crazy man's claims had affected his mind. Besides, with all the disappearances and deaths, his grandparents were concerned about him being out after dark.

After undoing the chain, Scooter pushed open the gate and began scratching. He needed more Calamine lotion; this itching was driving him crazy. After that, he'd eat. Then if it was all right, he'd visit Mr. Chandler.

Scooter wanted to know about the crazy man and his claims. Thinking about the crowd's accusations and the strange visitor saying Mr. Chandler knew vampires in LA sent chills along Scooter's spine. Did that mean Mr. Chandler might be a vampire?

"I don't think Mr. Chandler's a vampire," Scooter asserted aloud.

Flash barked in agreement. Judge Grandpa said Flash was an excellent judge of character. Not only that, but Scooter and Judge Grandpa had looked up *vitiligo* in the dictionary.

That told him a lot. Enough to know he didn't want to be a doctor — too many big words. They got stuck in one's mouth. *Vitiligo* was a skin disease that caused a loss of pigmentation. That explained why Mr. Chandler looked as he did and why he didn't come out during the day. In extreme cases, the person was virtually allergic to the sunlight, burning very easily.

When Scooter stepped through the gateway, the woods suddenly grew silent. Dead silent. Not one frog croaked. The insects seemed to have abandoned him.

"Weird," Scooter said, then shivered. "Flash," he began, looking down at the Lab. "Flash, what's wrong?" The Lab didn't move. He was so still he might have been petrified. His stare was directed at a lakeshore house to their right. Scooter followed the dog's gaze.

Movement at the Jaystone's house seized their attention. No one was supposed to be staying there. But in the gathering darkness, he could vaguely see someone standing on the front porch. Scooter felt he was being watched. His dread intensified. Was it that man? Or the kidnapper? Or a thief? The window was still broken. Whoever it was, Flash didn't like him.

"W — who's there?" Scooter called out.

"Hello, Jonathan. It's just me," his grandfather said, stepping from the shadows and descending the porch steps.

Flash growled, the sound coming from deep within his throat as if he were going to explode.

"What's wrong with you?" Scooter asked Flash. He patted his companion. Flash's hair was stiff.

"You're late, young man, and you've missed dinner," Judge Grandpa said, his voice steely.

"I know. I'm sorry, but . . . " Scooter began.

"No buts, Jonathan. No sorrys. I'm assuming you made the decision to be late, right?" His grandfather walked closer.

Even in the darkness, Scooter saw his expression; it was grimly stern — an expression he'd seen all too often.

"Yes, but it's because . . . "

"Your grandmother and I worried about you. Very worried. With all that's going on, you should know better. Now lock the gate and come on."

As Scooter closed the gate and reset the lock, a chilling breeze pierced him as though he'd been goosed by winter's handmaiden. "Whoa!" Scooter rubbed his bare arms rapidly. "Did you feel that?" Scooter asked his grandfather, who was standing right behind him.

"Feel what?"

"That . . . " The wind was abruptly gone, but the coolness remained, settling around him like a cold comforter. "Never mind." He glanced at Flash. "I'll bet you didn't feel it either."

Flash hadn't moved. Mesmerized, he stared at Judge Grandpa.

Scooter turned and bumped into the fence. The other gate shook, and his bicycle fell atop Flash. The Lab started, then darted off as if spooked, disappearing into the woods.

"HEY! FLASH, COME BACK HERE! I . . . I don't understand," Scooter told his grandfather. "FLASH! He's never done this before. FLASH!" he pleaded.

"Let him go," Judge Grandpa told him. "He'll come home when he's hungry."

"But . . . "

His grandfather gripped his arm firmly and began leading Scooter down the driveway.

"Hey! Your hands are like ice, Grandpa," Scooter complained.

His grandfather chuckled.

Although the chuckle sounded normal, Scooter was chilled.

"Part of getting older," Judge Grandpa replied. "So where were you this evening, young man? Where did you go after you rushed out of the VFW?" His stare was piercing.

Scooter felt he saw right through him. He shivered, then looked for signs of a pipe. So far, so good. No pipe, so the discussion wouldn't be too long. Scooter explained about Garrett, how he had looked and acted. How strange everything was.

"That is . . . odd." Judge Grandpa wore a puzzled expression.

They walked for a moment in silence. Ahead, there was a glow through and above the trees. The front floodlights welcomed them back home. Scooter heard something rattle and thought someone was at the front gate.

"What's going to happen to Mr. Chandler?" Scooter asked.

"I hope nothing."

"But that crowd was very angry. Mob-like."

"Mob-like is not a word."

"Oh, right. Still, I overheard some of them talking about going out to the Pickup Ranch and questioning Mr. Chandler. It sounded like. Well, as if they had torture more in mind than asking questions," Scooter said. He looked around for Flash. Where was he? What had spooked his faithful companion?

"I have faith cooler heads will prevail," Judge Grandpa told him, then patted him on the shoulder.

Scooter shivered.

"Sheriff Knight warned them about taking the law into their own hands, then scheduled a deputy to stay there tonight and keep a watch on the place."

"I was hoping to go back there tonight."

"Why? Weren't you just there last night?"

"I have some questions to ask him."

"About writing? You could call him."

"No, about a visitor he had last night. A crazy man with a really — interesting voice."

"A crazy man?" Judge Grandpa asked. He almost sounded offended.

"Some guy from LA that supposedly knew a friend of Mr. Chandler's. Claimed he was a vampire."

"My, I guess you aren't the only one with an overactive imagination," his grandfather mused. "Being a vampire does sound rather ludicrous."

It was fully dark now, the night having swooped in like a predator after prey. The amber moonlight reflected off the water, splaying through the trees and creating long shadows darker than the rest of the night. The woods were still silent — so silent he could hear a leaf fall.

"Ever had a feeling something bad was going to happen?" Scooter asked.

"A premonition?" his grandfather asked.

Scooter nodded.

"About Mr. Chandler?"

Scooter shook his head. "About you and Grandma."

"Really?" His grandfather appeared amused.

The forest parted, giving way to a clearing as they neared the end of the peninsula. The back of the house was dark, but the front was well illuminated. With the floodlights on, the darkness was pushed back nearly one hundred feet. Scooter thought there was something odd about the shadows, as if they were concealing a large body.

His grandfather patted him. "Don't worry, Jonathan. Nothing is going to happen to me. Now, put your bicycle in the garage, and let's go inside."

Scooter rolled his bicycle into the black maw of the garage. He quickly turned on a light; everything looked fine. He turned off the light, then stepped back outside.

His grandfather walked toward the front, but Scooter paused. "FLASH! COME HERE, FLASH!" He called several more times, struck by the eeriness of his echoing voice. The woods were still quiet, as if holding its breath, waiting for something to happen. Something bad. Scooter shivered.

"Come on, Jonathan. He'll come home when he's hungry."

"Okay," Scooter replied dejectedly. He followed his grandfather along the walk.

"I think we should call the sheriff about Garrett and his behavior. What do you think?"

"Sure."

"Oh, I have a surprise for you," Judge Grandpa said as he walked up the steps and opened the screen door to the porch.

"Really! What?"

"Someone has come to visit you. Someone special." Judge Keyshawn ushered Scooter inside the screened-in porch.

Scooter was thoughtful. "Don't tell me! Let me guess. Hmm. Mr. Chandler, maybe?" He pulled open the sliding glass door to the house.

His grandfather was close behind him. "No, but he should be here soon. Jonathan, what do you know about vampires? What have you read? Seen?"

Scooter thought that was a strange question. "Oh, legends and books say they're not alive. They're undead. People are turned into vampires by other vampires who bite them and drink their blood. Vampires live on the blood of humans. They need it to survive. Let's see, what else? They can't be seen in mirrors or photographed. The light of the sun will kill them. So will staking them through the heart. Crosses repel them. I don't know about other religious icons."

"And they can change shape, right?"

"Yeah, they can turn into bats and wolves. Maybe even spiders. Things of the n . . . " Scooter stopped dead, struck speechless.

Grandmother and Judge Grandpa were sitting on opposite sides of the table, staring at each other. Neither blinked. Neither moved.

"Hey . . . uh," Scooter was confused. Judge Grandpa was behind him. But if this was Judge Grandpa, then who . . .

Scooter recalled Flash bolting. Hadn't they just been discussing changing shapes? Morphing forms? Petrified with fear, Scooter was unable to turn, barely able to breathe.

"Some special vampires can change into many shapes. These vampires can look at a person and know their history. How they lived. What they like. What they don't like. They even know their innermost thoughts and idiosyncrasies. In a sense, they are dopplegangers — doubles of those whose shape they've stolen."

Scooter tried to breathe. His heart was racing so hard, pounding so loud, he could barely hear. He tried to turn again but could not. He knew who stood behind him.

"I've called Mr. Chandler. I told him you wanted to see him. That it was very urgent."

Scooter felt cold fingers brush through his hair. Shaking seized him.

"Do not be afraid," the voice behind him said. It was deep and compelling. "Mr. Chandler has a special fondness for you. Maybe he'll decide keeping you alive is worth coming back to LA to work for me."

His visitor was the crazy man who'd argued with Chandler. He'd called himself Mr. Shade and claimed he was a vampire.

Scooter stared at his grandfather. His visitor didn't just claim to be a vampire. Mr. Shade was a vampire.

Chapter Twenty

STRANDED

Frantic, the threesome heard the approaching motor and couldn't shake Russell's nightmare from their thoughts. Racquel looked around wildly, straining to find the oncoming boat in the darkness. Kristie peered intently in the direction they'd last seen Garrett's boat, hoping to catch the silvery gleam of the rising moon reflecting off the aluminum hull.

The motor still wouldn't start, so Russell hastily poured gasoline over it. The smell of gas was overwhelming.

"What're you doing!" Racquel screamed.

The oncoming motor's whine was growing louder. The boat was speeding closer.

"I can't see it!" Kristie cried.

Russell grabbed a rag and wiped down the engine. This

was unbelievable — too much like his nightmare. "Gasoline is a de-greaser!"

"SO?"

"I'm trying to unclog the engine!" Russell snapped. "SO NO SMOKING!" he told her. "Or we'll blow up!"

"Oh." Racquel put her hands in her lap, as if they'd been bad. "But we wanted to keep them in sight."

"We wanted to follow them!" Russell replied. "To find out where they're going! Not get run over!"

Russell wiped the engine, then threw the rag aside. He hurriedly grabbed the cord and pulled. The engine coughed. "Progress! Come on, baby!" He pulled again. The outboard coughed and puffed black smoke, choking him. In the stillness, the black cloud hovered over their boat. "I still don't see them!"

"Look harder." Racquel cried. "They're getting closer!"

"Come on!" Russell cried as he frantically yanked the cord again. The motor coughed. "DAMN IT! COME ON!" He pulled harder.

"Hurry, Russell!" Kristie shouted.

The sound grew louder — and closer.

"COME ON!" Russell urgently yanked the cord again and again. He didn't want to be run over again, even if the first time was in a nightmare. The motor finally sputtered, then caught, rumbling to a roar. "All right!"

"I SEE IT!" Racquel shouted. "I see it," she repeated, suddenly sounding much calmer.

"Where?!" Kristie asked.

Racquel pointed toward the shore. "There. See it? Mixing with those colorful lights along the shore? False alarm, guys."

"The wrong boat!" Russell gasped. He adjusted the throttle. He didn't want the engine to die again. The outboard sounded fine now.

"Yeah, the wrong boat," Racquel said. "It has lights. It

should sound like it's going away from us soon. See?"

Kristie nodded. The red and green signal lights passed a set of colorful party lights along the shore. The navigation lights continued southward, away from them.

Russell finally saw it, too. "Whew!!" He breathed a sigh of relief. Then he coughed on the gas fumes.

"You okay?" Kristie asked.

"I am so glad I'm not psychic," Russell chuckled.

"I could use a cigarette," Racquel moaned.

"NO!" Kristie and Russell cried in unison.

"Okay! Okay! Let's get going. Let's find Garrett!" Racquel said.

Kristie looked at Russell. "They're long gone by now," she said.

"I don't care! We'll find them," Racquel decreed.

Kristie shrugged her shoulders, then said, "It's hopeless. Let's tell your Dad. He might have better luck."

"No!" Racquel cried. Her piercing stare demanded that Russell do as she wished.

"I agree," he replied calmly.

"We can't tell Dad!" she screeched.

"Why not?" Russell asked firmly.

"Because he won't let you see Garrett? Because he'll ground us? Heck, you may never see Garrett again anyway. Something is wrong with him. And this," he waved to the lake, "this is a fool's errand. If you're so old and wise, you'd realize that! You'd know we need help. Garrett needs more help than we can provide."

Racquel started to say something, then her mouth snapped closed. There was iron in his voice she'd never heard before — and despite the stress, he wasn't stuttering. Finally, she shrugged and said, "What do you know, anyway?"

"I knew how to get this motor started," he replied hotly. "And it's going to take us to the nearest phone."

"Which is?" Kristie asked.

"Scooter's grandparents' place isn't far from here," he told her.

"Let's go!" Kristie encouraged him. "It's the best way to help Garrett and the others."

Racquel said nothing as Russell turned the craft around and steered toward the Keyshawn's peninsula.

Chapter Twenty-One

NIGHTMARES COME TRUE

Hands neatly folded, Scooter sat calmly in a chair by the break-
fast table — just as he'd been told. His eyes stared unwillingly
at the back of the vampire who looked like Judge Grandpa.
Mr. Shade looked out the window.

The real Judge Grandpa sat at the table too, staring emp-
tily at Grandma Keyshawn. They appeared to be asleep with
their eyes open.

Scooter had simply looked Mr. Shade in the eye, and
something seized his body and took possession of it. He'd
known better. He'd tried not to look into the vampire's eyes,
but something compelled him and pulled his eyes to the dark
one's.

A cauldron burned deep within those eyes, an unquenchable fire — a desperate thirst.

Why hadn't the crucifix protected him from the vampire? What would happen to him? Would the vampire feed on him? Feed on Grandma and Grandpa, too?

As fear blossomed in his stomach, Scooter was nauseous. He tried to stand, even move just a little. He was as alive as a breathing stone. Despite all his urging, his body failed to respond.

Was this how a stroke victim felt? Or someone on drugs? Scooter hated it.

"He should be here by now," Mr. Shade said. He turned to look at Scooter. "You must not be as important to him as I thought. He has no family and few friends. I'd hoped he'd bonded with you. You know, the son he never had. Someone to benefit from his wisdom and experiences."

Mr. Shade sighed. "Oh, well, if he didn't take me seriously and doesn't come, then I shall just have to feast."

He walked past Judge Grandpa, running a finger along the elderly man's neck. "You shall be the first, Judge Keyshawn. You are old, but strong of will. That'll make for a revitalizing nectar, even at your age."

Mr. Shade walked into the kitchen. It was green and yellow and cheery with flowered wallpaper and curtains, but the vampire's presence darkened it. Despite the potted and hanging plants, the place had a lonely, desolate feel — the dead among the dying. A dark haze overshadowed the entire downstairs.

Nothing looked right, seemed right, or felt right. Scooter kept telling himself this was a nightmare like Russell's — so realistic you couldn't believe you were dreaming. This had to be a nightmare! Had to be! Vampires didn't exist!

"I imagine y'all — such a quaint and useful word — y'all, are wondering what's going on? Why is this happening? Happening to me? Why is he doing this?" Mr. Shade said as he walked into the kitchen and pulled back the curtain to look outside once more.

"First, you might as well accept that this is not a nightmare. You are awake." Mr. Shade turned to look at Scooter.

His smile was cruel and looked alien on Judge Grandpa's face.

"I am a vampire, and I am called Mr. Shade. Lucius Shade. You are mortal and therefore sustenance. I didn't come to Gunstock specifically for you, though. No, I came for Marcus Chandler. A very good friend of mine is an actor and also a vampire. He has acted in some of Chandler's more morbid movies." Mr. Shade chuckled.

"You see, Chandler and friends developed a new way to film. Computers are such marvelous inventions, aren't they?" he went on. "With their help, vampires can now be filmed. My story can finally be told on the big screen."

"Can be told?" Scooter blurted.

"Ah, you are strong-willed, too. Young and stubborn." Mr. Shade smiled. "One way or another, Marcus Chandler will write, produce and direct my life's story, and I shall act in it. For who knows better how to be a vampire than a real one?"

The vampire paced back and forth. Judge Grandpa's usually stooped walk was now arrow-straight, his stance that of a young man. "And if he doesn't come," he said as he turned to look at Scooter, "you shall all die. If it is any consolation, it is quite painless. Death is a release from the agonies of life."

Panic surfaced, and Scooter's heartbeat raced as would a sprinting stallion's. He thought it might burst from his chest. The thundering in his ears sounded like someone pounding on an old castle's door, desperate to escape the pursuing dragons.

Despite his fears, somehow Scooter's breathing remained calm, almost meditative. How could that be? He was starting to get dizzy. Is this what dying was like? He'd heard that your hearing went last! Would he be struck blind next!

"I will not make you into vampires. Few are worthy of such a gift. And truthfully, competition could be a problem.

See, we believe in Malthus's theory of overpopulation. Besides, if there are too many vampires, too many people might die. Then, open-minded souls might begin to believe we are more than a legend or a myth."

With nowhere to go, nowhere to run, Scooter's fear fed upon itself, growing and festering. It summoned all sorts of terrible fates — all worse than the one before.

Where was Mr. Chandler? Didn't he care? Where was Flash? How could his best friend desert him? Scooter prayed for somebody, anybody, to be the cavalry. Why wasn't the crucifix Russell gave him helping?

"My patience is wearing thin, as it always does when I hunger. Your grandfather will sustain me until Marcus Chandler arrives." Judge Grandpa's double walked over to stand beside the original. Mr. Shade stroked Judge Grandpa's throat.

Scooter's panicked thoughts gained speed, whirling a million miles a minute but always interrupted with . . . I'VE GOT TO DO SOMETHING!

Again, Scooter desperately tried to move, but failed. The room seemed to shrink, becoming tighter, smaller, no larger than a coffin that stretched forward to his Grandfather. He could only see darkness — and Mr. Shade leaning over Judge Grandpa.

Scooter prayed, begged and pleaded. He mentally battered against the walls with his mind fists, but the barriers were too solid. Too strong.

Scooter's mental hands scrambled, his fingers questing for any type of crack, a secret door, a concealed vent — ANYTHING! He tried to throw himself forward. Nothing worked. NOTHING! PLEASE!

Mr. Shade placed his hand on Grandpa's shoulder, then tilted his head sideways to expose his neck. The vampire leaned forward, teeth barred, then they parted slowly.

"NO! STOP! NOoooo . . . " Scooter struggled, vibrating like a machine on the verge of exploding into a thousand pieces. Flash! Where was Flash?! Where was Mr. Chandler?

"Eh?" Mr. Shade straightened. "I do believe I hear something." The vampire glanced back to Scooter.

The cavalry maybe? Or Mr. Chandler?

He sniffed the air like a bloodhound. "Yes, I believe it is Mr. Chandler. I shall go greet him. Surprise him."

Mr. Shade walked past Scooter. Scooter couldn't stop his eyes from following and pulling his head along with them.

Mr. Shade went down the hall, past the bath and storage room to leave through the garage door. He left the door open behind him.

The garage was dark, a gaping maw, growing larger and larger, until it seemed ready to consume Scooter. STOP! Scooter wanted to scream. He had to get control of himself. With the vampire gone, his overwhelming presence absent, maybe he could move. Maybe he could escape.

The porch door opened, then Scooter heard footsteps. The front door slid open . . .

"Scooter!" called Mr. Chandler.

Scooter's hopes were buoyed when he saw Chandler come in the room.

"Mr. Keyshawn! What's going . . . Damn! That Mr. Shade is a dangerous crackpot!"Mr. Chandler moved to his side. "Let's get out of here before he comes back!"

Scooter wanted to tell him to hurry! Mr. Shade might be back any time. Scooter briefly felt hands on him to help him rise, then they quickly pulled away.

He wanted to shiver but could not. Scooter tried speaking again. He wanted to tell him to help Judge Grandpa first. He tried to speak, but still he couldn't. His lips were frozen, and his tongue was thick and sluggish.

"Scooter, help me here," Chandler told him. "Try to stand."

He stepped in front of Scooter. "Scooter, what's wrong?"

Scooter stared closely at Mr. Chandler.

"Come on! Get up!"

Scooter looked into Mr. Chandler's eyes. There was an unquenchable fire burning there. It came and went, as if playing hide and seek, but the flames were still there.

"Ah! Very good!" The vampiric doppleganger smiled a smile Chandler could never manage. "You have discovered me! Children are so precociously bright these days. As you have now learned, we can take on any shape! It makes getting near our prey so much easier. We look into their souls, see who they wish to see most and don the trappings of their desire."

Mr. Shade stared at Scooter. "You wonder why I did that to you, aren't you?"

Mr. Shade stepped back and laughed. "Another thing you may not know about vampires. True vampires like myself also feed on fear and terror. It has such a heady aroma." The vampire breathed deeply. "But it does not sustain us. Only blood sustains us."

Mr. Shade walked to the window. As he neared it, his clothes and body began to alter shape and change color. He was growing thinner, younger and more healthy appearing. His hair became fuller and red-hued, reminding Scooter of himself. Even the vampire's clothes were a duplicate of his own!

"I might as well give up on Marcus," the vampire sighed.

When Mr. Shade turned around, he looked exactly like Scooter — tall, gangly, redheaded and freckled. "Remember what I said about terror? Well, you shall get to watch yourself kill your beloved Judge Grandpa."

Chapter Twenty-Two

INFERNO

Scooter desperately wanted to close his eyes but couldn't. They felt glued open. He couldn't bear to watch himself kill Judge Grandpa, even if it wasn't truly him. But it was his fault his grandparents were going to die! All his fault! If he hadn't tried to join the Graveyard Armadillos, this never would have happened! He never would have met Mr. Chandler, and most important, never met Mr. Shade.

Scooter had given up hope and was praying when he heard the screen door open.

"Hey! Is anybody home?" It was Mr. Chandler. "Scooter? Judge Keyshawn? Anybody home! I received a phone call from a crazy . . . "

Mr. Shade straightened. "Come in! Come in!"

Appearing frazzled and windblown, Chandler peered inside. "Scooter?" His wide eyes moved back and forth between the sitting Scooter and the one standing near Judge Keyshawn. "Two of you?"

"So you've come to rescue this boy?" Mr. Shade asked, sounding like Scooter and pointing to the real Scooter.

Chandler appeared confused.

"Is he special to you, Marcus? I can call you Marcus, can't I? We'll be working together, won't we? You will be hearing my life story; and quite a tale it is, too. One of life after death."

"Mr. Shade? I . . . I don't believe this," Mr. Chandler stammered.

Scooter could see Chandler's knees shake and his lower lip quiver.

"It is I," Mr. Shade replied. "Here within young Keyshawn's facade. As I said the other night after our little scuffle, I am a vampire. I am stronger than you. Death, like any predator, has no meaning to me but as sustenance. I fear nothing for I am already dead."

He smiled a cruel smile Scooter couldn't imagine seeing in a mirror, even a fun house mirror.

"Because of these things, you shall do as I desire."

"I don't understand."

"I told you I have infinite patience," the vampire said. "Sooner or later, we will do this my way. I'd prefer sooner. If we wait too long, the movie of my life will be a two-parter, and the sequel rarely compares favorably to the original. Unless we make three. Then there is some hope."

"You are Shade!" Chandler gasped. "Really Shade . . . But you look like —"

"I am a true vampire," Mr. Shade replied in his own voice. It resonated deeply throughout the house, as if a low drum beat. "With death comes the loss of form, merely leaving thought and hunger. I can look as I desire."

His form wavered, then appeared to melt like wax. After

a moment, his clothing and flesh re-formed, looking just like Marcus Chandler — a tall, gaunt man with pale, blotchy skin, thinning gray hair and bright, blood-red eyes.

Chandler's mouth opened, then closed. He couldn't find the words.

Scooter knew how he felt. Stunned. Disbelieving. Unsure if he were awake. Praying he wasn't awake.

His stare riveting, Mr. Shade walked toward Chandler. "You will do as I ask, or these three, then more, will suffer the consequences. Nearly a dozen have already sustained me. Five have died. Their deaths were true."

"I . . ."

"You will return to LA with me, write and direct my life and unlife's story," the doppleganger smiled. "Won't you? Would it help if I said please?"

Chandler appeared to be lost, groping for words — groping for what to do. His hands were at his throat, fumbling for something under his shirt.

Scooter was afraid the vampire would mesmerize Mr. Chandler, too. Soon Mr. Chandler would be paralyzed, turned into one of Shade's many puppets.

Although Shade's stare wasn't directed at him, Scooter felt its power and magnetism. He sensed a vacuum where Mr. Shade stood, a draining, as though life was being sucked into blackness — into a bottomless pit of despair.

If he could mesmerize Mr. Chandler, Scooter thought, why threaten him?

"I hear your thoughts, young Keyshawn. I could simply 'charm' Mr. Chandler into doing as I desire, but creative thought is dampened when shackled. My life's story should only be done by one of the best at his best."

"I told you, I don't make movies anymore," Chandler maintained.

"Not even to save these three?" Mr. Shade stared at him — Chandler staring down Chandler. "I can read you. You will,

Marcus. You will acquiesce." The vampire reached out to the moviemaker.

"I . . . I am not afraid of you," Chandler said as he yanked a crucifix from under his shirt. The silver cross gleamed even in the dim lighting.

Mr. Shade's smile vanished as he stepped back.

"I visited Reverend Candel after your last visit. Just in case there was a shred of truth to your story." Chandler pulled a second and longer wooden cross from his pocket.

"Then you believed. Amazing. My kind finds great power in disbelief."

"If . . . If one can imagine something, then it can exist, even beyond the mind's eye," Chandler replied.

"Then you see me as I am. You must produce my story! You simply must!"

"I think I see the truth because I am near death."

"My story would win you many Oscars."

"I'm not interested in Oscars. I'm interested in life. Free them! Free them now!" Chandler demanded. He shoved the wooden crucifix forward.

Scooter felt his bindings slacken, but his fear had not yet departed. It whispered to him: You're trapped. How can you fight something dead? Give up. You're already dead.

"Even if I do free them," Mr. Shade replied, "I will not leave this area, until you come with me, Marcus. More will die. Their deaths will be on your conscience."

"I am not afraid of dying," Chandler stated firmly. He held the cross before him.

"Killing you would accomplish nothing," Mr. Shade replied.

Scooter's fear heightened as the vampire walked over to him. Go away! Scooter thought.

Mr. Shade, still looking like Mr. Chandler's twin, cupped Scooter's chin. The vampire tried to hide the pain of touching him, but his shaking hand gave him away. "I give you one minute to decide, Marcus."

"There isn't much of a decision to make, is there?" Chandler said dejectedly.

"I thought as much." Mr. Shade nodded. "Give me your word. A vampire can bind you with your word."

The vampire changed shape, morphing into a tall, handsome, broad-shouldered man dressed in a crisp black suit. Above dark, piercing eyes, his brows were wide and upswept as if they were the wings torn from a raven. His hair was darker than ink and styled in a medieval page cut.

Mr. Shade appeared much as Scooter had imagined him, yet much, much younger. He looked to be in his thirties. At first Mr. Shade's expression was cruel, the features cold and sharp, then he smiled. It did not reach his eyes. His black eyes grew larger, now dominating his face.

Although not directed at him, Scooter felt the vampire's gaze.

"Your word, Marcus." Mr. Shade's smile was chilling.

With a scrabbling of claws on linoleum, a golden blur appeared from the garage as Flash bowled over Mr. Shade. Flash knocked the vampire across the room to land at Chandler's feet. Flash scrambled after him.

Chandler yanked something from his pocket, then poured it on Mr. Shade's face. "Another blessing from Reverend Candel!"

The vampire screamed and clutched his eyes. As holy water splashed and ran across Mr. Shade's face, his features grew distorted, as though the flesh were melting. His nose pulled away from the bone and slid down the side of his face, slipping along his cheek to his neck

Flash renewed his snarling attack, snapping wildly at the vampire's legs. Mr. Shade kicked him away. Flash rebounded and bit into his arm, refusing to let go, ferociously thrashing back and forth.

Scooter felt his spirits soar. His mental bindings slackened more and more. With new-found strength, he fought against Mr. Shade's spell.

Suddenly Scooter found himself breathing better. The room seemed to expand, becoming less stifling. The oppressive weight holding him lightened, but his poison ivy itching returned with a ferocious intensity that Scooter somehow found thrilling.

He couldn't just sit here! Flash and Judge Grandpa needed him! DO SOMETHING! DO IT NOW! Scooter railed, pushed and pulled, fighting doggedly against the vampire's weakened will. He grew more and more angry at his futility. HE SHOULD BE FREE NOW!

Mr. Shade swatted Flash away like a fly. The Lab was hurled across the room, slamming into the kitchen cabinets. He lay unmoving, his head at an odd angle.

YOU KILLED MY DOG! YOU WON'T KILL JUDGE GRANDPA! Scooter willed himself to stand, but only his hands moved and his legs quivered. Fight harder! Scooter felt the pressure lessen, his load lightening as the weight fell from his mind. The itching was driving him crazy. But he must free himself. DIDN'T GRANDPA TELL HIM LOVE WAS STRONGER THAN HATE! THEN WHY WASN'T HE FREE?

The elderly moviemaker pulled out a second vial. With an angry roar, the vampire swiped at him, taking Chandler out at the ankles.

Mr. Shade jumped lithely to his feet. "You will do as I wish!" he raged, kicking Chandler. "But first you shall watch these others pay! Your cursed cross won't save them!"

"If water works, how about the Good Book?!" Judge Keyshawn cried, grabbing his *Bible* from the bookshelf and swinging it fiercely.

Mr. Shade reeled from the blow, staggering forward. JUDGE GRANDPA WAS FREE!

Scooter was suddenly free, too. He sprang to his feet so abruptly he was surprised. Then, he stumbled drunkenly across the kitchen, crashing into a china cabinet. The doors rocked open and several bowls and plates slipped free. "Ouch!" Scooter covered his head. Silverware and knives followed the falling dishware. Hey! Silver! He knew it affected werewolves but what about vampires?

Judge Keyshawn swung the *Bible* again.

Mr. Shade whirled, catching the Judge's wrists. The Judge twisted them and something snapped. Scooter's grandfather cried out. The *Bible* fell to the floor.

Mr. Shade winced as he kicked the book away. Then, moving with the speed of a viper, the vampire snatched Judge Keyshawn by the throat, lifting him high off the ground. "Say goodbye to your world!"

Scooter threw a carving knife. It flipped tip over handle, spinning brightly, until it stuck in the vampire's back.

Mr. Shade let out a wail.

Scooter grabbed another knife.

Mr. Shade hurled Judge Keyshawn aside, sending him crashing through a window. "You have all made me very angry!"

Scooter threw another knife.

Mr. Shade caught it, then began advancing on him.

Scooter heaved a third knife.

Mr. Shade caught it, too, snatching it easily from the air. "Silver doesn't bother a vampire," he informed him with a voice colder than a wintry grave. He threw both knives back at Scooter.

Scooter ducked. The knives sailed over his head, barely missing him. Then he fumbled for his crucifix.

The vampire grabbed Scooter under the chin and pulled him off his feet. With his feet dangling, Scooter stared directly into the angry eyes of Mr. Shade. His features were far from handsome now, grotesque with flesh gathered along his ears, chin and neck.

"Take off that stupid cross!" Mr. Shade shouted, pain filling his face, the hand holding Scooter smoldering.

From behind, Chandler attacked, striking with the wooden cross.

Mr. Shade grunted and dropped

Scooter rolled away — gasping for breath.

"SCOOTER, RUN!" Chandler yelled as he struck again.

The vampire's hair burst into flame.

"FLASH! TAKE SCOOTER OUT OF HERE!" Chandler ordered.

The revived Lab limped over to help Scooter. He nudged Scooter, whined, then gently took his hand in its jaws.

"We have to get Grandma!" Scooter told his golden companion.

They found her under the table. She seemed to have fainted. "HELP!" Scooter cried. "GRANDPA, HELP!"

Chandler struck again. Wherever he hit the vampire, Mr. Shade smoldered. Then, with a rippling flash of light across his body, the vampire burst into flames, becoming a human torch. Chandler cried out, horrified.

Mr. Shade lashed out and grabbed him.

Chandler's jacket caught fire.

Scooter tried to lift his grandmother, but he couldn't. He was too dizzy and weak. "Sorry Grandma." He grabbed one of her arms and dragged her toward the door.

In a fiery heap, Chandler and Shade stumbled into the couch, quickly setting it on fire. With a life of its own, the fire leapt to a nearby table, then ran up the curtains, heading for the ceiling. A lamp shade caught fire. The whirling ceiling fan whipped the flames into a frenzy.

"SCOOTER, RUN!" Chandler screamed again.

"You will do as I ask!" Mr. Shade demanded. He transformed into a flaming wolf, then snapped at Chandler, his teeth barely missing the moviemaker's nose.

"I don't care if I die!" Chandler cried. He struck with the cross again. "RUN, SCOOTER!"

Panicked, Scooter turned and slammed into the sliding

glass door. He staggered back a step and shook his head, trying to clear it. Stunned, confused and seeing double, Scooter struggled to pull his grandmother out the door. Flash guided him.

Scooter staggered off the porch, trying to be gentle with his grandmother. He glanced over his shoulder, then turned at the sound of a loud crackling noise.

The porch roof was now on fire. Everything inside was already aflame.

The furniture was ancient braziers. The carpet flamed, and the wallpaper peeled away like burning skin. A flaming lamp fell close to the door and shattered.

The ravenous roar of the fire was deafening, threatening to consume everything as the downstairs and porch grew darker, choked with smoke. The black fumes roiled along the ceiling and billowed free in any direction they could as they sought escape.

"MR. CHANDLER! GET OUT OF THERE! THE WHOLE . . ."

A large cracking sound shocked Scooter, followed by a deafening rumble as the ceiling crashed inward.

Chapter Twenty-Three

RACE WITH A DEVIL

Scooter gently placed Grandma next to a tree, then checked on Judge Grandpa. He was breathing raspily, and his pulse was weak and thready. Scooter worried about him. Usually, he wouldn't dare move him, but Grandpa was too close to the inferno.

Scooter dragged him away from the roaring blaze, laying him next to Grandmother. He looked at them, then at the burning house. Mr. Chandler was still inside.

Should he go back inside to rescue Chandler? Or call the fire department?

"Flash, what do you think? Call the fire department? Or save Mr. Chandler?"

The Lab darted toward the house, then back and forth.

"Back inside, eh?" Scooter took a step forward, then studied the burning house for an instant.

Acrid black smoke poured from the lower windows and roiled out from under the porch roof before billowing skyward. Through the kitchen windows Scooter saw fire cavort about, devouring whatever it touched. What could he do to stop this?

From across the lake, he heard a commotion. Someone else had noticed! That made the decision for him. Mr. Chandler was inside and needed help. Scooter hoped he wasn't too late.

Taking several deep breaths, then, keeping low to the carpet, Scooter darted onto the porch. He kept low, nearly crawling to the open sliding glass door, where he peered inside.

With all the smoke, he could barely see anything. The waves of heat nearly drove him back.

"MR. CHANDLER!" Scooter called out, then coughed. Opening his mouth was not a good idea. Neither was breathing. But Scooter didn't give up. He kept trying to find Mr. Chandler within the inferno, but between the charcoal plumes and the darkness, Scooter couldn't see anything. "MR. CHANDLER!" He coughed again.

Scooter thought he heard someone moving. Or something. He hoped it wasn't Mr. Shade. Did fire destroy vampires? They didn't have bodies to die.

How could he help Mr. Chandler? Well, he couldn't just stand here! Scooter desperately needed an idea. The house wouldn't last much longer.

He needed water. The hose! Scooter turned to run back outside.

As if on cue, the front windows exploded. Glass and flames belched outward; shards whistled through the air like bullets and fiery fingers, snatching at anything and everything.

Scooter ran to the side of the house and grabbed the

hose. He spun the spigot all the way open, then sprinted back to the porch, hauling the hose with him. When he reached the steps, water spurted from the nozzle. Scooter started inside, then stopped.

The huge opening where the sliding glass doors had been reminded him of the mouth of a fire-breathing dragon. Things were getting worse. The porch carpet and wooden trim were now on fire.

Scooter turned the hose on the carpet, dousing it heavily. Then he turned the stream of water on himself. "You stay here!" he told Flash. "I'm coming, Mr. Chandler!"

Spraying water in front of him, Scooter crawled to the shattered doors. He sprayed inside the house. It did a little good, dousing a few flames and pushing others back, but the fire still raged. A wind whipped through the broken windows, and he briefly got a glimpse of the place.

Red and yellow flames engulfed the downstairs. The walls were blackened and bleeding flames as though mortally wounded. All the furniture was either charred and smoldering, or blazing away as though tossed upon a bonfire. He felt helpless, even hopeless.

Wait! Scooter thought he saw something move. He turned the hose on it and hoped.

Flash barked excitedly. Contrary to orders, the Lab was right behind him.

Chandler struggled to remove a flaming table that had fallen on his legs.

Scooter was elated. He was still alive! "STAY!" Scooter told Flash.

The Lab looked upset but sat down.

Once more, Scooter reversed the direction of the hose, thoroughly soaking himself. He rushed outside. He took several deep breaths to hyperventilate, then darted inside the raging tinderbox.

As if happy to see him and ready to set him afire, the

smoke eagerly engulfed him. Scooter forged blindly forward, cutting his path with a waving wall of water. The heat struck him harder than a blacksmith's hammer, and he crumpled to his knees. He soaked himself again, then kept going, crawling to where he remembered seeing Chandler.

Scooter heard Flash barking. He seemed close to panic. Scooter felt panicky, too. His lungs were aching.

"Scooter?" Someone coughed. "I can't move my legs!" Chandler coughed again.

Scooter cracked open his eyes. He was right next to Mr. Chandler.

Scooter drenched him with water, then dropped the hose and added his strength to Chandler's efforts. Together, they pushed the table away, freeing the elderly moviemaker's legs.

Scooter's lungs felt ready to burst. He grabbed Chandler and hauled him to his feet. Scooter's eyes stung, and he closed them again. His lungs screamed for air, but he dared not breathe. Spots danced across his inner eyelids. He grew dizzy, barely able to stand.

Not much longer, Scooter told himself.

Flash barked wildly, encouraging him to come on! To hurry!

Scooter used the barking to guide him to the front door.

Leaning on each other, Scooter and Chandler staggered onto the porch. Blinded by tears, Scooter tripped. They fell down the steps onto the sidewalk and tumbled onto the grass. They lay gasping, wheezing and coughing as they sucked in sweet, fresh air.

After a minute, when he could almost breathe normally and could see again, Scooter said, "Mr. Chandler. We have to get you to a . . . " Scooter couldn't finish.

"That bad, lad?" Chandler groaned.

Scooter nodded.

Chandler was blackened and burned, his face puffy and swollen, burned red and smeared with charcoal streaks. His still smoldering clothes, now just rags, appeared to have been gnawed by some fiery beast.

"You'll have to help me move. Then call the fire department," Chandler managed.

Scooter nodded and helped Chandler to his feet. "Wait, no need to call. I hear sirens."

They had only taken a couple of steps when there was a slow, crumbling noise.

Scooter turned and watched as the upper walls of the house buckled inward. In slow motion, the top of the house imploded, collapsing upon itself. Fire geysered skyward, reminding Scooter of a giant fireworks fountain unleashed on the Fourth of July.

"I wonder if that . . . " Scooter began.

A wailing scream ripped the night as a fiery projectile burst from the house. It skipped off the porch, through a screen, then bounced on the ground several times before coming to a flaming stop in the grass.

Scooter couldn't believe his eyes. It was Mr. Shade . . . or what was left of him. He was charred and still burning, warped and twisted, now looking only vaguely human.

How could he be alive?! He wasn't, Scooter told himself. Hadn't been for a long time.

Mr. Shade's clothing was gone, revealing more bone than flesh. What skin was left was blackened and shriveled, clinging in globs resembling old rubber.

With eyes wide, Flash barked wildly, backing up with every terrified bark.

Mr. Shade stared at them with red, murderous eyes. "Kill you both!" His teeth seemed huge, more shark than human. As Mr. Shade began to rise shakily to his feet, his hands changed, elongating into unnatural claws.

"Run to my boat!" Chandler yelled hoarsely.

Flash seemed to agree, tugging on Scooter's shirt.

"Moving water injures them. It might not chase us there."

"The hose! We can . . . "

"No! Only naturally moving water. Lakes, streams, rivers and such. Now come on!" Chandler pulled him toward the shore.

"But Grandpa and Grandma!" Scooter cried.

"He doesn't care about them!" he replied. The sirens grew louder. "And in minutes, the fire department will be here!"

Scooter went along reluctantly at first, then looked back over his shoulder. Fear spurred him on.

A shambling creature of fire and melting flesh, Mr. Shade doggedly pursued them.

Leaning on each other, Scooter and Chandler, accompanied by Flash, stumbled across the front yard toward the gazebo. At the lake's edge where a wall of large stones protected the shore during winds and high water, the trio jumped down onto the mud and lurched toward Chandler's Baja speed boat.

With a helpful shove from Scooter, Chandler managed to crawl into the front of the boat. He slipped across the front seat and scrambled into the driver's seat of the Baja.

Scooter pushed against the bow, but nothing happened. "It's stuck!"

"Come on, Silverscreen!" Chandler yelled as he started the engine. The motor whined, then suddenly roared to life, the water churning and bubbling.

Scooter put his shoulder against the boat and heaved again with all his might, his feet slipping and sliding in the mud. Silverscreen didn't budge.

"IT WON'T MOVE!" he yelled.

Flash whined.

Scooter felt the vampire getting closer, wondering which part the nightstalker would enjoy shredding with its talons.

Barking ferociously, Flash whirled to face the oncoming danger.

"Keep trying!" Chandler yelled.

Flash barked, urgency in his voice.

Pushing so hard he thought his muscles would tear and the veins in his head would explode, Scooter felt the boat finally move a little. Harder! PUSH HARDER! Scooter saw red and grew dizzy. Abruptly his screaming legs straightened, and the boat moved, sliding a foot or two.

Scooter couldn't resist glancing over his shoulder. It was a mistake.

Still smoldering and silhouetted against the sky, the vampire reached the top of the rocky slope. "Flight is hopeless." Mr. Shades' claws clicked together; and his cold, cruel eyes sought Scooter's, attempting to hold him.

Scooter felt himself being drawn from his body. Flash bit him. "OW!" Scooter felt like himself again.

"Hang on!" Chandler cried and throttled forward. The motor roared, the boat shuddered, then slid quickly away from shore. Flash jumped in. Scooter hung on, dragged into the cool waters of Lake Tawakoni.

Mr. Shade bounded from rock to rock, landing near Scooter and lunging for him. The vampire's claws bit deeply into the flesh of Scooter's leg, dragging them both through the churning wake of the boat. "The only place you're going, young Keyshawn, is to oblivion!"

Scooter desperately hung on. Letting go was sure death.

Silverscreen dragged them farther into the water. Scooter's arms ached. His hands began to slip.

Flash leaned over the edge, grabbing his shirt and holding him.

Mr. Shade screamed, letting go and quickly splashing back to shore.

"Whew! That was close, Flash!" Scooter moaned. He was too weak to pull himself into the boat, but the Lab ensured he didn't go anywhere.

On shore, the vampire was raging in frustration and anger.

Chandler suddenly appeared above Scooter and grabbed him, hauling him inside. Together the trio fell into the bottom of the boat. It continued unpiloted, chugging backwards toward the middle of Lake Tawakoni.

"Are we safe, Mr. Chandler?" Scooter asked. He crawled to the passenger's bucket seat and slumped into it, completely exhausted. Flash rested his head in Scooter's lap and was rewarded with stroking.

"You should call me Marcus. But frankly, I don't know," Chandler replied. "I have imagined such horrors but never imagined them being real. Really real. Here and now. The legends are not legends but real. Deadly real."

Scooter stared numbly back to shore. His grandparent's home was no longer a house but a giant, guttering torch. Black smoke roiled from it, blotting out a stretch of the sky and a handful of stars. Most of the structure had crumpled into a pile, but some of the glowing red husk remained.Several nearby trees had caught fire and one had toppled over, nearly landing on the house. The inferno's radiance ignited the entire area, casting the burning light of a false dawn across both land and water.

Sirens grew louder. Scooter thought he saw flashing lights on the road leading to Siete Hombre Estates. "Let's go back. I have to see if Grandma and Grandpa are all right. They need medical attention! You need medical attention!"

"Do you think Mr. Shade is gone?" Chandler asked.

Scooter started to say yes, then something caught his attention. His eyes found a shifting shadow on the shore where Mr. Shade had been raging. It must be a trick of light, Scooter thought. Where there had been a distorted human shape, now stood a beastly horror, still changing, growing larger, its tattered wings expanding wide and stretching into the night.

"LOOK!" Scooter shouted and pointed.

Leaving a trail of smoke behind, the vampire launched itself airborne, wings flapping as the nightstalker flew toward them.

"It's coming after us!" Chandler jammed the gear shift

forward into high, spinning the wheel around, and heading into open water.

They raced across the glittering lake and cut across placid waters toward the golden moon. The wind tore at them, whistling over and under the windshield.

They couldn't fight the vampire, Scooter thought, but maybe they could outrun the monster!

Scooter glanced at the illuminated gauges. The tachometer needle reached into the red.

"Are you wearing a crucifix?" Chandler yelled over the wind.

Scooter nodded, then reached under his shirt. "It's gone!"

"Damn. I have mine, but . . . Look under there!" He pointed underneath Scooter's seat where a satchel waited. "A surprise for Mr. Shade."

Scooter opened the satchel. Along with another wooden cross, two stakes and a mallet were several glass vials.

"More holy water. Reverend Candel thought it strange I wanted so much."

Scooter grabbed the crucifix, then stuck a vial of holy water in his pocket. Next he glanced over his shoulder.

Against the burning backdrop, the monstrous creature closed quickly. Mr. Shade was far from human now, a misshapen mockery of a bat with long limbs ending in large claws and warped wings far too long for the rest of the body.

"You steer," Chandler told Scooter and left the seat.

Scooter took the driver's seat and the wheel. "Where're we going?"

"Anywhere, just away from that," Chandler pointed toward the smoking bat, "and toward the middle of the lake."

Chandler grabbed a vial, then moved to the rear of the boat. He lifted the back seat and removed an oar. Then he smashed it on the side of the boat, cracking it. With a little work, he had a crude spear — another weapon to use against the vampire.

The monster bat suddenly appeared overhead. Screeching like a banshee, the smoking horror swooped over the back of the boat, claws ripping and shredding clothes and flesh as it attacked Chandler.

Scooter glanced over his shoulder, staying hunkered down and close to the windshield, his chest against the wheel. What was he supposed to do?

Flash whined.

Chandler swung the oar awkwardly and missed.

The giant bat banked, then circled around, ready for another attack. The creature disappeared, blending in with the ebony waters. Suddenly it reappeared, strafing in low across the stern. The bat-thing flew around Chandler, cavorting and teasing.

The moviemaker struck and jabbed frantically, futilely slicing the air.

The Shade-beast suddenly tipped a wing, then swiped with a claw, sending the oar sailing into the water.

Scooter yanked the wheel hard to the side, steering to port. Chandler was knocked off his feet. The winged horror suddenly sailed past Scooter, flying over the windshield and screaming in frustration.

Flash jumped, snatching at it — but missed.

"Where is it?!" Chandler cried. "I don't see it!"

Scooter straightened the boat and looked in every direction for the undead monster.

The beast suddenly appeared again, soaring over the bow and almost glancing off the windshield.

Scooter ducked.

The air ripped as the creature raced past Scooter and slammed into Chandler, driving him against the rear seat. His head snapped back, hitting the padded sun platform and stunning him.

The monstrous beast landed on the back of the boat,

then began to change shape. Once more he appeared as Mr. Shade, but now he was larger, and instead of fingers he had taloned claws. Scooter gaped, disbelieving.

Flash snarled and leapt to the attack.

"FLASH, NO!"

Without looking, Mr. Shade backhanded the Lab, sending Flash overboard.

"FLASH!" Scooter yelled. He whirled and threw his vial.

It smashed off Mr. Shade's shoulder, soaking him in holy water. The vampire screamed, then began advancing.

Scooter jerked the wheel starboard. Chandler slid across the seat, crashing into the side. Mr. Shade was thrown off balance for a moment, then continued to advance slowly. Scooter turned the wheel the other way. The vampire stumbled, but regained his balance.

"Nowhere to go, young Keyshawn!" Mr. Shade was suddenly upon him, claws under his throat and slamming Scooter back against the wheel.

Scooter dropped the cross and heard something crunch.

"You shall pay for this with your life!" Mr. Shade seized his head and forced it back, exposing his throat.

Evil red eyes and huge, glistening fangs loomed close like flashing knives — dominating Scooter's world.

Scooter couldn't move. He was held fast as though in a vise. He uttered his most sincere prayer.

With a smile, Mr. Shade eased closer, the vampire's fangs parting the flesh of Scooter's neck.

Scooter felt pierced to his soul, the pain rushing and burning through him. In an instant, Scooter felt nothing. Apathy seized him, and he watched dumbly as he died.

Strangely, Scooter noticed a glow around his hand — a glow that was fading — but nothing around Mr. Shade. The vampire was darkness, a devouring black hole and enemy of life. No amount of light could fill it. Mr. Chandler had a light around him, too, but it was very faint and barely visible. Almost as weak as my own, Scooter thought. He felt himself drifting and being lifted.

Mr. Shade shifted, then cried out and hopped to the side. He kicked at something, moving the dripping satchel out of his way. The vampire cursed, then looked back to Scooter. "I believe you are dying for me." He eased closer, lips parted, fangs large and dripping red with blood.

"I got 'em!" Chandler cried as he looped his necklace over Mr. Shade's head and yanked back as though wielding a garrote.

"Yaak!" Mr. Shade croaked. He couldn't speak — couldn't breathe. The silver crucifix dug into the vampire's throat. Mr. Shade released Scooter and snatched at the necklace. The vampire's flesh began to blister and burn, then melt once more. The nightstalker's eye sockets drooped, sliding down its face to become jowls.

Chandler pulled harder. The cross sank deeper into the vampire's throat, cutting into his skin. Mr. Shade's talons scrabbled for the chain, but the crucifix had sunk too deeply into the soft flesh. The elderly moviemaker jammed a knee in the vampire's back and pulled with all his might, trying to decapitate the nightstalker.

Mr. Shade's dark eyes were desperate, no longer locked on Scooter. A hint of flame rippled across his body.

Scooter was dizzy but suddenly free. FREE! He looked around dully for the cross he'd dropped. It had to be here somewhere! Where was it?!

Mr. Shade burst into flames. The wind whipped past him, tearing at the flames and burning Chandler, but Chandler didn't let go.

"DIE FOR GOOD, DAMN YOU!" Chandler screamed over the wind.

Mr. Shade clawed futilely over his back, unable to reach Chandler with his flaming talons.

Scooter forgot what he was doing — what he was looking

for — and numbly watched the combat. They were going to win! Mr. Chandler was going to kill it! Kill it for good!

The chain suddenly snapped. "NOoooo!" Chandler cried as he staggered backward, slamming against the back seat and sprawling across the sun platform.

Mr. Shade lurched forward.

Scooter shuddered. They were dead. His hand bumped the key in the ignition.

"Die!" the monster roared.

Scooter turned the key and hoped Mr. Chandler was right. The engine died. The boat abruptly slowed, wallowing in the water.

The flaming vampire, now a flaming torch, hit the side windshield and flipped over the starboard side.

Scooter's head hit the windshield. He saw stars. He heard a loud splash before total blackness engulfed him.

Chapter Twenty-Four

THE VAMPIRE HUNTERS

As Scooter awakened, the gentle slap of water against the boat was the first sound he heard. Except for the lapping and a whisper of a breeze, the night was peacefully silent.

Scooter groaned and rolled onto his side. His head and back hurt. His neck throbbed. From the left side, pains darted in every direction. When he breathed, his lungs burned. His entire body ached and throbbed like an orchestra out of synch.

Unfortunately, the past few hours hadn't been a nightmare. They were real — deadly real. Scooter opened his eyes. It was still dark. He thought his vision was blurred, but it was difficult to tell. He had a sudden, unnerving sense of *deja vu*, taking him back to Friday night and the woods around the Pickup Ranch.

Soft splashing joined the rhythmic slapping of water against the boat. Scooter became wary and strained to hear, listening intently.

Swimming? Something swimming closer?! Was something getting into the boat? That thought jump-started his fear.

"What do you think it's doing out here?" someone asked, the female voice carrying across the water.

Something — a beast — huffed.

Scooter sank back in relief.

"Let's look. It probably just slipped loose and floated away from the dock."

"With the keys in it? We should be so lucky." This voice was bitter.

The voices sounded familiar — but caught in the hazy limbo after unconsciousness, Scooter couldn't identify them. Lord, how he hurt, Scooter inwardly groaned. What had happened?

Memories rushed back in a horrible flash: Judge Grandpa, a vampire? No, Mr. Shade, the vampire. Mr. Chandler's arrival, the fire, the chase, the . . . the horrible bat-thing. Flash being thrown overboard.

Scooter sat up abruptly and conked his head on the dash. "OWW!"

No, this wasn't a dream. They never hurt this much. Nightmares scared you, but they didn't hurt like this.

From somewhere nearby, but not on board, a dog barked.

"Did you hear that?" a voice whispered.

"Flash, be quiet!"

The Lab barked repeatedly, calling out to Scooter.

Flash?! Scooter tried to stand but couldn't. He looked around the boat. He was alone. Where was Mr. Chandler?

"Maybe he recognizes the boat," a feminine voice said. "We wondered why he was swimming out in the middle . . . Hey! Maybe Scooter's in that boat!"

"Right," a venomous female voice replied.

"Well, let's check it out anyway," the boy said.

There was the sound of something — some things — repeatedly dipping into the water.

Rowing! Then Scooter suddenly recognized the voices. It was Kristie, Russell and Racquel! Why were they out here? It didn't matter. They had Flash! Flash was okay! Scooter agonizingly hauled himself to his feet.

"Hey! Something's moving!" Kristie cried.

A flashlight beam blinded Scooter. He covered his eyes. "Hey, guys," Scooter managed weakly.

"W . . . who are you?" Racquel asked.

"It's me! Scooter!" he called out. "Hey, Flash!"

The Lab barked excitedly in reply.

"I think I'll survive," Scooter replied.

"SCOOTER!" Kristie cried.

"What're you doing out here?" Russell asked, rowing closer.

"It's a long story. Come tie off," Scooter told him and staggered to the port side of the boat. The Silverscreen had drifted against a sandbar and was partly beached.

Waiting for Kristie and Russell to row next to him, Scooter studied the sky. For the most part, the heavens were clear, a fading ribbon of sparkling black from east to west. The moon neared the western horizon, a hint of gray illuminated the eastern horizon, and predawn light touched a few scattered dark clouds.

Scooter leaned over the boat, almost falling in, and splashed water on his face. The cool water felt good. He wondered if he was burned as well as battered and bruised.

"Oh, my Lord!" Kristie whispered as the boats gently thumped together. "Scooter, you look horrible!" she exclaimed, the beam of light moving across his body.

"Thank you," he replied wryly. " I'm just glad to be alive."

"What happened?!" Kristie asked.

Flash barked, then leapt, nearly landing on top of Scooter.

Scooter fell back, and they hugged. He squeezed the Lab, who whined, then started licking him all over his face. "Phew! Your breath is horrible! And you stink! Have you been eating vampire?" He noticed a glow around the Lab, a bright green radiance. Flash looked healthy enough, considering the circumstances.

"Flash is okay, I think," Kristie told him. "Just battered and bruised, but he should probably see a vet. Now, what happened? What are you doing out here?"

"Man, Scooter," Russell began as he tied off to a grommet. He also was surrounded in an aura of light. "You do look abused! And you stink, too! Phew!"

"I'll tell y'all everything in a minute! First, I'm so glad you found my dog!" Scooter told them.

Flash barked in agreement.

"Did you hear or see anything?" Scooter asked. "Or anyone else?"

"No," Kristie replied. "At least not for hours." Her aura was mostly golden.

Scooter glanced at Racquel. Her amber glow was streaked with red and black.

"Mr. Chandler is missing." Scooter bit his lip. "I'm afraid he might be dead."

"D . . . dead?" Russell stammered. They were silent for several long moments.

"He fell out of the boat?" Kristie asked. "Like Flash did?"

"Yeah," Scooter grunted noncommittally. "What time is it?"

"Just before five," Russell replied.

"How long ago did you find Flash?" Scooter asked.

"I don't . . . " Russell began. "Maybe three or four hours ago. We stopped to rest. I am so tired of rowing. My arms are killing me."

"Scooter, will you tell us what's going on?" Racquel demanded. "Then we can fire up this boat and go find Garrett."

"What are y'all doing out here?" Scooter asked.

"I'll tell you after you tell us what happened to you," Kristie promised. "Why are you in a strange boat?"

After a deep breath, Scooter told them everything. His words ran together as he talked about going home and meeting his grandfather who was really a vampire pretending to be Grandpa. Before they could ask questions, he explained the nightstalker's ability to change shape.

His speech grew faster when he spoke of Mr. Chandler's arrival, the combat, the house burning to the ground, and Mr. Shade bursting from the fire. By the time Scooter was recounting their race to the boat, while being pursued by the bat-like creature, they looked disbelieving. He continued on, graphically describing the fight, Flash being hurled overboard, being bitten by the vampire, and in a desperate move, turning off the engine to stop the boat.

For a long time, nobody said anything.

Scooter knew they didn't believe him. "I woke up alone, just a few seconds before you guys got here." He didn't tell them he could see a glow around each of them. Nothing inanimate glowed, so he wondered if it had something to do with being alive.

"Vampire," Racquel sniffed.

"Why did it leave?" Russell asked, at least feigning belief.

"Mr. Chandler said running water hurts vampires," Scooter replied. "When the boat stopped, it was thrown into the water."

"Let me look at your neck." Kristie did, her touch was gentle as she gasped, "It looks like a vampire bite, I guess. Let's see if I can find a first aid kit." She found one in Silverscreen's glove box and began administering an antibiotic cream. "This is becoming a habit."

"I wonder what kind of infections I can get from a vampire?" Scooter wondered aloud.

"Right, a vampire," Racquel clucked.

"Garrett said Mr. Chandler was a vampire, and you believed him," Scooter countered.

"If Garrett told her smoking made you rich, she'd believe it," Russell told him. He knelt and picked up a blackened chain with a silver cross on it. "Whatever happened, I think we should push the boat off the sandbar and get help. Contact my dad and tell him everything. He'll help us."

Scooter thought something about Russell had changed, but he couldn't pinpoint what. He glanced at Racquel. She didn't appear happy, but then she rarely did.

"Sounds like a good plan to me. As we go, I'd like to look for Mr. Chandler," Scooter told him.

They worked the boat off the sandbar, then started the engine without any trouble. As they tried to backtrack the boat's path to the Keyshawn's place, they kept a lookout for Mr. Chandler.

The wind was cool. The gray of dawn had brightened. The low-lying clouds along the horizon now dappled with swaths of pink and peach.

Russell told Scooter why they were out on the lake and about their repeated engine troubles — the third time being the final time.

As Russell finished, Scooter thought he saw something on a sandbar. "Hey! Look over there!" Scooter pointed. He hoped it was Mr. Chandler and that he was alive!

Scooter steered to the far end of the small sandbar, cut the engine, then coasted onto the sand. "Mr. Chandler! Mr. Chandler! Are you all right?!"

Flash leapt out of the boat, then bounded across the sand. Scooter tried to follow and stumbled. Kristie caught him. Russell glanced at Scooter, then climbed out.

Mr. Chandler looked dead, his clothing burnt and covered with dried blood. His hair was singed and matted; and his pale, blotchy skin was ashen with numerous cuts and bruises.

Russell was hesitant to touch him. He remembered what Scooter had said about the vampire changing its appearance to trap people. Was this really Mr. Chandler?

"Wha . . . " Chandler moaned. Then he rolled over to look blearily at Russell. "Who are you?" he whispered.

"A friend of Scooter's," Russell replied.

Chandler was looking past him. "Silverscreen!" he rasped. Chandler tried to get to his feet but couldn't stand. "Is IT dead?! Is Mr. Shade dead?" he called to Scooter.

"I don't know," Scooter called back. "I hit my head and blacked out." The glow around Mr. Chandler was faded and gray.

"Then it was thrown into the water, too," Chandler told him. "Vampires despise water. Legends claim natural bodies of water can wash away the undead's soul." The injured moviemaker attempted to stand again.

"Can someone give me a hand?" Russell asked. "Racquel, he needs help."

She jumped out of the boat, sinking in the sand, then walked over to Chandler. She was reluctant to touch him.

"Take an arm," Russell directed.

"We have to make sure it's dead!" Chandler croaked. "We must be sure! Everyone's lives depend on it!"

"We need help, sir," Russell told him.

"They'd never believe us," Chandler moaned. "I wouldn't. Not if I hadn't seen IT!"

"I don't believe you," Racquel agreed.

But Kristie and Russell were beginning to believe.

With Flash leading the way, they guided Chandler to the boat and helped him inside.

Chandler hugged Scooter. "Glad to see you're alive, boy!"

"I thought I was a goner. When I woke up and found you gone, I thought . . . "

"You know we have to find Shade and slay the nightstalker immediately. There's no time to waste."

"We have to find Garrett," Racquel countered.

Scooter answered Chandler's questioning glance, explaining about Garrett and the others. "I think the vampire might be controlling them. Puppets, you know. Thralls," Scooter told him. "Mr. Shade can hypnotize people. Take control of their bodies. Maybe even their minds."

"I guess that's possible," Chandler agreed. "That way he would know what's going on in town during the daylight."

He glanced to the east. The sky had brightened considerably with a golden radiance. "It's almost sunrise. I don't do well in the sun." Chandler grabbed a hat from a compartment, then he shook the satchel. "A pair of vials left."

"What are those?" Kristie asked.

"Holy water. It hurts Mr. Shade, or any other vampire for that matter," Chandler replied. "Let's hurry back to my place. We can quickly refuel, then begin hunting for it."

"We need more help," Russell maintained.

"Do you really think anyone would believe us? Believe the truth?" Chandler asked. "I make horror movies. You four are kids. They wouldn't believe us. No way. No how. They'd think it was just a fantastic tale. A scary flight of fancy."

Scooter nodded sadly. "Unless Grandpa and Grandma are all right."

"We'll phone from my house," Chandler agreed with a weak smile. "Now, let's get out of here. I'm too tired to drive. Can you drive, Scooter?"

He glanced over to Russell, who looked envious.

"Don't be afraid to throttle it all the way forward," Chandler told him. "We're racing against daylight now!"

Scooter turned the key and fired up the engine. It settled quickly into a purr, so he throttled forward, giving Silverscreen a lot of gas.

Racquel wasn't prepared for the fast start and was thrown back. "HEY!!"

"If Grandpa and Grandma aren't all right, I'll get you,

Mr. Shade," Scooter swore quietly. "I'll drive a stake right through your black heart!"

About twenty minutes after the sun had risen, they raced into the Chandlers' dock at the Pickup Ranch. Scooter's docking was a bit rough, but Chandler didn't seem to care. He was driven by the lack of time. Although the others weren't sure what was going on, Scooter understood. The sands in the hourglass were minutes of daylight trickling away.

They helped the exhausted moviemaker stagger to and climb into a red pickup parked near the shore.

"Are you sure you should be driving?" Racquel asked as they bounced along the rutted dirt road at over forty miles an hour.

"No," he replied. "Not sure of much anymore, but I know we must find and destroy Mr. Shade!"

Once they arrived at his house, Chandler called the hospital. As he finished speaking and hung up, he said, "Your grandparents are unconscious, in serious condition, but the doctors expect them to be all right."

"They're alive!" Scooter exulted. He had feared the worst.

"Unfortunately, they can't confirm our story," Chandler told them, putting on a huge field hat. He had paused to put on thin, white pants and a long sleeve shirt with a scarf around his neck. "We must find Mr. Shade today! Find IT now!"

"Why the big deal? The big hurry?" Racquel asked.

"If we don't find the vampire today, it will find us tonight!" Chandler's eyes glinted feverishly as though he were deranged. "We know too much about it! Our biggest ally is daylight. It is now or never! We must find and destroy Mr. Shade!"

"He's *muy loco*," Racquel said. "Shouldn't we get him to a hospital? He looks gnarley."

"You are ignorant, distrusting and prideful," Chandler told her.

"Listen here, buster . . . "

"Can't you save the tirade for later?" Kristie asked Racquel. "I've had it with your outbursts." Her voice changed, and Kristie appeared haughty as she said, "If you're so much more mature than all of us, why don't you act your imagined age instead of acting like a spoiled brat?"

Racquel reacted as though slapped.

Russell smiled.

"How do we find Mr. Shade?" Scooter asked.

"Russell, you said that this Garrett fella's boat was crossing the lake?" Mr. Chandler asked. "Or heading for the islands?"

"The islands would be a good place to hide," Scooter said.

"Y. . .yes, there are old f . . . fishing shacks on some of them," Russell agreed. "D . . . do you think they were taking those kids to him? T . . . t . . . to . . . "

"Yes," Scooter replied, fatigue and dread heavy in his voice.

"To sustain Mr. Shade."

"The islands, eh?" Chandler mused aloud. "They'd be relatively safe from intrusion, and it could fly there. People would think they were seeing a bird. And bats are common near lakes."

"What do we do if we f . . . find Mr. Shade? I . . . It?" Russell asked.

"We either stake it through the heart or drag its coffin into the sunlight," Chandler replied.

"What about you and the sunlight . . . " Scooter began.

"I've protected myself as well as I can. With the top up, I should be all right." He donned sunglasses. "Come quickly, we must refuel, then find Mr. Shade before it's too late. Are y'all with me? This is not a game or a cool adventure. This is deadly serious."

Scooter nodded grimly.

Flash's bark squeaked; he sounded nervous.

Kristie hesitated, then said, "I'll go. When my parents get hold of me, I'm dead anyway. Why was I out all night, Dad? Why I was chasing a vampire." She sighed. "But if this is real, I know my dad would do the same in this situation."

"L . . . let's do it," Russell agreed.

"I want to find Garrett," Racquel said acidly. "If he's working for this Mr. Shade and finding him takes me to Garrett, then that's fine by me."

"Here, everyone put on one of these," Chandler told them. He gave Racquel and Scooter crosses hanging from leather thongs. "Everyone have one?"

Russell and Kristie nodded. He'd been wearing one because of his dreams, and she always wore one close to her heart.

They packed more stakes, an axe, a shovel, a small sledgehammer and some flashlights. Then they filled up two five gallon gas containers from a large tank near the barn and drove along the dirt road to the dock. After refueling Silverscreen, they climbed in, ready to go.

Scooter steered away from the dock, then throttled full-forward. Silverscreen surged ahead, the bow rising skyward, then settling as they raced into the bright day in search of darkness.

Chapter Twenty-Five

DAY STALKERS

Scooter was driving in a dream; Silverscreen steered itself as though the boat had a mind of its own. Scooter had no idea how long they'd been cruising at full speed — maybe half an hour — but the six islands were now finally in sight.

The clumps of land, the calm olive green water, and the distant shores with their blurry trees and small houses felt different — looked different, even other-worldly, to Scooter. The wind and the droning of the motor separated him from everything, almost as if he were watching a movie in a circle theater.

The sun climbed a little higher during their journey, staring across the lake like a baleful yellow eye. The water's surface caught the fading light, glistening magically with white-gold highlights. Sometimes Scooter was mesmerized by the sparkles.

We need the light, he thought, to kill Mr. Shade. But they only had ten or eleven hours left at best. Would that be enough? What if Mr. Shade wasn't hiding on one of the islands?

Scooter tasted something bitter and figured his stomach was rebelling. He'd eaten quickly at Mr. Chandler's house, woofing down whatever was handy. Would he eat again? He'd never had that thought before. Would he see another sunrise?

He glanced at his friends; Kristie, Russell, and Racquel all were deep in thought. They stared across the water, wondering what dangers this day might bring. Mr. Chandler was curled up in a shady corner, his hat pulled down and a towel draped over him. Flash put his head in Scooter's lap and whined fearfully.

"What are we going to do when we find this . . . this Mr. Shade?" Russell asked. "Arm ourselves with flashlights, holy water, crucifixes, and march in and s . . . stake him through the heart?"

"I'm scared, too," Scooter said grimly. "If I wasn't scared, I probably wouldn't be here."

"It's not a him, and it should be sleeping," Mr. Chandler told them without looking up. Under his flapping hat, he appeared asleep. "We can carry its coffin or whatever it rests in out into the sunlight. Are there any caves on the islands?"

"None that I know of," Scooter replied. He looked at Russell, who nodded in agreement.

"Then Shade is hiding either in a shack on an island or in a house along the shore," he said. "I hope it's hiding on an island. Finding it along the shore would be like searching for a needle in a haystack."

"Be careful," Chandler told them. "Shade will probably have armed guards. I don't know what kind, but your friends may try to kill you."

"What!" Racquel cried. "Garrett would never harm me! Never!"

"He will if Mr. Shade has control of him," Scooter replied. He rubbed his neck; it was throbbing. "If Garrett's charmed, he'll do what the vampire wants. Don't trust him."

Scooter wondered if he himself could be trusted. After all, he'd been bitten. He'd spoken briefly to Russell and Kristie about keeping a close eye on him. He still didn't tell them that he saw a glow around them. He feared they might mistake it for something evil, when it seemed to be such a wonderful gift.

"Maybe touching them with a cross will break the spell," Kristie ventured.

"We can hope," Scooter replied.

"Scooter, you look tired. Just in case some . . . just in case, can you show me how this works?" Kristie asked. "How to start and drive the boat?"

"That's a good idea," Chandler said. "Everyone should know."

"Sure," Scooter said. He stopped the boat and turned off the engine. "Sit here." Scooter stood and motioned to the driver's seat. She slid by him and sat. "This will be the quick version. Russell, can you see?"

"Yeah."

Scooter showed them how the lever worked, shifting gears from neutral to forward and back, and how to choke the engine — to give it more gas to start easier. Two buttons on the grip had to be depressed to shift into forward or reverse. It was easy to throttle and accelerate. The farther she pushed the lever, the more gas the engine received, and the faster it would go.

Scooter wished he had more time; just being close to Kristie was nice; but he could feel the sun racing across the sky. "You drive for a while," Scooter told her.

She started the engine, let it run for a minute, and then shifted into drive.

"Give it more gas!" Scooter encouraged.

"Okay." She shoved the lever forward.

The engine roared, and Silverscreen surged forward, throwing everyone backward. Scooter would have fallen if he hadn't been hanging onto the windshield. The bow rose skyward, then lowered as the boat planed across the water.

"That works," Scooter said.

After a while, they repeated the process with Russell. Racquel watched as though bored by the whole thing. Chandler dragged out the life vests and gave them each one. Racquel sat on hers. Kristie hugged hers like a teddy bear. Russell reluctantly switched places with Scooter and walked through the split in the windshield to the bow.

After a few more minutes at top speed, Scooter announced, "We're getting close." He nodded toward the islands.

They were nearing the first of a half dozen clumps of land surrounded in every direction by glass-smooth water. Only a couple islands were big enough to house or hide much of anything, but they all had tall grass and a few trees.

Scooter decided to circle the first one, then head for the two largest islands. Maybe he was just delaying the inevitable. "Look for a boat or anything odd."

As they circled the first isle, Mr. Chandler said, "I don't understand why anyone would think I'm a vampire." He shook his head, then asked, "Did any of you really think I was a vampire?"

"You look . . . different," Russell answered slowly.

"I'm an albino." Chandler's voice was cold.

"I know."

"The articles in the paper said you shun the sunlight," Scooter added.

"Words can sure take on many different meanings, especially if someone is wielding poetic license," Chandler said.

"Garrett said you were one," Racquel said. "He's the leader of our gang. And the pictures of you that Scooter took didn't turn out."

"Ah, yes. I found one. The film was bad."

"That's what he said people would think."

"That's because it's true. The problem with gangs, and sometimes any group, is that not enough individual thinking goes on."

There was embarrassed silence.

"She thinks Garrett's the coolest thing to ever walk the earth," Russell said. "She thinks if she fawns over him he won't want anyone but her."

"RUSSELL!"

"Well, it's true. She's already brainwashed, guys."

Racquel was so mad she simply let out a screech.

"That's mature," Kristie said quietly.

Racquel unleashed a withering stare in her direction.

Kristie smiled sweetly in response.

Scooter smiled, too. He could hardly believe Russell; he'd never seen him stand up to his sister before. True, the water had some odd effect on him, eliminating his stuttering; but he had never acted this assertive. Maybe he was finally fed up. About time!

"Mr. Chandler, we're sorry," Kristie said. "Very sorry. We were just looking for adventure. Stupid, I know, but true."

"Scooter already explained. I remember being young. Funny," he mused, "when you're young you want to be an individual, so you join a group of like-minded people and dress like them just to be different. Then, if someone isn't one of your gang, it becomes a problem." He laughed. "Then later, you don't like different things at all. You get comfortable with the way things are. Me, I've always been different and in the minority. Didn't y'all wonder how they took my picture, or those articles in the paper?"

Embarrassed, Kristie looked away, then met Scooter's eyes.

He was ashamed of himself, remembering his thoughts, especially the first time he'd seen Mr. Chandler. He had looked like a monster. Scooter had no trouble imagining him as a vampire, especially after seeing Mr. Shade as Mr. Chandler. But then, he shuddered, he'd seen himself as a vampire, too.

"Scooter, why are we doing this?" Russell asked suddenly.

"Because it's the right thing to do," Kristie replied for him.

"Right, Scooter?"

At times like this Scooter hated knowing what was right. Judge Grandpa said knowing what was right, not liking it, and doing it anyway was a sign of adulthood. It didn't sound like fun at all.

"If I thought there was even a shred of a chance someone would believe me," Scooter began, "I'd tell the sheriff. But I don't think they'd believe us. I have such a vivid imagination. And remember the wild story the Mochries told Kristie's dad? They gave several versions. People would think this was just more of the same, a tall tale being spun."

"Mr. Chandler is with us," Kristie pointed out.

"So he's a weird old man with a wild imagination. I know that Mr. Shade was at the ranch Friday, but who else does? Vampires don't leave footprints. Anyway, Russell, I have to or I'm dead," Scooter finished as he rubbed his neck.

Russell swallowed heavily. "Well, I'm with you. I wouldn't want to lose my best friend."

"Thanks, bud. Oh. Seen anything?" Scooter asked, suddenly realizing he'd completely circled the island without ever looking at it.

They all shook their heads.

"Should I go around again?" Although he didn't see any, Scooter felt things on the islands — creatures of some kind. They . . . felt small. Maybe birds.

"Garrett isn't there," Racquel said petulantly. "Go on. I can feel where he is."

They passed another island; this one so full of white birds it appeared covered by snow. A few of them flew away as the boat sped past.

Scooter didn't even bother to check that isle. He believed birds would shun a place if a vampire was hiding there. Besides, he didn't feel Mr. Shade.

"He's not there either," Racquel told him. "Keep going."

Scooter nodded and steered for the closest of the large islands. Many trees and a hummock in the center provided plenty of cover warranting an investigation.

"Won't they hear us coming?" Kristie said. "Should we paddle in?"

"The vampire will probably feel us coming," Chandler replied, his voice sounding eerily hollow. "And its guards will be on alert. They would see us coming."

Reaching the north side, they saw a small, rundown shack made of rotting boards and planks. The windows were shuttered, and the door was closed, giving the impression it was long abandoned. The grass around it was tall, at least waist high in some places.

Scooter thought the shack emanated a sense of oppression and loneliness, as though it had once been well kept and often used. It might have had a dock once, but only wooden pilings were left.

"I don't see a boat," Racquel said.

"They could have hidden it someplace," Kristie thought aloud.

"I think we should check it out," Russell suggested.

"Just land and I'll look it over," Mr. Chandler told them.

"Right," Racquel said. "Pardon my doubt, but you can barely stand Mr. Death Warmed Over."

"We'll go with Flash," Scooter said, sounding bolder than he really felt. "He'll be able to tell, won't you, boy?"

Flash whined, then barked and nodded.

"He's such a smart dog," Kristie said, hugging him.

Flash smiled, his tongue lolling, then he licked Kristie. She laughed.

"Russell, help me land," Scooter told him.

Russell nodded, then walked up front. He motioned Scooter to go left, then right, guiding them in. When they neared shore, he sat on the bow. "Stop," Russell said, then jumped on land, catching the boat to slow their beaching.

"Okay, now what?" Racquel said.

"We check it out," Chandler told them. He opened the glove box and pulled out a gun.

"What's that for?!" Kristie exclaimed.

"Will that do any good?" Scooter asked. "Mr. Shade is already dead."

"Just in case there are guards of some type other than your friends."

The moment seemed to crystallize for Russell. He bit his lip, finally realizing how serious this might be.

Mr. Chandler picked up the satchel. After digging through it, he handed a vial to Kristie. "Scooter, grab that axe. Russell, the shovel. Keep a crucifix in your hands at all times," Chandler told them. He carried the gun and a wooden cross. "If we find Mr. Shade, we can carry his coffin out into the daylight — or we open a window, smash holes in the wall, ceiling — or whatever we can do to expose the nightstalker to the sunlight."

Scooter couldn't believe Mr. Chandler was going anywhere. He looked deathly ill and could barely stand on his own.

With Kristie and Russell's help, Chandler managed to make it ashore without falling in the water. Scooter didn't like what he saw; the glow around Mr. Chandler was dim, fading, and contained black spots. Kristie and Russell managed to guide him to a tree where he rested in the shade.

"I see prints in the mud," Russell said. "Someone was here recently."

"Vampires don't leave prints," Racquel snapped.

"Thralls do," Scooter told her.

Flash jumped on shore.

Scooter followed. "What do you think, Flash?"

The Lab stuck his nose in the air, then searched the ground, careful at first not to get too near the house. A low growl started deep in his throat, then gathered like rumbling thunder. With hair and tail stiff, the Lab approached the door.

As Scooter neared the cabin, Kristie and Russell joined him. "You're not going in there, are you?" she asked.

Flash stood at the door and barked repeatedly. Scooter could feel a dark presence and an absence of life. If there were guards, they were also dead. Or maybe, undead.

"W . . . well, t . . . they k . . . know we're h . . . here," Russell stammered.

Scooter motioned him around to the side, away from the front door. With a couple of blows, he destroyed the shutters.

"See anything?" Russell asked.

"No," Scooter replied. He didn't feel anything either, except an underlying sense of dread. Or was that his imagination?

"Let's do the other one, too." They smashed the other shutter, looked in the window, then walked to the front door.

"What'd you find?" Kristie asked.

"Nothing so far." Cross held out before him, Scooter turned the door knob, then stepped back. "Ready?" he asked.

"Y . . . y . . . yes," Russell stammered. Kristie and Racquel nodded.

Scooter kicked the door. It swung open and hit the wall with a loud thwack. Scooter felt Mr. Shade's presence — a heavy emptiness surrounded the vampire. It was vague, but it was here. Mr. Shade had been here before but was now long gone.

"Is Shade in there?" Chandler asked. He staggered from tree to tree, getting closer to them.

The cabin was a deserted, one-room structure, once used as a fishing hut. He saw a rickety bench, a worn table, and a broken cot with one end touching the ground. Old fishing poles hung from pegs in the wall.

"Nothing," Kristie said, sounding both relieved and disappointed.

Scooter still felt the vague ill presence. "They were here, not today, but earlier," he told them.

"How do you know it was them?" Racquel asked.

"Flash smells them." Scooter avoided telling them the whole truth. He could feel that Mr. Shade had been here. "And things aren't as dusty and dirty as they should be." He pointed to some marks in the ground. "It looks like somebody was dragged through here."

"Then let's keep checking," Chandler told them.

They returned to the Silverscreen. Scooter and Russell helped the weakening moviemaker, barely managing to get him inside the boat. When Chandler slumped to the floor, he looked dead.

"Are you sure you're up to this?" Scooter asked.

"I'll be fine. We can't quit! We must find the nightstalker!" Chandler replied.

"I told y'all you wouldn't find anything," Racquel said, briefly glancing at Chandler. "A waste of time and energy."

Scooter helped Kristie, then Flash on board. Scooter and Russell pushed off, getting a little wet in the process. As they drifted away from shore, Scooter climbed into the driver's seat. "On to the next island," Scooter told them.

He was relieved they hadn't found anything, but also scared. He knew his life was measured in minutes of daylight. They were fading away at a pace more suited to winter than the seemingly endless days of summer.

They cruised past another small island, this one barely above water with tall weeds and saplings sticking above the surface. It appeared to be a great fishing spot.

The biggest island was at least a couple hundred feet long and not quite as wide, and surrounded by a red dirt beach. All the trees were in the middle, overgrown and tightly clustered, as if snatched from a jungle. The shadows were deep and thick, easily concealing something in their dark cloak.

"He's here," Racquel told them quietly. "Garrett is here."

As they began to circle to the east, a dilapidated dock came into sight. Lonely pilings stood away from shore. Closer in, some of the dock was still intact, partly sunk into the water, creating a ramp that led to a deck and the front door of the rundown cabin. The front half was supported by pilings above the water, while the rest of the place had been built with the island as its foundation.

Tied to a piling was a john boat. "That's it!" Racquel said. "I told you!"

The cabin was much larger than the shack they'd just searched, probably with more than one room, and gave off a sense of waiting for something. Nestled suffocatingly among the trees, the cabin was covered in thick shadows. It appeared to be crouching, a brooding creature ready to spring upon its prey when least expected.

The lowest row of boards on the house added to the image of a beast; they were warped and twisted, easily imagined as teeth. Looking almost like fangs, newer boards had been added to the worn, gray-faded ones. The windows were covered from inside with something black. Scooter was reminded of a host of dark eyes staring at them; telling them to leave. Daring them to enter. Scooter knew this must be the place by the way it looked, and more importantly, how it felt.

"Someone's done some work on it," Russell pointed out. Lumber scraps were over near the bushes.

"Probably trying to keep out the light. I think this is the place," Scooter said. "Mr. Ch . . . I mean, Marcus, are you ready?" Scooter looked at him.

Mr. Chandler didn't move.

Kristie shook him lightly, then harder. "Oh, no." She checked his pulse, then breathing. "Thank God, he's alive." She shook him again. "But I can't wake him."

"Then we're on our own," Scooter said, his voice sounding hollow.

He looked at the cabin. He could feel Mr. Shade. He was in there, compelling Scooter to come inside and embrace oblivion.

Chapter Twenty-Six

DARK HOME

Scooter guided the boat through the disconnected pilings to a partly collapsed dock. Putting out a foot against the dock, Russell brought the boat to a slow stop. Kristie threw him a line, and he tied the rope around a piling.

For a long minute, no one spoke. The boat rocked gently, nudging the dock, then settled. The cabin appeared ready to collapse. The upper half of the building was bowed, as if it were squatting on thick legs, ready to leap from the brush. Overgrown trees, bushes and wild brush cloaked much of the dilapidated structure. Darkness enshrouded the place, protecting it from daylight with a veil of shadows.

New boards were nailed across the windows and used as supports low along the base of the building. This gave the cabin a sinister grin, straight board teeth mixed with boards grayed and warped over time. The ramped dock leading to the front door looked like a long bleached tongue. Step on it, and it would snap you into its maw.

"Do you really think Mr. Shade is here?" Kristie asked, her voice strained. "Maybe somebody's just repairing the place. Or remodeling."

"Don't be a moron," Racquel replied. "It's the same boat Garrett was in." She nodded to the john boat.

"Mr. Shade is here," Scooter said as he rubbed his neck with one hand. In the other, he held a silver crucifix. He recalled Kristie saying the holy cross had staved off Mr. Shade's control. The one Russell gave him hadn't worked earlier.

"I feel him. Can't you?" Scooter asked, nodding toward the building.

Flash whined, breaking the uneasy silence. Scooter patted him.

Russell swallowed uneasily, then said, "I th . . . think I c . . . can feel it."

"Waiting won't make this any easier," Scooter said, "or safer, either. Too bad we can't burn down the place. That'd be safer," he murmured. "And that would take care of all of Mr. Shade's cover."

"But Garrett's in there!" Racquel screeched.

"And we don't know who else," Kristie reminded him.

Scooter nodded. He knew. He could feel life and death waiting inside. Perhaps Garrett, BJ, CJ, and others were here — the pawns of Mr. Shade. "Just wishful thinking."

"What do we do now?" Russell asked.

"Walk in the front door with our crosses out?" Racquel suggested.

"They'd be expecting that," Scooter began. "Let's look around first and come up with a plan. Be creative. Russell, you're a good shot, aren't you?"

"I'm better," Racquel said.

"Russell, why don't you carry the gun? Just in case," Scooter said.

"Why won't you let me have it? Because I'm a girl?" Racquel asked.

"No," Scooter replied. "Because you couldn't shoot Garrett to save yourself."

She glared at him.

Scooter grabbed the satchel and the axe, then climbed out of the boat.

Flash jumped, joining him on the dock. His tail tucked between his legs, he whined and looked at Scooter.

"Because we have to," Scooter told the Lab.

"Fight on the side of angels, right?" Kristie asked with a wan smile.

Scooter nodded, then helped Kristie onto the dock. She carried a vial of holy water. He heard her whispering a prayer and Russell humming to calm his nerves.

"Let's go!" Racquel said. "I want to know what's going on!" With grim determination, she pushed past Scooter, heading for the derelict house.

"She's in a h . . . hurry to d . . . die," Russell said as he moved beside Scooter. "Racquel, wait! Wait up!"

"Watch your step!" Scooter yelled. "It doesn't look very solid."

She was already at the door, trying the knob. "It's locked," she said, frustration heavy in her voice. "Let's break it down! Shoot the lock off!"

"Dream about this?" Scooter asked.

"No," Russell replied. He stepped on a board that bowed and squeaked under his weight. He quickly stepped onto another one.

"Any premonitions?" Scooter asked.

"Just grim."

"There goes that theory. Think they might have guns?" Scooter suddenly asked.

"B . . . BJ probably would," Russell stammered. "Garrett might. Knives, too."

Flash sniffed at the doorway, whined, and barked excitedly as he backed up. His nose wrinkled from the smell of something foul. His hair stood on end. Evidently he expected something to burst through the door at any minute.

"We could kick it down," Russell suggested.

"You watch too much TV," Scooter replied. "I have an axe."

"We could try a window like last time," Kristie suggested.

"Sunlight would be a big help," Scooter agreed. "But we can't do the windows this time," he told her as he inspected them. Many layers of chicken wire created a thick mesh across the windows. "It's been protected." Looking toward the roof, Scooter backed up. The trees in the area made getting atop the structure easy. Maybe the roof wasn't as well protected.

"I have an idea," he said. "Let's get away from the front door." He walked around to the left side of the cabin, off the dilapidated dock and onto the island. Kristie and Flash followed. "Russell, keep an eye on the front door."

"What are you going to do?" Russell asked.

Scooter nodded toward the roof. "Up."

"HEY!" Racquel cried.

The door suddenly opened, and two dark blurs burst from the darkness of the cabin. The Dobermans were malformed with big, blood-red eyes. Their ears were pointed like a devil hound, and their oddly long legs ended in claws as if the beasts were part tiger.

Flash rushed in, intercepting one and slamming into it, sending the huge beast sprawling. It scrabbled for footing, then tumbled off the dock.

The second black beast knocked Russell over and kept charging. Russell landed hard, losing his grip on the gun. It bounced away, skipping across the dock.

The beast slammed into Scooter, driving him back. He reeled a few feet before collapsing under the weight of the dog. Scooter landed hard, knocking the wind from him; but he held onto the axe.

The snarling beast snapped at him. To avoid the huge jaws, Scooter threw his head back, smacking it on the dock. Stars danced before his eyes. He saw two dogs attacking now. Their red eyes were huge, and their sharp teeth dripped green froth.

Which was which? Or had a second suddenly joined the first?

Scooter quickly chose one, shoved the axe handle in its mouth and pushed with all his might. The beast gagged, its fetid breath making Scooter nauseous. He wrestled with all his strength, then it let go and danced back.

As the Doberman rebounded to attack, a golden blur barreled into the black beast, sending it sprawling. The malformed dog reacted with unnatural speed, rolling quickly to its feet, ready to fight.

Snarling, the two dogs clashed. The huge Doberman drove Flash backwards and landed atop the Lab.

"My dog! Don't hurt my dog!" Scooter yelled as he swung his axe. His first blow landed on the beast's head with a sickening crunch. Its eyes rolled, then it shook its head to shrug off the blow. Scooter hit it again.

Flash scrabbled to his feet.

Scooter moved in for another strike, hoping to knock it into the water. Give them time to think of something.

"Get away from it!" Racquel yelled.

"But . . . " Scooter looked back.

Rachel raised the revolver.

"Don't — " Scooter began, seeing visions of Racquel hitting Flash.

The gun spat fire. Shots rang out, stopping everyone. The unearthly Doberman shuddered, took several wobbly steps, then collapsed onto the dock.

"Look out for the second one!" Kristie yelled.

The slick black beast raced toward them, its claws digging into the wood. A board squeaked under its weight as it leapt forward. Racquel dropped it with a shot.

"Good shot!" Russell exclaimed. "Damn good! Dad would be impressed!"

Racquel smiled ever so slightly.

"Oh, Flash!" Scooter grabbed his dog and hugged him. "Thanks, Racquel," Scooter told her. Surprising him, she just shrugged and smiled.

"I've never seen anything this horrible looking," Kristie said. "It looks . . . warped. Twisted."

"D . . . don't get near it. J . . . just in c . . . case it's faking," Russell cautioned.

"The door is closed, again," Racquel pointed out.

"Wish I could keep it closed," Scooter said. "Racquel, watch the door. Shoot anything or anyone who comes out."

"Scooter!" Kristie exclaimed.

Scooter couldn't believe he'd said that, either. He'd been under the vampire's control once. He doubted he'd survive a second time.

"Racquel, you're such a good shot, if it's a person, wing them in the leg or foot," Scooter suggested. "Protect yourself. This isn't a game."

She nodded. Her expression was grim.

Scooter carried the axe to the trees, then looked for just the right one. After finding it, he climbed up, then along a thick branch almost resting atop the roof. He balanced on the branch, lying across it.

"How's it look?" Kristie asked.

"Ready to collapse," he replied. "I wouldn't stand on it."

Scooter leaned over and began hacking at the tattered shingles where the wooden roof was exposed. Shingles crumbled. Wood chips flew, fluttering in the breeze. Lying on the branch made it difficult to get in a good swing. He was glad it wasn't very sturdy. After several blows, he had put a hole in it. "Success!"

"Can you see anything?" Kristie asked.

"No," Scooter replied. "Racquel! Russell! How's the front door?"

"Nothing so far."

Scooter continued working, widening the gap. He found a second spot and began chopping away. Soon he made a second hole. "I still can't see anything." He climbed to the ground, then headed up another tree. He repeated the process, putting two more holes in the roof.

"See anything yet?" Kristie asked.

"It looks deserted." He could see a little better, circles of light on a dirty wooden floor, but nothing else. His senses told him differently. He felt someone inside — someone living. Even more powerfully, he felt Mr. Shade's presence. It was compelling him to climb down. To come inside. Scooter shook his head.

"Are you okay?" Kristie asked

"Yeah! I wish I could climb down onto . . . Hey!" The branch shifted. Scooter lost his balance and began to tumble.

"Scooter!" Kristie cried. Russell came running.

Racquel glanced from the door to the roof, then back. The door opened. Darkness stared back at her. Scooter had just knocked holes in the roof, so daylight should be streaming in.

Racquel saw something move in the doorway. The darkness shifted. She had a flash of intuition. "Garrett?"

Pale faced but with a winning smile, Garrett stepped partly from the shadows. Only his face and hands were visible.

Racquel was taken aback by his appearance. He reminded her of Marcus Chandler. His eyes were ablaze. His eyes . . .

"Come in," Garrett implored, his voice silky smooth and compelling. "Racquel. I have missed you. I need you, Chaquita. Come." He stepped back into the shadow. Only his face and a beckoning finger were visible; the rest of him was wrapped in darkness.

"I'm coming," Racquel said, walking forward. "I'm so glad you missed me."

"RACQUEL! STOP! WHERE ARE YOU GOING!" Russell raced after her. "She's going inside!" Russell grabbed for her as she stepped into the darkness. The door slammed into his outstretched hand, then he crashed into the door.

"What's going on down there?!" Scooter called. He'd climbed back on the branch and regained his balance.

"They have Racquel! She just walked inside!" Russell cried as he bounced to his feet.

"Then we have to hurry!" Scooter said. He looked around. This wasn't working out like he'd hoped. He debated cutting down a tree, hoping it would land on the roof and let in more sunlight. They wouldn't expect that. He'd just have to pray the rickety house would support a falling tree so that no one inside was crushed.

A shot sounded, and a section of the roof exploded. Wood fragments flew. "What . . ." Scooter was surprised as a bullet zinged past. He lost his balance, falling off the branch.

"Scooter!" Kristie cried.

Scooter tumbled onto the roof. It creaked and groaned under his weight, but held. "Whew!" he sighed.

"Scooter, are you all right?"

"Yeah, this isn't as rickety as it . . ." The roof suddenly collapsed. As though swallowed, Scooter disappeared into the darkness below.

Chapter Twenty-Seven

EXPOSED

"**S**COOTER! SCOOTER!" Kristie cried frantically as she scrambled up the tree.

Barking wildly, Flash jumped up against the trunk, as though trying to climb the oak.

"What's happening up there?!" Russell yelled as he continued to pound on the cabin door.

"Scooter fell through the roof!" Kristie peered across the top of the roof, then climbed higher until she could see down the hole that had swallowed Scooter. "Scooter's gone! I don't see him!"

"Then they've got him and Racquel! We have to help them!"

While Russell pounded away, the door suddenly and silently swung open, revealing a portal into darkness. "K . . . K . . . K . . . Kristie, the d . . . door just opened!"

A breeze wafted from inside. It smelled ancient and rotten like a long-closed tomb. Except for the earthen smell, Russell was reminded of the time he'd opened a chest belonging to his great-grandmother.

"WAIT!" Kristie cried as she hurriedly slid down the tree.

"We have to save them! I can't desert Scooter, again! And Racquel . . . " Russell took a step forward.

"That's what they want you to do," Kristie called to him.

"What choice do we have?"

"We can still go back and get help."

"By then it might be too late." Russell turned on his flashlight. The beam barely penetrated the darkness; a heavy black fog seemed to fill the room. "I thought Scooter chopped holes in the ceiling."

Kristie was behind him now, looking over his shoulder. "He did. They must be in another room, farther in."

Flash stood next to them, trembling, his tail between his legs. He whined, then inched forward inside the cabin. With the beams of their flashlights leading the way, Kristie and Russell followed closely behind. They had only taken a few steps when the Lab's stance stiffened. Flash began barking angrily.

"What do you see, boy?" Russell asked. Their beams played across a black, impenetrable curtain. "I don't see anything. What should we do now?"

Scooter groaned. His back hurt even more now. Hot wires ran down his legs, and his feet burned as if pricked by hot needles. What happened? Where was he?

He rolled over and opened his eyes. Darkness surrounded him.

The last thing he remembered was falling out of the tree. He must have crashed through the roof. Scooter suddenly realized he was inside the house. Inside the house with Mr.

Shade! Fear seized him, grabbing him and shaking him with skeletal paws. Scooter's heart raced, and he had trouble breathing. How could it be dark? He'd cut holes in the roof.

Was it night? Cool sweat ran down his face and neck, sliding along his back. Had he been dragged into another room? Where was everybody? Where were CJ, BJ, and Garrett? W. . . where was the vampire?

Scooter fingered his throat. At least he hoped the cross around his neck would protect him.

Somewhere nearby he heard voices; they sounded muffled.

"Glad you could make it, Chaquita." That sounded like Garrett. "Tai has something special for you."

"W . . . what?" Racquel's voice shook. "Who's Tai?"

"We'll be young forever. You'll be beautiful forever. Just like her."

"You're delirious, Garrett. Let me help you," she pleaded.

"Aw, Chaquita. You wait and see. One more night, and we'll be free of our parents. Isn't that what we've always wanted? To be free?"

Scooter felt around, searching for his flashlight or his axe. He had a dreadful, sinking feeling neither was close by. He was in trouble, deep trouble. The holy water, the mallet and the stakes were outside. He had to get out of here! Darkness was his enemy.

"Are you talking about running away?" Racquel finally asked.

"In a sense. But more than running away from our parents. Running away from our lives. Our boring, everyday ordinary lives. We can be different from everyone else."

"I thought you didn't like different . . . "

"Even better, Chaquita, we can be different and better!"

"You're crazy! Hey, let me go," Racquel railed.

Scooter heard a loud slap.

The first slap was followed by a second, but this slap was

even louder — harder. Racquel whimpered.

"Got some things I want to teach you," Garrett said with a smile. "You're going to love them. Tomorrow you'll look at everything differently. I promise."

Scooter stopped searching. Carrying an ancient stench, a chilling breeze wafted over him. He sensed a presence. A vacuum. Death. A hole where there should be life. Should be something! Anything!

Scooter tried to cry out, but the sound leaving his lips was a hoarse wheeze. Drenched in sweat, his heart pounded so loudly he could barely hear. Mr. Shade was here! In the room with him!

With a shaking hand, Scooter grasped the cross around his neck and prayed.

Kristie pushed her cross forward. The darkness receded, slinking back like a wary, reluctant creature. Kristie took a step forward, inside the cabin. The ebony curtain receded some more, but it seemed tensed, even cornered.

Flash inched forward, a steady guttural growl deep in his throat. Suddenly, the darkness reached out, grabbing the Lab, and pulling Flash within the black wall.

"Flash!" Kristie screamed and stepped forward.

Another black tentacle lashed out, snatching Kristie's hand. She was so shocked, she almost dropped her flashlight. Kristie yanked back, trying to pull herself free; but the ebony snake dragged her slowly toward the black curtain.

"Help! Russell!"

Russell hit it with his cross. Burned, the dark tentacle snapped back into the black wall.

Flash had grown silent.

"Flash?!" Kristie called out.

A pair of hands silently darted from the ebony curtain, grabbing Russell and snatching him into the darkness.

"Russell!" Kristie screamed.

Something stepped out of the abyss.

Starting at his nose, then across his face and chest, the darkness peeled away from the figure.

"BJ!" Kristie exclaimed, leaping backwards.

The Mochrie boy's smile was filled with evil intent. His eyes danced maliciously in the light.

The darkness bulged, and a second figure stepped out. "CJ!"

BJ snatched at her, grabbing her arm.

"Don't touch me!" She struck him with the flashlight.

BJ dropped to the floor like a sack of potatoes.

CJ darted forward, grabbing at her.

Kristie whirled and raced for the door.

"There's nowhere to go, Kristie!" CJ hollered, chasing after her. "There is no escape!"

Kristie was faster. She reached the door first, diving through it. The worn and ragged boards tore at her as she rolled across the dilapidated dock. Without looking behind her, Kristie leapt to her feet, ran down the dock, and jumped into the boat as though it were a magic carpet ready to whisk her to safety.

Kristie glanced over her shoulder. No footsteps hounded her. There was no sign of CJ or BJ. Had the darkness enveloped them? Darkness still waited just inside the door; it seemed alive, even breathing, waiting for her to return.

What was she going to do? Kristie refused to go back in there. That was suicide! There had to be a better way.

Maybe Mr. Chandler would know. "Mr. Chandler! Mr. Chandler! I need your help!" Kristie moved to his side and shook him lightly. "Mr. Chandler! We need you. Scooter needs you!"

Kristie shook harder.

"You have disturbed my rest." Mr. Shade's omnipresent voice echoed throughout the room.

Scooter couldn't see him, but he could feel the vampire staring down on him.

Crimson eyes suddenly appeared in the darkness. They glowered like hot coals in a deep pit. "You have caused me much trouble. But I do thank you for bringing Marcus Chandler to me. If he survives the day, come the night, he will be mine."

Something grabbed Scooter by the collar, choking him and lifting until eye to eye with Mr. Shade. The vampire's eyes changed color, now blood-red moons in a baleful night's sky.

Scooter flailed his feet and hands, striking at his captor. Each futile blow felt as though it had passed through icy water.

"So pitifully weak," Mr. Shade told him, "but such a pain in the — dare I say — neck."

Scooter smelled something burning. In an instant, he was dropped.

The eyes lowered, growing closer to his. They flickered as if Mr. Shade were in pain, then hardened, an intense, cold fire ignited in them. "Take off that cross."

Scooter felt seized by a hundred hands.·

Hunger burned within the nightstalker's eyes, but it was now overshadowed by an imperialness. Mr. Shade was accustomed to being obeyed.

Scooter struggled against Shade's command. But Scooter's shaking hands were removing the cross against his will. As it passed his lips, he kissed the cross and managed to utter a prayer.

"I command you! Take it off!" His voice resonated. The walls trembled. For a moment, the command resonated in Scooter's ears. "You have no will of your own. Your will is my will. Your soul is my soul. I have already tasted of you. You cannot resist. You will not resist!"

Scooter felt himself losing his grip. He was becoming numb — becoming distant. It was getting harder and harder to think. The cross threatened to slip from his hands. With his last ounce of will, he cried out, "Flash! Kristie! Russell!"

Scooter slipped away further. He tried to get bullheaded

and stubborn. He thought of his grandfather and grand-mother.

"Take it off! I command it!" The eyes were larger now. The darkness was gone. All Scooter saw was the darkspawn's eyes, big and red, a pair of fireballs exploding to engulf him.

Scooter was suddenly lost. A fog arose around him, thickening in the fire. Scooter felt as if he were floating away, drifting from his body.

Now he looked down on himself. Somehow he could see in the darkness. An ebony figure even darker than the darkness hovered over him. The vampire leaned forward.

Scooter dropped the cross, then clutched at the chain. With a mind of its own, his hand continued to lift off the necklace.

"Tear it off!"

Scooter heard the boat engine start. They were deserting him! He was dead. He would never go riding or fishing on a sunny day. Never draw his comic book. Never kiss Kristie.

Outside in the boat, Kristie was frantic. Mr. Chandler was still alive but unconscious and barely breathing.

She turned on the radio but nothing happened. Stupid, she told herself. Kristie flipped a button with the word 'radio' under it. Static sounded from the speakers. She grabbed the handset and began calling out, "Mayday," as she'd seen done in the movies. "I need help! We need help! We're on the lake! At Fisherman's Island! Help, please!"

No one responded.

Kristie was torn by indecision. She wanted to escape. She wanted to help her friends. She didn't want to die. She was too young to die. Her friends were too young, too.

She started Silverscreen, recalling the steps Scooter had shown her.

"What's going on?" Chandler moaned.

In a torrent of words, Kristie explained.

Somehow, Chandler pulled himself into the passenger

seat. He wearily looked at the house and dock. "Nobody answered your radio call?"

"Not yet." Kristie bit her lip.

"Then we don't have much time to save Scooter and the others. The crucifixes didn't work?"

"We couldn't get close enough."

"Then . . . sunlight . . . " he began. Then his eyes suddenly rolled back, and Chandler shuddered and collapsed.

"What do I do?" Kristie screamed. Tears of frustration streamed down her face. "Tell me!"

"Flash! Kristie! Russell!" she heard Scooter cry out.

If she ever needed an angel, she needed one now. How could she get sunlight into the house? Kristie wondered. She couldn't carry it. Reflect it in with a mirror like the gnomes in the movie Legend? She didn't have a mirror — except the rearview mirror. It wasn't big enough. It would only work in the front room. She needed more sunlight to spread throughout the cabin!

She couldn't bash in the windows or make more holes in the roof. Scooter had taken the axe with him.

Make a hole? A scene from Disney's *Beauty and the Beast* came to mind: Belle's father's invention crashing through the door to save him. Kristie knew what she must do!

She had to pretend she was crazy, that's all. Or a heroine in a movie. She wouldn't let the vampire have her friends. She couldn't!

Closing her eyes, she remembered what Scooter showed her. She pulled back the gear shift, putting the boat into reverse The motor roared. Water churned, but they didn't go anywhere.

Kristie heard a scream. Scooter!

Desperate now, Kristie gave the engine more gas, pulling all the way back on the shift. Silverscreen jerked but still didn't move back. Up front, the rope stretched straight and tight.

Stupid girl, she told herself. Kristie eased the boat forward, then quickly scampered to the bow. She untied and unwound rope, then hurried back to the steering wheel.

Kristie put the gear shift in reverse. This time, the boat slowly slid away.

She backed until she cleared the dock, then turned the boat and headed for open water.

Did she hear Scooter scream again?

Kristie jammed the throttle all the way forward, spun the wheel, and headed back toward the cabin. As the bow leveled, the craft gained speed and raced forward.

Kristie desperately hoped she was in time. Hoped they were still alive. That she had good aim. That she didn't kill herself.

She steered for the part of the dock that was half in and half out of the water, creating a crude ramp. She glanced at the speedometer. The needle passed twenty. Then raced pass thirty, reaching for forty. She stared at the dock. She was almost there. This was crazy!

Kristie prayed, closed her eyes, and ducked under the instrument panel. Mr. Chandler had already slumped to the floor of the boat.

With a crash, a squeal and boat-shuddering jolt, Silverscreen slammed into the sagging dock. The boat rocketed out of the water, flying toward the house like a missile. The engine roar became a metallic whine as propellers whirled through the air.

Silverscreen momentarily coasted airborne. Time seemed suspended. A thunderous crash filled the air, deafening Kristie as her world fell in. The second impact jarred her far more than the first. Her head hit the steering wheel. Her teeth clacked together, and she saw a flash of light followed by falling stars and a deep blackness as if the sun had been eclipsed.

With a spray of splinters, drywall and debris, Silverscreen exploded through the front wall like a catapulted giant spear, then shot across the dark room. The boat struck the second wall which ruptured in a hail of wooden shards and drywall dust. The boat careened sideways, knocking a massive hole through the cabin, and skipped across the dilapidated deck.

The decrepit platform crumbled under Silverscreen's weight, collapsing into the water. The boat shifted to the starboard, threatening to roll over, then slid into the water.

Everything shook. The walls, floor, and ceiling quaked mightily. An earthquake? Scooter wondered. Then, as though smashed by a huge fist, the wall behind Mr. Shade erupted. Debris ripped through and past him, leaving him unharmed but slashing across Scooter.

The house leaned and listed forward, toward the lake. The ceiling creaked, then gave way. Like dominoes falling, it collapsed in stages. More and more of the roof fell as the cave-in accelerated.

Scooter suddenly saw light. Sunlight warmed his face; he could feel again!

Beams of sunlight splayed through the dust, piercing the vampire. Mr. Shade screamed; his eyes wide and wild. The nightstalker's mouth was open in a silent, tortured scream. Smoke poured from his clothing and hair as though it would burst aflame. Mr. Shade's flesh began to melt and run, then darkened and blistered. The vampire's form rippled, then erupted into flames that danced and devoured, eating away at the undead beast.

His flesh quickly seared away, leaving only bones that snapped and crackled, then burned and blackened. With a whoosh, the fire suddenly extinguished, and the charred skeleton crumbled into a pile of dust.

Scooter stared dumbly at the ashen spot in the patch of sunlight. The front half of the cabin had collapsed, and sunbeams formed in the dusty haze. Scooter rubbed his eyes, unsure of what had happened.

"Who dropped the bomb?" Scooter asked. He looked around for a fallen tree but didn't find one.

A flurry of movement followed a golden blur. The next thing Scooter knew, Flash was licking his hands, face and neck.

"Yes, I'm alive!" Scooter laughed. "I'm alive, really." Flash didn't stop, so Scooter gave him a big hug, then pushed the Lab away so he could rise to his feet. Pain raced down his legs, flaring in his knees and feet. Scooter quickly sat back down.

To his left, he heard weeping. Through the debris and a stretch of cracked drywall, Scooter saw Racquel cradling Garrett. He looked unconscious. BJ was lying nearby, staring vacantly into the sunshine. Not far away, his brother was crumpled in a heap. Russell knelt next to him.

"Hey, Russell! Buddy!"

"You're alive! Yee-haw!" Russell cheered. He scrambled through the wreckage to help his friend.

"You're all right!" Kristie cried as she crawled through the devastation, bruised and bloody. She jumped over a downed support beam in the front room and ran toward them.

"Kristie!" Scooter yelled. "Our guardian angel!"

Flash woofed.

Kristie ran into his arms, and the threesome hugged. Flash jumped on them, licking anyone he could.

"Is the monster dead?" Kristie finally asked.

Scooter nodded. "Mr. Shade is dead. Really dead this time!" He pointed to the ash heap. "That's all that's left of the vampire. Now, what happened?!" Scooter's hand motion was all encompassing.

In a breathless rush, Kristie told them everything.

"Kristie, you're great! What an idea!" Scooter kissed her on the lips.

After a long moment, Kristie sat back, beaming brightly. "I think everything is going to be all right now."

Chapter Twenty-Eight

UNKIND WELCOME

They found an unconscious girl and boy among the wreckage.

"I recognize them from church school. It's Elvin and Karen LaRoche," Kristie told them. Both kids had neck wounds — nasty gifts from Mr. Shade. "They need a doctor. And soon."

"Like just about everybody else," Russell replied. He and Kristie carried them to the boat.

Scooter couldn't lift anything; he could barely stand. Walking in the water wasn't so painful or difficult. He swam around, checking out the boat's hull. "It's scraped but looks fine. Now the propeller, that's a different story altogether. It's badly bent, but will probably work if we creep along."

"It's gonna be slow going and very crowded," Russell said. "Gonna have to stack the zombies like firewood," he joked.

"Just be glad you're alive," Kristie said as she glared at him. "Hey, Garrett came in a boat. I wonder where it is?"

"I think I see it." Scooter pointed. The craft was underwater, crushed under the collapsed dock.

"I guess we all pile into one boat," Kristie murmured, sounding distressed.

"That's ten of us," Russell tallied.

Flash barked.

"Okay, eleven of us," he amended.

"Anyone have any ideas?" Scooter asked. Russell shook his head. "I'm going to try the radio again." He climbed into the boat.

After convincing Racquel to leave Garrett for a minute, the threesome carried CJ, then BJ out of the house and into the boat.

"I don't like the looks of this," Russell said.

"Good thing we're mostly kids and a dog," Kristie said.

Scooter sighed. "I wish I could think of something else. No one is answering the radio. I don't want to stay here, and I doubt anyone else does either. We need to get to a doctor."

"And soon," Kristie repeated as she climbed in last. The boat sank even lower, the water just below the gunwales. "Let's go." She and Russell pushed the boat away from the ruins of the dock. Water splashed over the side as Silverscreen drifted away from shore.

Scooter eased the boat into reverse. It shimmied and shook, but the propeller didn't clank as he worried it might. The engine sounded fine. When Scooter shifted into forward gear, Silverscreen shook even more and wallowed in the water. "It's going to be difficult to plane out," he informed them.

"You have plenty of gas," Russell said, looking over Scooter's shoulder.

They plowed ahead, pushing the water aside instead of

riding atop it. A huge wake spread out behind them as if they were a shipping barge.

Nobody seemed to mind the closeness. Kristie sat on the floor leaning against Scooter, her head on his leg. Scooter was glad to be alive. Touching someone made him feel safe.

He glanced at BJ and CJ. They appeared to be in shock, sitting and staring blankly ahead. The LaRoches were about the same. Garrett, cradled in Racquel's arms, was still unconscious with a nasty lump on his head. Chandler appeared unconscious.

"Russell, want to drive?" Scooter asked.

"You bet!"

They switched positions, and Scooter moved up front.

While Russell drove, Scooter and Kristie cuddled. Flash put his head in her lap. She laughed and began petting the Lab.

Russell smiled and began singing a song called, *Truckin'*. Kristie joined him; and they serenaded the group with several songs, including a few rousing gospel hymns. Howling with a deep, warbling bass, Flash joined Kristie on *Zippitty Do Da*. It was a wonderful day.

When they reached the sandbar, Russell used a rope to tie their old john boat to a grommet on the back. Scooter, Kristie and Flash climbed into the towed boat, letting Russell chauffeur them. He looked almost as happy as Flash, who had moved to the bow of the john boat, pretending to be a maiden head. The Lab's eyes were closed, his tongue lolling, and his ears flapping in the wind, carefree and dreaming of flying.

The trip to Chandler's dock at the far south end of the lake took over an hour, but the singing made time fly. Before they knew it, they had arrived at the ranch. When they pulled up to the dock and crawled out, they discovered they were bone weary.

"I'm beat," Russell said.

"Me, too," Scooter replied. Kristie had to help Scooter, whose leg felt afire and couldn't bear much weight. "To a pulp. Better than the alternative, though."

A frown on his face, Flash looked concerned, circling and getting in their way.

"It's okay, boy. I just need to see a doctor and get some rest."

"Pile everyone into the truck, and we'll ride to the house." Marcus Chandler groaned as Russell helped him ashore.

The moviemaker had just awakened. He was covered with towels, one was even wrapped around his head. He reminded Scooter of a modernized sheik. "Someone else will have to drive."

"I will," Russell volunteered. He guided the elderly moviemaker into the front seat.

"You're a veteran now." Scooter laughed.

Oddly enough, Racquel didn't even complain that she was older and should be driving. All her attention was on Garrett. Her cheeks were tear-streaked and stained. With Kristie's help, she steered Garrett into the back seat.

Russell and Kristie carried the LaRoche kids, maneuvering them into the back of the vehicle. The Mochrie boys were no longer in shock, but they were silent and nearly lifeless. Russell and Kristie guided the zombie brothers into the back of the Dodge pickup.

Flash jumped into the front seat next to Chandler. While Kristie and Scooter crowded into the back, Russell climbed into the driver's seat. Chandler gave him the keys. "REALLY!" he managed without stuttering. He'd always wanted to drive without his dad around.

"Just take it slow," Chandler told him.

Russell beamed as he started the pickup. "A speed boat, now a truck! Dreams do come true!"

As proud as any peacock, Russell drove them along the gravel road towards Chandler's house.

"Hey, look at all those people!" Russell exclaimed. "How'd they know we were coming?"

A huge crowd surrounded the house. Cars and trucks were parked all over the place as if at a party.

"There must be at least fifty of them," Chandler groaned. "I don't like the looks of this."

Scooter scrutinized the crowd. Something didn't seem quite right. "I don't think they're a welcoming committee. Hey, Russell! I think I see your dad! He's on the other side of that crowd." Scooter pointed. "See him on top of the car? He has a bullhorn."

Russell squinted. "Yeah! I see him. I'm driving there."

"Check out the signs," Kristie pointed out.

"It reminds me of a protest demonstration," Scooter agreed.

The placards and signs were hateful:

"Go back to California!"

"Vampires Stay in LA!"

"White Power!"

"White for Might. Right for White!"

Others were even more profane and racist.

"I have a bad feeling about this," Racquel moaned.

"Oh, no!" Scooter exclaimed.

The crowd noticed the Dodge. They pointed at it and waved their signs. Several people suddenly rushed toward them.

Scooter recognized Mr. Nathans, Mr. Hernandez and the assistant to the mayor, Mr. Cauthon. Then, more people followed, like lemmings jumping off the cliff — one after another.

"They've got bats and clubs and shovels and rakes . . . " Kristie began.

"I fear it's a lynching mob," Chandler moaned. "Ms. Emmitt warned me, but I didn't believe her. I guess I thought more highly of the people of Gunstock than she did, but I was wrong. She was right! Hurry! Drive away! Drive directly to the hospital!"

Russell had just stepped on the gas when Kristie screamed, "You can't! You'll dump us out!"

A rock struck the windshield, chipping it. Other missiles followed. In moments, it sounded like they were driving in a torrential hail storm.

"Keep going!" Chandler yelled.

"I'm heading for my dad!" Russell shouted.

People jumped in front of the pickup, but Russell kept creeping forward, hoping he didn't kill anyone.

The mob pressed against the pickup, swinging bats, signs and rakes, bashing it viciously. Through the pounding and thudding, Scooter heard many voices. People were yelling profanity and calling Chandler's name.

"Show yourself, coward!"

"Get out here, boy!"

Scooter read more signs. They called Marcus Chandler a murderer, kidnapper, bloodsucker and far, far worse.

Flash barked loudly as if demanding they listen to him, the voice of reason.

"Hey, there's a dog and kids in there!" somebody shouted.

"He's captured more kids!" someone else bellowed. "Open the door!"

The pounding intensified.

Russell blew the horn, startling several who fell off the hood.

"He's sacrificing kids!" a woman screamed hysterically. "They're dead in the back!" This was followed by more angry shouts. Something hard and heavy struck the front windshield forcefully; and it cracked, spider-webbing completely.

Russell couldn't see anything. Too frightened to stop, Russell drove until he hit solid metal with a thump and a thud.

In a boomingly amplified voice, they heard Sheriff Knight shout, "Get away from the truck!" This was followed by several shots in the air.

Grumbling and complaining, people reluctantly backed away from the truck. Their faces were angry, with murder in their eyes, and their fists were clenched white.

The driver's door was suddenly yanked open. "Russell! What in heaven's name is going on here?" Sheriff Knight asked. He looked at the occupants. His eyebrows rose when he saw what appeared to be bodies in the back. "Racquel!" Sheriff Knight flung open the back door. He and his daughter hugged. "Are you all right?"

"I'm fine, Father, but Garrett isn't. He got hit on the head and . . . and . . . " She didn't finish, not knowing how to explain. "I don't know about CJ and BJ. They need a doctor!"

"We're afraid Mr. Chandler might die from sun exposure," Scooter added.

"Lewis, call for an ambulance! And call Emory! We may need more than one!" Sheriff Knight cried.

People pressed around him, shoving the sheriff and Racquel against the truck.

"Everybody get back! Lewis! Call for backup!"

"Are those my sons?" Mrs. Mochrie shouted, fighting her way to the rear of the pickup truck. "What's happened to them?"

"I'm trying to find out, Pearl," Sheriff Knight told her.

"We want action! We want Chandler!" Jake Gunn yelled. Aaron Nathans joined him, then others did too, starting a chant.

The Gunn brothers pushed their way toward the pickup. Each carried a sign in one hand and a big stick in the other.

The sheriff eyed them warily. "Stay back, boys. Let us find out what happened."

The crowd quit pushing, but they were on the edge, ready to rush forward at any moment — ready to tear Marcus Chandler apart.

"Russell! Racquel! Please tell me what's going on? And

Scooter! Is your grandfather going to be glad to see you!"

"Grandpa's all right? What about Grandma?!"

Sheriff Knight nodded. "They're both fine. I just spoke with the Judge. Now, tell me what's going on here!"

The crowd eagerly pressed forward to hear every word. Russell looked around, then began explaining, speaking without stuttering. Chandler chimed in with Racquel, Kristie and Scooter also adding bits and pieces.

Their words were greeted with numerous gasps, guffaws and other sounds of disbelief.

"Lies, all lies!" Jake Gunn yelled. "It's a cover up because Chandler is famous. If he was just a rancher like Peters . . . "

The two deputies moved in and eased back the crowd. Those who wouldn't go easily were forced back.

"Russell, start over and tell me again what happened," Sheriff Knight demanded.

When the jumbled story was completed again most people agreed with Merl Cauthon when he said, "That's utterly ridiculous. Total hogwash! Preposterous! A cover up that won't wash!"

Sheriff Knight shook his head. "Russell, I have to agree with them," he said sadly.

"Chandler's the vampire," someone in back shouted. "Not some imaginary person called Mr. Shade."

"He can't be a vampire," another responded. "It's broad daylight."

That brought a short silence, until someone muttered, "Murderer."

"He murdered Missy and the others!"

The demands and name calling started all over again.

Scooter recognized many of the people besides Cauthon, Nathans, and Hernandez: the rancher, Mr. Peters; Mr. Ringly from the grocery store; Mr. Carlson who owned the gas station, Mr. Short from the power company and Mr. Evans with the water company, and many others. Some of their wives and kids were with them. Scooter couldn't believe how they were acting. He saw light around each of them, and many times it was red-streaked or spotted with black. He wondered if the red was anger and the dark splotches fear.

"What about Missy and Debbie?" Sheriff Knight asked.

"Mr. Shade . . . the vampire got them," Russell replied.

"Now, Russell . . . " Sheriff Knight began.

Garrett suddenly awakened, pulling away from Racquel. His movements were lightning fast and surprising, all she could do was gasp as he said, "You will pay for your disbelief! Pay with your lives! Tai exists, and she is powerful! As Tai killed Missy and Debbie to survive, she will do the same to you all!"

The mob fell silent, stunned by Garrett's sudden outburst.

"Who is Tai?" the sheriff asked.

"The same vampire," Scooter began to explain. "She — he — could make herself, I mean, himself look like anyone. Even you."

"Now, Scooter, that might be good material for comic books but . . . " Sheriff Knight started.

Flash barked indignantly, demanding those words be taken back.

"Don't start with me, Flash."

The Lab snorted, then lay down, legs crossed and looking away with his nose pointed into the air as if to say humans could be so stupid at times.

Garrett wasn't done ranting. "Unless you worship her as BJ, CJ, and I do, she will come for you! She is the mistress of the night, defier of death! There is no stopping her . . . " His own words suddenly seemed to hit home. Garrett looked confused. "Stopping her . . . She is truly dead, isn't she?"

"We destroyed her, Garrett," Racquel said. She hugged him fiercely. "You're free."

"No . . . she can't be destroyed. How? I don't want to be free! We had a better life ahead!" Garrett suddenly collapsed in Racquel's arms. They would have fallen if a deputy hadn't stepped in to help.

"He was ranting!" Jack Gunn yelled.

"That murderer has drugged them," Tom Gunn added, helping to whip the crowd into a frenzy once more. "Chandler's a drug dealer, too!"

"Russell, Scooter, one of you please tell me the truth," Sheriff Knight pleaded. "This is not a game."

"But there was a vampire," Russell contended.

"Mr. Shade killed Missy and Debbie and enthralled Garrett and the Mochrie brothers," Scooter told them. "He tried to kill Grandpa and me last night! Obviously, nobody believed him."

"Enough of this bull," Jack Gunn bellowed. "We'll deal with Chandler ourselves!"

The crowd pushed forward again, overwhelming the sheriff and his deputies. Sheriff Knight was knocked to the ground. Someone hit him on the head, stunning him. Deputy Lewis pulled someone down on top of him. The other deputy slumped against the pickup, then slid to the ground.

Russell tried to start the truck. Before the engine had finished turning over, he was pulled out of the truck.

Martin and Hernandez grabbed Scooter and snatched him out of the Dodge. Scooter cried out in pain as fire flared through his back and down his legs.

Two rough-looking men jerked Kristie from the truck as she screamed. "Mr. Martin! Mr. Hernandez! Stop! You're hurting Scooter. Let him go!"

When they didn't, Flash bit them, and they dropped Scooter to the ground. Snarling and with jaws gnashing, the Lab moved to help Kristie next.

The Gunn boys hauled Chandler to the front porch of his house. "Hang him," Jack yelled. A rope was thrown over a rafter beam along the underside of the porch and all was readied.

"Let's have justice," Jake chimed in as his brothers bound

Marcus Chandler. They looped the rope over his head.

"No!" Scooter cried. "This is wrong! Listen to us! He didn't do anything wrong! He tried to help us."

"You're just a kid," Mr. Peters told him. "No one listens to you. You and your wild imagination, boy."

Scooter had never been so mad, so mad he ignored the danger and the pain in his back, and fought his way forward, pushing and shoving people out of the way. Russell and Kristie joined him, but it was hopeless.

"Hang him!" a woman cried.

Jake and Jack pulled on the rope, hoisting Chandler high in the air.

Chapter Twenty-Nine

LIGHT OF REASON

"**S**top this!" bellowed a voice from the crowd. A pair of people pushed through the throng: an elderly man with a priest's collar helping another with a cane. "You're acting like sheep, or fools, letting yourselves be led astray by those criminals!" The man pointed his cane toward the ranch house porch where the Gunn brothers held Marcus Chandler between them.

"It's Grandpa!" Scooter shouted. In a sea of chaos, Judge Keyshawn stood defiant, calling for reason. He was battered, bruised and bandaged, which seemed to heighten his stature. As Scooter rushed toward him, his heart swelled with pride.

"Marcus Chandler is not a murderer or a vampire," the Judge continued. "One's been proven and the other is simply ludicrous."

The Gunn brothers paused, unsure what to do next. For a moment, the large crowd grew silent. People shuffled restlessly. Nervous hands were clasped guiltily.

"For years you have trusted me to judge based upon evidence, on fact, and not runaway emotions. Something none of you are doing here today. Step back for a moment. Remember things are not always as they first appear. That is why we have trials with evidence. Not guesses and circumstantial fragments, but concrete proof.

"If there is a shadow of a doubt in any of your minds, I urge you to stop! Stop now! Ask yourself: Can I live with blood on my hands? Especially the blood of an innocent man who has done no harm? Are you attacking him solely because he's different from you?"

No one moved, except Scooter and Flash who were rushing to Judge Grandpa's side.

"Let's look around for a moment. Alvin," Judge Keyshawn pointed to Mr. Ringly, "have you ever had aliens land in your back yard?"

Alvin shook his head.

"Aaron claims he has. Maybe Aaron's an alien. You never know about those E.T.s. Either way, Aaron's certainly different. And look at Herb, here." The Judge waved toward the tall, bareheaded man who owned the gas station. "He's been bald since he was seventeen. Anyone else here been bald since they were seventeen?"

Someone chuckled. "His genes are different, I'd bet."

"And Martin here. Well, one leg is shorter than the other, and the heel on one shoe is bigger. You gonna hang him for that? How about Jeremy Evans? He has a birth mark on his face. Then there's Ramon here. His name even sounds different, doesn't it? Well, in case you haven't noticed, Ramon Hernandez is Hispanic, and he's tan without getting any sun. Isn't that true, Ramon?"

The man nodded, looking very sad. His wife tugged on his arm, urging him to leave.

Judge Keyshawn looked over to Pearl Mochrie. "And Mrs. Mochrie, well, she's a female. Same species and color but of the opposite sex. That makes her very different, more so than the others I've already mentioned, unless Aaron really is an alien."

Someone in the background guffawed. Another person snickered.

"I am not!" Aaron yelled. "Herb, you know me. I went to kindergarten with you!"

"Almost failed, too, if I remember correctly,"

Herb replied with a smile. "Before we lynch Aaron here, let's look at the Gunn brothers. Anyone else ever been to jail? Herb, have you ever assaulted anyone? Ramon, you ever raped anyone? Pearl, you ever run over anyone in your car?"

"She couldn't in that Pinto," someone in back snickered.

"How about you, Ethel?" the judge asked Mrs. Ringly.

She shook her head.

"No? Then why are y'all listening to these men? Why are y'all joining them?"

Scooter reached his grandfather, and they hugged. "I know you're scared," the Judge continued. "I was frightened for my grandson last night. Afraid I'd lost him. Just remember, once you kill someone, there is no turning back. No second chance.

"So stop and think for a minute. If you don't stop, you'll all be accessories to murder. You'll be guilty just like the Gunns. Criminals! Don't think you can get away with it because you're in a crowd. I know who you are! Father Candel knows who you are, as does Sheriff Knight and his deputies! I ask you this: If you murder Marcus Chandler, are you going to kill the rest of us, too?"

Besides the Gunn boys, not one of the crowd would meet the Judge's gaze. They were all looking to the ground or at the sky. They even seemed too chagrined — too embarrassed — to look at each other. Herb dropped his sign.

"Y'all should be ashamed of yourselves," Reverend Candel added. "The authorities have found Mr. Chandler innocent. If you don't have faith in Judge Keyshawn and Sheriff Knight, then we need to have a long talk, as well as some reading from the Good Book! Remember, you will be judged by your actions!"

There was a lot of grumbling and milling about. Carlson turned around and headed to his pickup. Cauthon quickly followed. Dragging their signs as if they were a ball and chain, Ramon Hernandez and his wife joined them. Others watched them leave, then a few more shuffled off toward their vehicles.

"Mom?" CJ suddenly climbed out of the Dodge truck. "Mom, what's going on?" Pearl Mochrie hugged her son.

"What happened to you?" she cried.

BJ also climbed out of the truck. "The Pinto broke down at the Pilot Point graveyard. There was this beautiful woman; she bit me." Mrs. Mochrie grabbed him by the ear "Ow!"

"Who cares about vampires!" Jake Gunn bellowed and began tugging on the rope. "A vampire didn't kill Jo — Chandler did." Jake moved to hoist the rope. Only Jack moved to help him. Even brother Tom stood back, arms folded across his chest.

"Let go of that rope!" Sheriff Knight yelled. Jack and Jake kept hoisting.

Sheriff Knight fired a warning shot into the air. People jumped back. A few covered their eyes and cringed a little. "Jake! Jack! Stop now or I'll shoot!"

Chandler's feet were off the ground, kicking the air. Red eyes bulging, his hands grasped the rope, trying to hold himself aloft so he could breathe.

A shot rang out. Jake Gunn staggered back, winged in the shoulder. He let the rope drop from his hands.

Chandler dropped back to the ground, then he collapsed

onto his knees, gasping for a breath.

Jack also let go and raised both hands skyward. The deputies moved in to help Chandler.

"Jake, Jack and Tom Gunn, you're all under arrest for attempted murder. The rest of you will cease and disperse," Sheriff Knight said. "Now go home!" He looked around carefully at everyone. "If y'all aren't gone in the next two minutes, we'll arrest whoever's still here."

The rest of the crowd slowly headed back to their cars. Their heads were hung low, and their eyes were downcast. Doors slammed and engines came to life. Ever so slowly, a line of cars and trucks moved along the gravel road, heading back towards Gunstock.

"Father!" Kristie rushed forward. "You won't believe . . ."

"Come here, sweetheart!" Reverend Candel called to her. "I'm so glad to see you!" They hugged each other, squeezing tightly.

"How are you?" Scooter asked his grandfather.

"Battered and bruised," he said with a weary smile. "Just like your grandma, but we'll be fine. I'm not sure which I believe less. What happened here or when our house burned down. You say that man was a vampire? I don't remember much about it. It seems like a nightmare now."

"I'll tell you all about it," Scooter said. "You probably won't believe it, but I'll tell you anyway."

"What about Jo?" Tom Gunn shouted as the deputies handcuffed them. "We demand justice! I don't believe no vampire killed her."

"You haven't heard the last of this," Jack said menacingly.

"Oh, yes, we have," Sheriff Knight replied sternly. "You boys will be in jail for quite awhile, if I have my way. It should be a quick trial."

More sheriff cars arrived, and an ambulance wailed in the distance.

"Ah, peace at last," Marcus Chandler said, rubbing his

neck as he stood in the shade of the front porch. "The darkness has been destroyed, and the light of reason has won again," he finished wryly. "I just wish it were so."

"Well, no one will bother you for a while," Sheriff Knight said. "Not after this embarrassing scene. And if they do, call. We'll be on the lookout."

The ambulance pulled up and paramedics loaded Garrett and the LaRoche kids inside. Racquel went with them. After getting assurances that Reverend Candel and the Judge would drive Russell home, Sheriff Knight took Marcus Chandler to the hospital. Kristie, Scooter, Russell, and Flash climbed into Reverend Candel's car.

"Funny how things work," Judge Keyshawn said. "If y'all hadn't hassled Mr. Chandler, we might never have discovered Mr. Shade and more might have died. Something good came from bad. That doesn't even include putting the Gunn boys back in jail. Nope, something good from something bad. That doesn't happen very often. But things don't always appear as they really are, either. Maybe in dealing with Mr. Shade, we learned a few things about ourselves."

"Yeah! No more secrets!" Russell promised. "They're trouble. I thought it was my fault for not speaking up earlier."

"Hey, perk up! We're heroes!" Kristie said as she hugged them both.

Barking, Flash nosed his way in.

"We saved BJ, CJ, Garrett, Mr. Chandler, the LaRoche kids and probably the whole town! With the help from a guardian angel or two," she added, glancing at her dad.

"And I got to drive!" Russell said. "A speed boat and a truck!"

They all laughed.

"It's going to be a great summer!" Scooter announced. "I don't need a gang when I have great friends like you two. Three counting Flash."

"Yeah!" Russell agreed.

Kristie hugged him again.

"Things can finally return to normal," Judge Keyshawn said, "until next year when y'all start driving. Then life will get scary again." He laughed. Everyone in the car joined him.

Scooter looked forward to relaxing, riding, fishing, and berry picking. And doing some writing, he thought. He felt inspired. Maybe he'd write and draw a comic book about what had happened! Yeah! He could do that! He could picture Mr. Chandler on the cover, surrounded by all those buried pick-ups.

Fog swirled around Mr. Chandler and . . .

Exciting Selections From:
Stealing Time

Gretchen's arms were tired, but her beautiful blue eyes sparkled as she laughed delightfully. Her apple-cheeked face reflected the sun's radiance. With just a glance, one could have mistaken her ponytail for a streaming halo.

"I love riding Kalyde II."

The Magic Bicycle, named after an alien, was a bright red blur. Gretchen and Danny pedaled in perfect time, synchronicity and imagination propelling the bicycle faster until it stretched into a crimson streak. Kalyde II was barely visible. The boulevard's center line blinked rapidly. Telephone poles along the hilly route appeared to shrink into skinny posts of an endless picket fence.

A loud caterwaul sounded from Danny's left. Riding within reaching distance, the calico feline Murg, his sister Sarah, and star-born friend Kah-laye-dee rode the other magical bicycle. The second magic gift from "Kalyde" was sky blue with white trimmings.

**

"How do you plan to hide among the Terrans?" Murg telepathically asked.

"An old trick but tried and true," Krindee replied with a

smile. "I will take the guise of a cat. Cats are known for having unusual personalities, making it easy to blend in."

"Easy to be a cat. Easy to blend in." Despite being on her back, Murg's tail snapped this way and that.

**

As Danny moved away, a bluish glow spilled under the door. He watched as it crept toward the bedroom door, threatening to radiate out into the hall. Hoping nobody could see it, Danny tried to block the light. As if sentient, the glow wavered knowingly, then darted back under the closet door.

Murg just sat back and watched it all. "Relax, Danny. Just be as calm, cool, and collected as I am."

When Danny opened the door, his father towered there, looking down with a dark gaze. Behind him, a pretty woman and a pair of stern men in dark suits crafted from the fabric of black holes waited impatiently. A menacing air surrounded the trio, hawks ready to dive upon unsuspecting prey.

**

The tattooed rider roared along Danny's other flank. Writhing snakes breathing fire covered his arms. "We got ya Chase!" Page yelled, the cigarette sticking to his lower lip. They grew closer. Moved tighter. Page hefted his bat. "Batter up!"

Danny quit pedaling and stopped on a dime. In a cloud of dust and bouncing rock, the riders blew by him. Danny pivoted and turned behind them, heading for an unfinished house.

Reggie cursed and steered back around. Muscling his motorized horse, Page followed.

"I don't believe it!" Page cried. "Get him, Vargas!"

The orange-haired boy was closest now.

Danny noticed his rifle was larger than a normal bb gun.

"I think that's a 410 shotgun!"

Danny steered for the boards ramping to the front door. The shotgun roared.

**

What if Chase had been serious? Spike wondered. The alien bicycle had repaired itself, just like the tandem. "I'd love to have a piece of E.T. technology. That'd be worth big bucks. I could sell it and move out ."

Spike ran his hands along the tandem's frame. It seemed to undulate under his hand. Spike laughed. Was Chase's imagination infectious?

Spike touched the seat. Nice padding. Must be comfortable.

The seat. Spike smiled evilly. "This will do just the trick!"

**

Murg hissed. "Danny, keep quiet and stay very, very still."

Although the mammoth shade appeared to be mostly shadow, Danny could see Mr. Pickett all too clearly. Darkness wrapped around Spike's stepfather as a massive, black overcoat. The shadow of his baseball cap hid all but his eyes, which gleamed readily in the cold moonlight. In one huge hand Mr. Pickett held a dark flashlight; in the other, he carried a rifle, its metal glinting silvery.

As if knowing they were near, Spike's step-father slowly approached the threesome. Mr. Pickett suddenly paused, looked around, then knelt to check the ground. Danny thought he saw the large man sniff as if a wild animal tracking prey.

"He's looking for tracks." Murg thought. "Hunting something."

When Mr. Pickett looked up, Danny could see his face. Spike's stepfather appeared furious, his chin tight and wide.

Gaunt lines cut dark across his ghost-white flesh. His eyes seemed to have taken on a reddish hue, pinpoints of laser sight seeking a target.

"He's hunting us!" Danny started to shake.

**

Day faded to night and returned again the next morning, and by lunch, Danny still hadn't seen Spike or felt Xeno. Danny hoped to find Spike in the library, but doubted Thugman would be there. He was somewhere in the past, lost Danny hoped wistfully. But where? Unfortunately, even with Spike absent, Danny felt his life wasn't going to settle until he resolved matters.

For a moment, Danny felt a kinship with one of Marvel's first popular comic book characters, Peter Parker, the Amazing Spider-Man. Danny was amused to think he was living a secret life, just like Superman and Iron Man.

**

"I see. So you and Krindy stood and pedaled all the way home?" Christina looked skeptical.

Danny nodded, then felt trapped. Sinking. Fast.

"You were sick and you stood all the way home? Your stomach was bothering you, you were cramping and you stood and rode all the way home? Do you want to stick to that story? You know what, maybe Cynthia is right!" Christina snapped. "IF so, I'm an idiot!"

"Shush!"

"Shush yourself! I'm sorry. This will only take a second. Danny, when you want to tell me the truth, come see me."

"Christina . . ."

She held up a hand to forestall him. "When you feel like trusting me with the truth, Danny, I'll listen. Okay? That's the best I can do right now."

Danny tried to find words as he watched her go.

**

"Thank you for your faith, Father. I shall not fail you." Drawing her sword before her, Jeannette d'Arc rose from bended knee and strode toward the sorceress. "Be gone foul demon."

"Aside child, or you shall share the fate of these armored churls."

"I do the will of the Lord. Angels bring me charges. You are not the first vile English woman to set foot upon my land. As the hand of God, I will first cleanse my homeland of you, then the rest of the English barbarians!" Light as bright as the sun sprang from her rings, engulfing her hands and running along her sword. When the holy fire reached the tip, the blade exploded with white flames.

Morgan Le Fay grimaced, then directed her staff at Joan of Arc. The dark lightning struck Jeannette's white shielding, shattering as obsidian upon marble.

The Maid of Prophecy charged. With both hands, Jeannette swung her blazing sword. Morgan countered, wielding the staff to block. The forest shook as blade and staff clashed again and again, black and white lighting flickering across the trees. Branches shook and snow tumbled to the ground in great heaps, sounding as giants stalking the woods.

**

A second pair of green eyes accompanied the first. Yellow orbs joined them, then twin eyes the color of blood appeared along the circle. More and more faceless eyes silently gathered. Soon, a hundred glowering eyes surrounded Stonehenge.

"What are they?" Danny asked.

As if one, the floating eyes moved forward. Dark shapes appeared, the eyes now no longer disembodied. The wolves sat, staring at Danny. A chill skittered along his spine.

**

Standing on the Boston street corner Spike waited for Babe Ruth to leave Yankee Stadium. A team of horses hauling a wagon of ice passed by, kicking away a cloud of dust. Spike waved away the dust, looking for the Babe's funky, bright red "horseless carriage".

Before Spike had waited for the Babe outside the park, but now that Ruth's popularity had swelled, the gate area was crawling with kids. The brats made it difficult for him to spend any time with the baseball legend, so Spike moved to this corner.

**

Spinning and whirling, Danny rose and fell as though riding a white tornado. He couldn't see anything, the whiteout all-engulfing. "What's happening?! Murg? Murg?! Where are you?!" Danny felt hemmed in, the nothingness growing tighter. Was he dead?

Out of the blinding blaze, Kalyde II suddenly stormed into a hot, humid place, the rain fired as hard as bullets. Wet vines slapped them, green ships lashing. With a thought, Danny erected the force field. "Whew! We're alive!"

"And in a jungle," Krindee replied. The Siamese backed away, staring at the bushes as they slapped the protective globe and slithered by.

"That was the dumbest thing you've ever done!" Murg snapped. Her damp fur stood like a porcupine's quills. "You damaged the time tunnel!"

Exciting Selections From:
The Magic Bicycle

First Ride

As the bicycle raced faster and faster, the world around them blurred into a whirlwind of colors. Danny felt lighter and was sure the bicycle had lost contact with the road. But he still felt safe.

A roaring sound like a thousand charging lions was followed by a tremendous clap of thunder. Bright, almost blinding, sparks surrounded them, then the world went white for a moment, then turned into a hazy grayness as if they were riding through engulfing clouds. Danny suddenly noticed it was quiet. Where was the sound of the wind?

Clouds parted. They were riding atop a gleaming rainbow. Below were brilliant streaks of red, orange, yellow, green and blue. Forming walls along each side of them was an electric purple. It was so bright that when Danny looked at himself, everything he wore, even his skin, glowed brilliant violet.

Murg meowed loud and long. Danny looked over his shoulder. The calico was standing on his shoulder staring skyward. Danny followed Murg's gaze and found sparkling stars in the darkness above. They were riding across the sky to South Carolina!!

The world suddenly went white, then flashed brightly as if they rode directly into a star. The lions roared once more and the thunder cracked as if a giant hole was being ripped in the sky. Danny was disoriented for a moment, then he realized they had done it! In less than a minute, they had ridden from

Texas to the east coast near Myrtle Beach, South Carolina.

Alien Encounter

Danny tumbled head over heels as he crashed down the stairs, each step biting into him as he bounced. He covered his head as best he could and hoped he survived. His feet rebounded off the bannister and sent him cartwheeling over the edge of the stairway.

Danny landed on an old tattered mattress that cushioned his impact. Something warm brushed against his leg. "I'll live, Murg," Danny groaned. He opened his eyes and was shocked to be staring at himself. Crimson and azure light flashed through the boarded windows of the basement and splayed about the room, illuminating his double.

Jumping to his feet to flee, Danny conked his head on the edge of the steps. Stars seemed to fill his vision, falling across his double's face. Its expression had changed from imitating his surprise to capturing his pain. "Who . . . what are you?" Danny whispered.

Words sounded inside Danny's head, "Greetings. I am Kahlaye-dee, a stranger to your planet." Danny was amazed. Not a word has touched his ears, and the alien's lips had never moved.

Danny watched slack-jawed as the wondrous transformation took place before his eyes. His double's features changed, no longer mimicking Danny. The shapeshifter's form shrank, becoming thinner, although its head stayed the same size. Its flaming red curls disappeared, now replaced by short blue hair that stood straight up, reminding Danny of a classmate. Its skin had lost its fleshy color and now gleamed with a bronzed hue. The stranger's nose had lengthened, flattened and spread wide. Its — or maybe — his eyes were still blue, but now glowed from deep within the tall, recessed sockets of his elongated face. Thin lips curled as the skinny being smiled, then reached out to touch him.

California Ghosting
Selection from Chapter One
"Ghostly Hitchhikers"

Blasing didn't respond. He recognized when simply saying anything could provoke a confrontation. Blasing saw something out of the corner of his eye. "LOOK OUT!"

Angela looked back to the road and slammed on the brakes. An old man and his mule were in the road! Angela cringed, awaiting the bone-crushing thump and the sight of bodies flying.

Instead, the pack animal and its master passed through the hood, then the windshield. The ethereal prospector smiled a toothless grin and doffed his dusty cap as he sliced through the interior of the 4-Runner. The ghostly mule was less accepting, its eyes wide with panic. Suddenly, the rank smells of old sweat, dust and unwashed mule overwhelmed them.

After the 4-Runner squealed to a stop, Blasing whirled around, eyes popping wide. "What the hell was that?" He pointed at the grayed and somewhat translucent miner dressed in worn clothing. As if desert mirages, distorted background shapes could be seen through the spirit. The ghost was obviously angry, cursing and tugging on his mule's bit, trying to convince it to move. The pale beast was amazingly overloaded with transparent boxes and bags bound together as if caught in a large spider's web.

"Is that a ghost?" Blasing whispered incredulously. "Ms.

Starborne, I . . . ." His lips worked silently.

Angela watched Blasing struggle with the concept of wandering spirits, his handsome face a mask of stunned confusion and his eyes unsettled. He ran a hand through his hair, then his dark gaze met her unwavering stare; he seemed to have composed himself quickly. "I don't believe in ghosts." He didn't sound convinced.

"You will," Angela said cryptically, no longer looking at Blasing but feeling the weight of his stare. "Maybe he's . . . wandered away." According to Peter, this wasn't supposed to happen.

"Wandered away? From where?"

"I'll ask," Angela said, trying to sound casual as she began rolling down her window. Her heart was pounding, her palms were damp, and the urge for a cigarette was strong.

"Isn't that dangerous?" Blasing asked. The near accident was not a big deal, but she was acting as if this were an ordinary, everyday experience.

"It might be."

The ghost spat, wiped his mouth. "Lillybell! Dang it ya floppy-eared varmint. If I had my stick ya wouldn't be actin' like this!" The mule appeared offended, setting its ears back in preparation for the forthcoming struggle.

Angela cleared her throat, starting to speak, but was stopped by the ghostly prospector. "This is your fault, purdy lady. Why I oughtta . . ." He began stalking toward the car.

The mule snorted, then nosed its master, almost knocking him off his feet. The miner staggered, then whirled quickly, yanking off his hat and slapping his unruly companion. "Think you're cute, do ya?" Lillybell bared her teeth, then began heehawing and rocking back and forth. Madder than a hornet, the prospector threw down his hat and began hopping back and forth.

"You know, I've never heard of a ghost being this far away from the resort," Angela said tightly. Then she realized she'd let important information slip.

"You mean the Ghostal Shores Resort really is haunted?" Blasing asked. "Not just a gimmick like Disneyland?"

"This makes no sense at all," Angela continued uneasily, trying to ignore Blasing's hot stare. "Spirits are supposed to be tied to a person or a place, not wandering around looking for food and lodging."

"Ghostly hitchhikers. Right."

"Believe it," Angela replied.

"I wish I'd stayed in Tahoe instead of letting you drag me here. All I have to deal with there are drunks, jealous boyfriends and confused teenagers in hormonal overdrive."

Angela's eyes flashed, then narrowed; she bit back a retort, along with a childish urge to stick out her tongue.

It was probably wise to drive away, but Angela found herself morbidly fascinated. The old miner had moved behind his mule and was leaning against its rear, grunting loudly and pushing as hard as he could. The mule took two quick steps forward, then another sideways. The prospector fell on his face, partly disappearing into the ground.

Angela almost laughed but didn't, sensing the miner might turn his wrath on her. "Are you going to Ghostal Shores?" Angela didn't recognize him, so he certainly wasn't from the resort.

The miner didn't reply, instead he hauled himself to his feet and began digging into a pack. "Ya win, ya ornery beast." He gave Lillybell a sugar cube. "Lady, will ya kindly get your newfangled whatchamacallit out of the way? The first carriage that went by really shook up Lillybell, but you scared the hell outta her!"

Angela's anger swelled; she started to say something about walking in the middle of the road, then realized it was pointless. When you were dead, you didn't care about getting run over.

"I said get the hell outta here!" He began to walk menacingly toward them. "Nobody messes with JP Johnson!"

"Ms. Starborne . . ." Blasing began.

Without another word, Angela stomped on the gas pedal and the 4-Runner raced away.

Otter Creek Press, Inc.
P. O. Box 416
Doctors Inlet, FL 32030-0416

Telephone: (904) 264-0465
Toll Free: (800) 326-4809
Email: otterpress@aol.com

You May Order

Retail prices:
Softcover: $12.95 (U.S.); $14.95 (Canada)
Hardcover: $19.95 (U.S.); $24.95 (Canada)
Please include $4.00 per copy for tax, shipping & handling

Copies _____   Amount Enclosed _____

Name of Book _____

Name _____

Address _____

City _____ State _____ Zip _____

Otter Creek Press, Inc., accepts money orders and checks.

About the Author

William Hill

William Hill is a native of Indianapolis, Indiana, and first learned to read through comic books and adventure and science fiction novels.

Although not a military brat, he has lived in Kansas (Shawnee Mission), Tennessee (Nashville and Bristol — setting of *Dawn of the Vampire*), and Texas (Denton, Dallas, Richardson, and Cedar Creek — setting of *Vampire's Kiss* and *Vampire Hunt*). He has "serious" degrees in Economics from Vanderbilt University and an MBA from the University of North Texas.

Since realizing that the corporate world stifled creative thought and discouraged personal imagination, Bill has been employed as an alchemist in South Lake Tahoe and an EMT/Ski Patroller at a North Lake Tahoe resort.

Although his first writing love is magic-oriented fantasy, Hill's first and second novels — *Dawn of the Vampire* and *Vampire's Kiss* — were supernatural thrillers published by Pinnacle. *The Magic Bicycle* and *California Ghosting* were published by Otter Creek Press.

Bill and his lovely and supportive wife, Kat, currently reside in Lake Tahoe, Nevada. **Bill intends to write imaginative fiction and fantasy until dirt is shoveled upon his coffin.**